MYSTERIES *of* MARTHA'S VINEYARD

A Light in the Darkness
Like a Fish Out of Water
Adrift
Maiden of the Mist
Making Waves
Don't Rock the Boat
A Port in the Storm
Thicker Than Water
Swept Away
Bridge Over Troubled Waters
Smoke on the Water
Shifting Sands
Shark Bait
Seascape in Shadows
Storm Tide

MYSTERIES *of* MARTHA'S VINEYARD

Storm Tide

ELIZABETH PENNEY

Guideposts

New York

CHAPTER ONE

Priscilla Latham Grant was halfway to her cousin's house when the first raindrops fell. A gusting wind rattled the November trees, sending a few brown leaves spinning down.

"I hope the storm doesn't get too bad," Priscilla said to Jake, the red and white loveable mutt she'd adopted. He panted in reply. Jake loved riding in the SUV, no matter the weather.

At least it wasn't snow. November in Martha's Vineyard was a time poised between seasons. It could be gloriously warm and golden or frigid and foreboding. "If you don't like the weather, wait a minute," Priscilla muttered. She laughed. *I guess I'm a real islander now.* The phrase was common among New Englanders, and after more than a year on the island, she knew why.

A recent widow, Priscilla had moved from Kansas to the island when her aunt Marjorie unexpectedly left her a lighthouse, complete with a cottage. Even better, her new home included three wonderful cousins her age, a network of Latham relatives, and a rich family history. She was closest to her cousin Joan, and the opportunity to share impromptu meals like tonight was something she treasured.

She drove over a rise lined with venerable maples and spotted the cheerful light of Joan's house twinkling in the rapidly falling dusk. The days were so short this time of year.

"Here we are," she said to Jake. "Ready to see Sister?" A sharp bark and a tail wag greeted her words. Sister was the lively blue heeler mix Joan had adopted in the spring. The two dogs adored each other.

Joan came to the front door to greet them, holding Sister's collar so she wouldn't bolt. "I'm glad you could come," she called, a wide smile on her elfin features. Petite and trim, Joan wore her dark hair short.

"Thanks for having us." Priscilla went around to the back seat and grabbed the dish of half-baked roasted potatoes she'd brought as her contribution. They were her signature dish and would finish cooking in Joan's oven. She'd also made a square cake using home-made applesauce from Vineyard apples and a recipe from her mother's vintage cookbook.

One dish under an arm, the other in her hand, she let Jake out of the SUV. He dashed over to Sister, and the pair began their ritual of sniffing noses. Joan shooed them both inside, holding the door for Priscilla to enter.

"Something smells good," Priscilla said. She handed her pans to Joan and pulled off her coat, then kicked off the ubiquitous rubber-soled boots she wore from October to March. The hallway was small and cozy, like the rest of the house. Joan's furnishings and style were simple yet comfortable.

"I made my classic Boston baked beans," Joan said. "They take all day in a low oven." She led the way to the kitchen in the back of the house, followed by two leaping dogs, their nails clicking on the hardwood floors. After she set Priscilla's dishes on the granite counter, she asked, "Would you like tea? I can put the kettle on."

"That sounds perfect. I'm chilled." Priscilla rubbed her hands together with a shiver, noticing the trickles of rain down the picture windows overlooking Joan's garden. Three seasons of the year, the garden featured riotous English-cottage flower beds adorned with trellises and other features. Now the beds were forlorn, only a few bushes with red berries providing interest.

Joan filled the kettle at the sink. "I'll pull the beans out soon, and you can pop in your potatoes to finish up. We're also having spiral ham. I'll warm up slices for us." At the word *ham*, both dogs sat, tongues hanging out. The women laughed.

"Can Sister have a treat?" Priscilla reached into her sweater pocket for the biscuits she kept there for Jake. They weren't ham, but they'd do. At Joan's nod, she gave the dogs each one. Carrying them away in their teeth, both pups plopped under the table with groans.

The women joined them at the table, holding mugs of fragrant spice tea. Priscilla took a sip. "I can't wait to see Rachel in a couple of weeks for Thanksgiving." Her daughter, age thirty-three, was a project manager for a telecommunications firm in Kansas City.

"I'll bet." Joan's dark eyes twinkled. "How are things with her and A.J.? Are they still seeing each other?"

"Yes, they are. Although I think the long-distance aspect is wearing on her." A.J. was a tall, handsome, and, most importantly, kind FBI agent based in Boston. He and Rachel had met on one of her trips to the island.

"I'll bet. It must be hard." Joan's lips twisted in a sympathetic grimace. "Do you think he'll join us for Thanksgiving dinner?

He'd be welcome." The Latham cousins were planning a get-together at Joan's sister's house. Trudy had a spacious, hospitable home that could adequately host a large gathering.

"I'm not sure. I'll ask her next time she calls." Priscilla thought about the upcoming holiday. Thanksgiving was one of her favorites, a perfect combination of loved ones and a delicious feast. This thought led to another. "Are you entering the cranberry sauce contest?"

"Of course. The food pantry needs the support, especially at this time of year." Joan picked up a battered cookbook sitting on the table. "I've been browsing this for recipes."

Priscilla reached out a hand. "Let me see." There were more than sauce recipes, but she focused on that section. A recipe featuring blueberries sounded intriguing. "I think I'll get fresh cranberries from Sheila Weller." The Wellers had operated a cranberry bog on the island for decades. Candy Lane Confectionery, a bakery in town, used Sheila's berries for the muffins Priscilla loved. As for the blueberries, Priscilla had frozen some from a local farm.

"That's a great idea," Joan said. "I love visiting Sheila's farm. Much more fun than going to the grocery store."

"I've always wondered how they harvest cranberries," Priscilla said. The tart red fruit didn't grow in Kansas, but it was a major crop in Massachusetts.

"It's interesting, for sure." Joan stirred her tea absently, staring out into the soggy garden. Her eyes widened. "Look at that wind." As if in response to her words, the gale howled around the eaves of the house with an eerie, rising wail.

Priscilla looked out to see trees bowing in the wind, their branches waving. The tops of small saplings almost touched the ground. "Wow. It's really gotten stronger in the last few minutes."

"Let me check the weather." Joan got up and turned on the weather radio on the counter. The station gave regular forecasts and updates relied upon by coastal residents.

The droning voice conveyed a warning. A nor'easter had strengthened as it turned toward land, and the islands were in its path. Wind gusts over forty miles per hour and downpours were expected. "Travel is not advised," the voice said.

"You might be staying here for the night," Joan said with a laugh. "Let's pray we keep our power."

"I'm happy to stay if I have to." Since her dog was with her, Priscilla didn't absolutely need to go home. As for her property, the hundred-year-old lighthouse had endured many a storm, hurricanes included. What harm could a simple nor'easter do?

A thumping sound drifted into the kitchen. At first Priscilla thought it was a shutter banging against the wall, but then it resolved into fervent knocking.

"Someone's at the door," Joan said. "I can't imagine who."

From her seat, Priscilla could see the visitor when Joan opened the door, the curious dogs at her heels. A drenched young woman dressed in a light coat stood there, shivering. "I think I'm lost," she said. She rubbed her arms, teeth chattering.

"Why don't you come in and warm up?" Joan said. "We should be able to help you find the place you're looking for." Joan helped her take her coat off and showed her in, the dogs eagerly trailing their new friend.

Priscilla stood when they entered the kitchen. She introduced herself, as did Joan.

The young woman reached out a cold, damp hand. "Hi. I'm...Anne. Anne Edwards." She sniffed, then laughed. "Sorry. I think I'm coming down with a cold."

"No wonder." Joan bustled over to the stove to turn on the flame under the kettle. "Have a seat."

Anne pulled out the chair between Joan and Priscilla and sat, moving slowly as though her bones hurt. Jake and Sister vied for pats, and with a laugh, she gave them both a head rub. "They're so cute."

"They are," Priscilla said. "And annoying." Studying the new arrival, she noticed she had pretty, delicate features and almost milky skin. When she bent her head, Priscilla saw she was wearing a wig. Alarm lanced through Priscilla. *Is she ill?* Besides that clue, it was hard to tell, although Anne was very slender and almost frail. The wool sweater and slacks she wore nearly swamped her frame.

Joan placed the basket of tea bags in front of Anne. "Pick one." She whirled away to the cupboard and pulled down a mug. "Are you hungry? I can make you a sandwich."

Anne laughed. "My goodness, you're too kind. A cup of tea would be great. I had lunch not too long ago." She checked over the tea selections and chose one.

A minute later, she had her mug of hot water and was dipping the bag. Joan landed in her chair again. "So tell us, where are you headed?"

Anne took a sip before answering. "I'm looking for the Weller Farm. I've rented a cabin there."

Priscilla and Joan exchanged looks. "We were just talking about the Weller Farm," Priscilla said. "The owner sells cranberries. I didn't know she rented cabins."

"Oh yes," Anne said. "She has two or three. They look really cute online."

A retreat to a farm cabin sounded lovely, but at this time of year? Priscilla wondered what was behind Anne's visit to the island. Feeling it would be rude to ask, she refrained from questions. But she couldn't resist commenting, "I hope they're heated. It can get pretty cold out here in November."

"Oh yes. I made sure of that," was the calm reply.

Joan hopped up again and rummaged in a drawer. "I've got a map of the island here somewhere. It's easier to show you than tell you how to get there." She found the map and carried it and a pen back to the table.

Anne scooted closer to watch while Joan drew on the map, giving landmarks as well. "The dirt road to the farm comes up pretty quickly," Joan told her. "There is a sign but it can be hard to see, especially when it's dark." Lightning flashed, followed by a thunder crack so loud the house shook. "Or stormy."

"'It was a dark and stormy night...'" Priscilla said, watching the rain sheet down. The rainfall was so dense now, she couldn't see beyond a few feet. Jake whined, pressing his nose into Priscilla's hand. Like many dogs, he didn't like thunder. Sister went deeper under the table.

Their visitor stared out the window. "Wow. It's really getting bad."

"You might have to—" Joan's words were drowned out by another thunderclap.

Lightning danced in the sky, a little too close for comfort, Priscilla thought. "It's right on top of us," she said.

Joan stood and peered outside, her expression worried. Then she went to the back door and opened it to peek out for a better look. "Water is just streaming down the hillside. I've never seen anything like it."

The other two followed and took turns looking outside. Priscilla saw several frothy brown streams winding down through Joan's garden, moving so fast they made little waves when they hit obstacles. "They're tearing up your garden."

Joan's grimace and shrug were illuminated by another flash of lightning. "There isn't much I can do about it."

Thunder resounded again, but this time it was followed by a strange rending sound and enormous thumps and cracks that made their mugs dance on the table. Jake howled, and Sister joined in.

"Guys?" Anne said from her position by the door. "A tree just fell down."

"Let me see." Joan nudged her aside and, heedless of the rain, stepped outside onto the deck. "Oh my," she called. "It's one of those big old maples." She stepped back in, brushing the water out of her hair. "It fell across the road." She shuddered. "Thank goodness it didn't fall on my house."

"I'm surprised we—" The lights flickered and went out. "I was going to say, surprised we didn't lose power." Priscilla groaned. "The tree must have taken down the wires."

"This is crazy!" Anne said. "What if I'd been driving under that tree when it fell?"

That was a sobering thought. Priscilla breathed a prayer for all those traveling during the storm. Then she extended her prayers to the whole island. What if trees did fall on people's houses? They could be hurt or killed. Or have to fix their roofs and replace possessions ruined by falling debris or rainwater.

Joan snatched up the receiver to the landline. "Phones are out too." She found her cell and placed a call to the power company to tell them where the outage was. She disconnected with a rueful laugh. "It might be a while. The calls are just pouring in, they said." She studied the screen. "Hope my battery lasts a while."

Priscilla had the same hope regarding her own cell phone. But thinking of more immediate matters, she took a good look around Joan's kitchen, barely able to see anything in the dim, gray light. "I'm glad you've got a gas stove. At least we won't go hungry. Though we'd better keep the fridge closed." The rain was slowing for now, but an outage could take hours or even days to fix.

Joan found a candle and lit it. "I can make a fire in the wood-stove to keep us warm. We're pretty much all set." She set the candle on the table. "Can you tell I've been through this before?"

"Totally," Anne said. "In Boston, we don't have this problem too often. But it must be different out here." Then she clamped her lips shut, as though regretting revealing that much.

"It is," Priscilla said. "And to be honest, that's part of the charm." Yes, living on an island sometimes included events that weren't very convenient, like when the boats couldn't run due to weather. But she wouldn't trade her home for anywhere else.

Joan flitted back to the stove and pulled out the bean pot. "These are ready. You'll have to eat with us, Anne. I insist." She turned up the heat and slid the pan of potatoes into the oven, followed by a foil packet of ham.

"That's so kind of you." Anne's smile was wan. "I guess I picked the right house to stop at."

"I'll say." Priscilla injected warmth into her voice, hoping to make the young woman feel welcome. "Joan's doors are always open to stranded travelers."

Blue, red, white, and yellow lights flashed up on the road. Though the early dusk was falling, the strobes pierced the gloom like beacons.

"That was fast," Joan said. "They must have been in the area." She got up from the table again. "The storm has let up a little right now. I'm going out to see what's going on."

"Me too," Priscilla said. She had to admit to being curious about the fallen tree.

In the end, all three of them trudged outside, Anne wearing a borrowed slicker. They left the disappointed mutts behind for their own safety. Priscilla saw them watching out the window, the curtain pushed aside and their heads close together.

"Where's your car, Anne?" Joan asked. Priscilla's was the only one in the driveway.

Anne pointed to a small white sedan. "I parked on the road and walked down the driveway. I was afraid I might not be able to turn around."

Priscilla hopped over a stream of water cutting across the gravel. "That was smart. I hope I can get out." The dirt was much softer now and driving on it would only damage the driveway more.

On the main road, a power truck, the town road agent, and a police cruiser were parked near the fallen giant, their lights still flashing. Men in hard hats shouted to each other, and Priscilla heard the loud buzz of chain saws.

Priscilla spotted Officer April Brown, the only woman in the crew, and walked over to her. "Wild storm, isn't it?" She had to raise her voice to be heard above the saws. "I'm so thankful that tree didn't hit Joan's house."

April, watching the work with folded arms, nodded. "Yeah, and this is only the beginning. Another front is moving in." She smiled briefly at Joan and Anne standing a distance away, giving them a small wave. "Good thing the crew was close by. It's going to be days before we're back to normal." She sounded gloomy.

Priscilla sympathized. April had two teenage boys and a husband at home, but when emergencies arose, she had to work around the clock. It was part of the job.

Judging it was safe, Priscilla edged closer to the tree. The trunk was massive and gnarled, probably over a hundred years old. Instead of breaking off, as often happened during a storm, the roots had been torn out of the ground due to the soggy soil.

Priscilla spotted something in the crater created by the roots ripping free. *What is that?* It had a rounded shape and was large. Not a rock, since it was definitely white, not tan or brown or gray.

Seeing that April had moved to the head of the tree, she crept closer. Reaching down, she rubbed mud away, wincing at the stain on her gloves.

Then she yelped. The object had eye sockets. And now that she was closer, she saw sticklike limbs and outstretched finger bones. Something glittered on one phalanx.

She had found a skeleton.

CHAPTER TWO

W hat's the matter?" Joan asked, appearing at Priscilla's shoulder. "Some kind of animal nesting in the tree?"

Priscilla stepped back, hugging herself. "No." Her teeth began to chatter but not from cold. From shock.

Joan bent to examine the find, leaping back when she realized what she was seeing. "Oh my. There was a skeleton under that tree?"

"Apparently." Priscilla looked around for April. Then she noticed the white sedan was gone. "Where's Anne?"

"What?" Joan whirled around. "Oh. I guess she took off after I started walking over here. I didn't see her leave."

April was strolling their way, hands resting on her hips as she inspected the progress on the tree. Priscilla waved her over. April tipped her chin in inquiry when she drew closer. "Whatcha got?"

In answer, Priscilla pointed. She knew the moment April realized what it was by the widening of her eyes and her involuntary lurch backward. Her hand fished for her chest microphone and she called it in to dispatch.

"Did you know that was there?" she asked Joan. She studied the contour of the landscape. "It's on your property, right?"

Joan's brow furrowed. "That skeleton's probably a hundred years old. How would I know about it? It was under the tree all this time."

"We have no idea how old it is," April said. "Not yet." She stepped closer to the edge of the road. "And is this your property or not?"

"It is," Joan admitted. She pointed out her boundary lines. "I've lived here since my house was built, back in the 1970s. All the houses around here were built then. The land was part of an old estate."

Now that the initial shock had worn off, Priscilla realized something. Whoever the person was hadn't been buried in hallowed ground. He or she had probably been murdered. Grief and sorrow seeped through her body, making her weak. "I don't feel very good," she said.

April took her arm, and with a surprisingly strong grip, led her to the cruiser. "Sit down for a minute." She settled Priscilla in the front passenger seat.

"Are you okay?" Joan asked. "I thought you were going to faint."

Priscilla tried to laugh. "I thought so too, for a minute." She turned to April. "What's the protocol in a case like this, Officer?" Now that they'd discovered a suspicious death, it didn't feel right to call April by her first name.

"We've got to launch a full investigation." April peered up at the ominous clouds. "Which won't be easy in this weather. And, if the cause of death is foul play, then the state medical examiner will get involved. But with the ferries shut down, they won't be able to do much."

Another cruiser zipped up the road, lights whirling, and screeched to a stop. Two officers stepped out. Priscilla recognized Bill Denton and Ed Sequeira. "We got a call, April," Bill said. "You found a possible 10-55?"

April looked at Priscilla. "You going to be okay?" At her nod, April hurried off to join the other two. A minute later, the trio was standing by the crater, taking turns examining the remains without touching anything.

My gloves. Priscilla studied the muddy fingers. She never would have touched the skull if she'd had any idea what it was.

"10-55 is police code for coroner's case," Joan said. She worked part-time at the hospital as an ultrasound technician, so she'd heard it all over the years. "That makes sense, since it's an old skeleton."

"Did you see the ring?" Priscilla asked. When she closed her eyes, she could still see it etched in her brain. A circular diamond, surrounded by sapphire and diamond rectangles, radiating out like flower petals. The rain had obviously washed it clean, otherwise it would have been encrusted with decades of dirt.

"I did. Gorgeous." Joan bit her bottom lip as she stared toward the tree. "The skeleton has to be female, wearing a ring like that."

Rain had started to bucket down again. Ed trotted back to his cruiser and pulled a duffel bag out of the trunk. A minute later, the two men were setting up a tent over the remains. April went to confer with the road crew, who had gotten one lane cleared. They'd have to leave the lower part of the tree in place, in case evidence was caught in the roots.

April swung by, after talking to the men with chainsaws. "You can go back to the house, if you want. We'll be here a while. I'll come down and take a statement a little later."

"We have baked beans and ham if you're hungry," Joan said. "Plus tea and coffee."

"And my special potato dish," Priscilla added. Good thing she'd made a big pan.

"Sounds good," April called. She darted off, her attention on her case.

Joan scraped the remaining beans out of the pot with a rubber spatula. "These were a big hit. So were your potatoes." The police officers had taken a few minutes to eat, as had the road and light crew. Thankfully, power had been restored, and they'd driven off to another site, lights flashing.

Priscilla regarded the almost empty pan of potatoes roasted with bacon and broccoli, a recipe handed down by her mother. "I'm glad we could do something for them. They've got a rough night ahead."

The storm had circled back around and was now hitting the island full force. Priscilla stayed over at Joan's after learning that roads on the way home were blocked. Plus, according to the officers, motorists were being warned to stay off the roads. Getting caught in a flash flood or hit by falling branches were real possibilities.

Priscilla thought of the skeleton under the tent. *Poor soul.* "Who do you think that is out there?" she asked Joan. "You said the property used to be part of an estate?"

Joan placed the plastic container of beans in the refrigerator. "Yes. The Parker family owned all the land along here. Their first summer house was built in the late 1800s, and when that was torn down, they sold off some parcels." She shrugged. "To pay for the newer and bigger house, I guess."

"Were there any unsolved murders that you know of?" Priscilla poured boiling water into two mugs. With the amount of tea they'd been drinking today, it was a good thing Joan had decaffeinated choices.

Joan folded her arms, tapping one foot. "Not that I know of." She gestured. "Let's go in the living room. I have some island history books that might help us figure out who we found."

The other room was toasty, warmed by a fire in the woodstove. Both dogs had naturally gravitated to that spot and were sprawled out on the rug.

"They've got the right idea," Priscilla said with a laugh. After setting the mugs on the coffee table, she took one end of the overstuffed sofa. She glanced around the room, enjoying Joan's use of blue, green, and cream to create a restful space. Touches of deep pink in the upholstery fabric and accessories added zest.

Best of all, one of Aunt Marjorie's paintings hung over the mantel. This one depicted an island harbor touched by the setting sun. Priscilla allowed herself to be drawn into the scene, memories of summer on the island drifting through her mind.

"Here we are." Joan placed a stack of books on the coffee table. She handed one to Priscilla, then sat on the sofa beside her.

"What am I looking for?" Priscilla asked. To her delight, the paperback book had an old sepia-toned photograph of her lighthouse on the cover.

Joan chose a book. "Anything to do with the Parkers."

Priscilla leafed through, noticing the book was divided into sections. One featured photographs of magnificent summer homes, built by wealthy visitors in the late 1800s. She studied each photograph and caption carefully, looking for the Parker name.

Then she saw a turreted, shingled confection of a house with a group of Victorian-clad men and women standing on the porch. *The Parker house was built in 1880*, the caption stated. "Found it," she said.

Joan scooted closer and they both read the short paragraph about the house, its owners, and architect. Priscilla turned the page and found a photograph of a handsome young couple dating from the 1920s, judging by their hair and clothing. "'Elizabeth Morgan Parker and her husband, Vernon Parker,'" Joan read. "'Everyone called her Bitsy.'"

Bitsy was a beauty with short dark hair, a heart-shaped face, and large eyes. Vernon wore his hair parted in the middle, and had handsome if slightly heavy features. The smile on his face could only be called smug. According to the text, Vernon was a principal in an investment firm in Boston called Parker & Warren. Priscilla had seen that name somewhere recently. They must still be in business.

"Look at her hand," Joan said, her voice tight with excitement. "I thought I remembered seeing that ring."

On Bitsy's delicate hand, placed so gently on her husband's sleeve, was the ring the skeleton wore. Either that or its exact duplicate.

"What happened to Bitsy?" Priscilla asked, an electrified sensation in the pit of her stomach. They were on the verge of a major discovery, she just knew it.

Joan pulled another book off the pile. *Martha's Vineyard Mysteries*, read the garish title. "This book doesn't have the highest credibility but it's got some juicy stories." She flipped to the back and scanned the index. "Ah. Here we go."

Priscilla moved a little closer. The heading on the page said, *The Runaway Socialite*. "I have a feeling she didn't run away," she said.

"Me too." Joan cleared her throat and began to read. Despite the overly purple prose, the gist was clear. Vernon Parker claimed his wife Bitsy had run away with another man in 1932 as the explanation for her disappearance. In any event, he remarried a woman named Mabel soon after divorcing Bitsy, which was quite a scandalous move in that day.

"Maybe Vernon killed Bitsy and just told everyone she left town." Priscilla picked up the first book and studied Vernon's photograph. Was that the face of a killer? If so, not only had he murdered Bitsy, he'd smeared her reputation in the process by claiming she'd run away with someone else.

But perhaps she was rushing to judgment. Maybe Vernon honestly thought she had left the island, not knowing she was dead and buried in his backyard. She shared some of these thoughts with Joan.

"It's a puzzle all right," Joan said. "I don't think Bitsy had any children, so I'm not sure how they'll identify the skeleton. They'd have to find another relative for a DNA match. That might be difficult after all this time, almost ninety years later."

Priscilla considered. "They can determine age, gender, and health by examining the bones, right? That will give them a pretty good idea if it might be her."

Joan traced a finger over Bitsy's pretty face. "Something's telling me it is her. The location, the ring...who else could it be?"

"His second wife?" Priscilla said.

"No. I think she's in the cemetery with Vernon. The Parkers have a huge monument. For some reason, they're buried here, not in Boston."

Again, a memory niggled in Priscilla's mind. "I recently saw something about the Parker firm in one of those Boston magazines," she said.

Joan pointed to a magazine rack next to an armchair. "Look in there. I subscribe to a lot of regional publications."

Priscilla went over to the rack and searched through the issues tucked inside. She found the one she remembered, which featured "40 under 40" in the Boston business community. She brought the magazine back to the sofa. A couple of minutes later, she found the entry she remembered.

It featured two striking young women, cousins Whitney and Jordan Parker. Both had risen rapidly in the investment community ranks. Both were on target to become partners at Parker & Warren.

"Look at this," Priscilla said, showing Joan the article. "Do you think they're related to Vernon?"

"I'm not sure about Whitney," Joan said. "I haven't met her." She laughed. "But I've had a few run-ins with Jordan over the years, although she's mostly here only in the summer. She may not be forty yet, but she acts like her grandmother, a bossy, nosy woman if there ever was one. In Violet's eyes, there was only one way to do things—her way."

Morning brought clearing skies—and a parade of cars easing past Joan's house. Priscilla looked up at the road, where a cruiser's lights flashed. "I think we have curiosity seekers," she said.

Joan, busy cracking eggs into a bowl, glanced outside. "I'm not surprised." She winced at the sight of her soggy garden. "What a mess. I'm not looking forward to cleaning up."

Priscilla regarded the rivers of mud cutting through the flower beds and lawn. "I think you might have to wait until spring. And don't worry. We'll all help you." She was referring to her other cousins, Trudy and Gail. "We know how important your gardens are to you. And we enjoy them too." Joan's lovely gardens were admired by everyone who saw them. But today the passersby were rubbernecking at the white tent guarding the skeleton.

A skeleton. Priscilla still hadn't recovered from the shock of her grisly find. Hopefully the forensics team could find answers. No doubt they would excavate today and carry the lonely bones away until they could be buried properly.

A familiar black SUV approached, slowing to a crawl. The vehicle braked at the cruiser, the driver's side window unrolling to reveal Gerald O'Bannon, an officer in the Coast Guard. One of Priscilla's greatest surprises on the island had been Gerald's friendship.

Feeling like a giddy teenager, Priscilla moved into the living room after the vehicle continued down the road. To her delight, the SUV signaled and turned into Joan's driveway. She dashed back into the kitchen. "Crack a couple of extra eggs. Gerald is here."

Joan laughed as Priscilla zoomed toward the front door, the dogs leaping and barking behind her, like a small-time pied piper.

Priscilla waited until he was stepping onto the front porch before opening the door, using the time to smooth her hair in the hall mirror. There was such a thing as appearing too eager. "Good morning," she said. "You're just in time for breakfast."

"Now there's a greeting." Gerald grinned as he stepped inside. He pulled off a wool cap and ran his fingers through his thick hair. "Bacon and eggs?" he guessed with a sniff. "I'm in." He shrugged out of his coat, and Priscilla hung it on a peg. His rubber-soled boots followed.

The dogs lingered to give the footwear a thorough investigation, then followed to the kitchen, tags jingling.

"Hello, Gerald. Good to see you," Joan said. "What a storm, huh?"

"It sure was. We lost trees all over the island. Power's still out in some places." He nodded at Priscilla, who was handing him a mug of coffee. "Everything's fine at the lighthouse, though."

"Good to know," Priscilla said with relief. She'd been worried all night about the state of her property. She topped off her mug with coffee before popping slices of bread into the toaster. That was her contribution to breakfast preparations.

At Joan's invitation, Gerald sat at the table, giving Jake and Sister big helpings of pats and love. "I understand you had a little surprise last night."

Priscilla loved his habit of understatement. "I guess you could say that." She buttered toast and cut the slices in half while filling him in. "It was a huge shock when I realized what we'd found."

"I'll bet." Gerald's eyes were sympathetic.

Joan filled plates with eggs and bacon while Priscilla added toast and ferried them to the table. "We think we might know who it is," Priscilla said. "Right, Joan?"

"We have a theory anyway." Joan set a caddy holding home-made strawberry jam, blueberry jam, and orange marmalade on the table, then sat. "Let's say grace."

After Gerald led the prayer, the trio dug into the tasty meal. "This is really hitting the spot," Gerald said after they'd eaten in silence for a few minutes. The dogs hovered at his knees, hoping for a dropped bit of bacon. "Thanks for letting me barge in."

"Anytime," Joan said graciously, passing Gerald the jam caddy. "Back to our forlorn friend. She's wearing a gorgeous ring. One that Bitsy Parker wore."

"According to the history books, Bitsy disappeared in 1932." Priscilla took up the tale. "But we think it's her out there." She lowered her voice. "It's possible she was murdered and buried in her own backyard."

"That tree used to be on Parker land," Joan said. "Now it belongs to me."

The medical examiner's office had sent Dr. Evan Stanley, an earnest young man dressed for the cold weather in an orange quilted coat and matching wool hat. He pushed his glasses up with one thumb, studying Joan with steady gray eyes. "Tell me, Mrs. Abernathy, did you have any idea this skeleton was under your maple tree?"

Along with the examiner and two members of his crew, Officers Brown and Denton were on the scene. Gerald, Joan, and Priscilla had walked up after breakfast to see what was going on.

Joan sighed, having made this point several times to various law enforcement personnel. "No, I hadn't a clue. I've never had an occasion to dig around under the roots. And if I did, and had found a finger or toe bone, I certainly would have called the police."

"Of course, of course," Dr. Stanley muttered. He made a note on his tablet. "We'll be excavating the rest of the remains, and from there we should be able to determine gender and approximate age of the deceased."

"Can you tell how long the body has been there?" Priscilla asked. They had the ring to go by, but it was possible someone besides Bitsy had been wearing it.

"Sometimes," the examiner said. "It depends on the layers of the soil and if they've been disturbed. But with the rain we had yesterday, most of the information we might gather is probably lost."

Priscilla studied the saturated ground. He was right. After that disastrous deluge, the area where the skeleton lay was a mud pit.

"I did dig up something near the tree last summer when I was planting bulbs," Joan said. "A cuff link."

The examiner and his crew exchanged glances. "That might be somewhat helpful if you remember the approximate location you found it," a young woman said. "But since it's been removed from the site without our documentation, it will be useless as far as the law goes."

"But maybe it will help us, er, you, figure out what happened," Priscilla said.

"Maybe." The young woman sounded doubtful. "We'll take a look at it though."

"I have it right here," Joan said. She reached into her pocket and pulled out a small plastic bag holding the cuff link. "I thought it might be important, so I dug it out of my jewelry box for you to look at."

Priscilla had already seen the cuff link, which was gold with brown and cream inlay design. The medical examiner studied it before passing it to a colleague.

"It looks from the 1920s or '30s," April said, "but of course it needs closer study as to maker and origin."

"That's what I thought," Priscilla said. "Maybe it's the same vintage as the skeleton."

Before she could say more, a gold luxury sedan screeched to a halt beside the little group. A woman with shoulder-length blonde hair jumped out.

"I'm glad I caught you," she said to the medical examiner. "That skeleton is not Bitsy Parker. I have proof."

CHAPTER THREE

Dr. Stanley recovered quickly from the surprising intrusion. Adjusting his glasses again, he said, "We haven't determined who the skeleton is, ma'am. If you have any information regarding it, you need to share it with us."

"Don't call me ma'am." The young woman stamped her foot, which was clad in an expensive leather boot. She wore a matching suede fur-trimmed coat and hat, and gold earrings peeked out of her glossy hair. "I don't have any information about who it is, just who it isn't."

Jordan Parker. Priscilla recognized her from the magazine article, although instead of a sweet smile, a scowl sat on her pretty features.

The police officers had been letting Dr. Stanley take the lead but now Officer Denton held up a hand. "Hold on. Let's take a step back. The skeleton was only discovered last night. It hasn't even been fully excavated."

"That's right," Dr. Stanley's assistant said. "We aren't close to any conclusions yet. It will be a few days, at best."

Jordan pushed out her full lower lip. "I heard through the rumor mill that it *was* Bitsy. But it can't be. She ran away."

Priscilla had the feeling that the tree crew had spread the rumors. Certainly the police officers knew better than to speculate, especially if the deceased still had living family. Due to the distinctive ring the skeleton wore, Priscilla had a strong feeling that these were Bitsy's remains, but she kept her mouth closed. Let the medical examiner and the police take the heat. She had the feeling that if they reported something Jordan didn't like, she would strongly and publically object.

But she had to ask herself—why did Jordan care about a ninety-year-old case?

The forensics team got to work right after Jordan zoomed away, so Priscilla, Joan, and Gerald walked back to the house. "I'd better get going," Gerald said when they reached his SUV. "Thanks again for breakfast."

"Anytime," Joan said. "It was good to see you." She cocked her head. "Going to Aggie's for Thanksgiving?" Gerald's daughter and her family lived on the island.

He shook his head. "Not this year. They're going off-island to the in-laws." He forced a smile. "Can't blame them. The other grandparents deserve a turn." Gerald adored four-year-old Max and baby Ava. Priscilla had helped him babysit a few times and she'd seen how attached he was, and vice versa. They were cute, smart kids.

"Why don't you come to Trudy's?" Priscilla asked. "We'd love to have you join us again." Last year he had come to the cottage on Thanksgiving.

"That sounds great," Gerald said. "What can I bring?"

"Whatever you want," Joan said. "Trudy is doing the turkeys, so the rest is up for grabs. Let us know, and we'll add it to the list."

One of the cousins would prepare whatever was lacking after guests relayed what they were bringing. Everyone had a special dish.

Gerald opened the vehicle door. "I make a mean stuffing with oysters. I'll bring a big pan." He climbed inside.

"Oysters?" Priscilla suppressed a shudder. She couldn't imagine eating those with turkey. Her family always did the classic bread stuffing with onions and celery. If they felt wild, they'd add diced apples or nuts.

"It's delicious," Joan said. She waved at Gerald, who was starting up the SUV. "Let's have another cup of coffee. Then I'd better get going. I have the day off, but I have tons to do."

After the cup of coffee, Priscilla headed home. She drove the winding roads, her belly clenching with worry when she saw all the storm damage. A few people had trees land on their roofs, and some wires were still down, hanging in black loops. Gerald had said things were fine at the lighthouse so she hung on to that hope.

Holding her breath, she drove down the small lane to the lighthouse, releasing a sigh when she saw the white tower gleaming in the sun. At first glance, the cottage appeared intact, all the shutters still in place. "We're home," she said to Jake, her heart lifting in joy. Would she ever take this all for granted?

As she climbed out of the SUV and gazed at the ocean view, at the placid blue-green waves breaking on the rocky shore, she vowed to always be grateful.

Gratitude was the secret to a happy life, one of the older parishioners in her church back in Kansas had told her. The elderly woman had seen her share of misfortunes over the decades, but she had a serene, joyful countenance. Priscilla aspired to emulate her.

"'Rejoice always, pray continually, give thanks in all circumstances,'" Priscilla quoted aloud, the Scripture like balm to her soul. Standing strong on a rock, her house had survived the storm. Reflecting back over her own life, she had to admit the same was true for her. It was the Rock that made all the difference.

A certain number on the caller ID later that day made Priscilla's heart leap with joy. She turned off the vacuum cleaner and picked up the receiver. "Good afternoon, darling."

"Hi, Mom. Did you survive the storm okay? It was on the national news."

"We did." Priscilla sat down in her favorite armchair by the fireplace, joined by Jake, who flopped at her feet. "I was at Joan's for dinner, and Jake and I got stranded there." She described the storm and how it had brought down trees and made the power go out. This reminded her of Anne, and Priscilla wondered how she'd made out. Everything they'd experienced after Anne left had pushed the young traveler right out of her head.

"Ugh," Rachel said. "Wow, that sounds terrible. I'm glad a tree didn't hit the house."

"Me too. We did, um, make an interesting discovery." Priscilla had debated whether or not to mention the skeleton, but with the internet, Rachel might well find out another way. She'd be hurt if Priscilla didn't tell her first, since she could be a bit prickly that way. "We found a skeleton under the old maple tree across the road from Joan's. We think it might belong to a missing person from 1932."

Rachel was silent for a moment. "Seriously? A tree fell down, and there happened to be a body under it?" She groaned softly. "Trust you to find it." She was referring to Priscilla's habit of stumbling upon mysteries ever since moving to the island. She honestly didn't seek them out. Somehow they found her.

Priscilla didn't give Rachel any details about the discovery and how she'd actually touched the skull. That was something she was going to try to forget, so why upset her daughter? "A forensics team is taking care of it. They'll find out who it was and give her a proper burial."

Of course Rachel seized on the pronoun. "Her? How do you know it was a woman?"

"She was still wearing a ring." Priscilla described the ring and the research she and Joan had done. "We think it might be Bitsy Parker, who disappeared back then."

Rachel sighed. "Poor thing. I hope they can finally put her to rest." She paused. "Only a couple of weeks until I see you!"

Priscilla gladly accepted the change of subject. "That's right. I'm so excited. When do you think you'll arrive?" Rachel would fly to Boston and then take the ferry over to the island.

"Well...I wanted to talk to you about that." She hesitated. "I'm coming a few days early."

"That's awesome." Priscilla sat upright, startling the dog. "Are you coming here or staying in Boston?" Either would make her happy. She could pop over to Boston in a heartbeat herself.

"Um, Boston. Mom, don't take this the wrong way, but I have plans."

Priscilla's heart sank. "And you don't want to see me?" She heard the dejection in her voice and bit her tongue. Rachel was a grown woman, and nothing was to be gained by acting needy. She really didn't want her daughter to feel forced to spend time with her. That would be humiliating.

"It's not that, Mom. I-I'm going to be busy. Doing some shopping. And seeing A.J., of course." Her voice lifted when she said his name. "We'll see you on Thanksgiving though."

Ah, that was it. Romance. How could Priscilla stand in the way of that budding relationship? She'd never seen Rachel so excited about someone. Maybe—she broke off that thought and said, injecting warmth into her tone, "Of course you want to spend time with A.J. I don't blame you a bit. Just keep me posted about when you two will be arriving on the island."

Gratitude. After they disconnected, Priscilla reminded herself of her vow. Yes, she was grateful to have Rachel, and thankful she was coming for a visit, even if it was short. And of course it was natural for adults to have other priorities besides their parents.

But why did it sting so much? Obviously she needed more practice. "'In all things give thanks,'" she whispered.

Candy Lane Confectionery was packed the next morning when Priscilla arrived. She stood aside to let a few people exit with their white bags and to-go cups, then slipped inside. Trudy's distinctive laugh rose over the babble of voices, and Priscilla spotted her cousins and Uncle Hugh at a table in the corner.

After purchasing coffee and her usual cranberry-orange muffin at the counter, Priscilla wound her way through the room, nodding and smiling at people she recognized.

"Good morning," she said when she reached the table. She set her breakfast down then pulled off her wool hat and removed her coat. "It's crazy in here."

Trudy looked up at her, a teasing look in her sparkling blue eyes. "Everyone is relieved to survive that storm." She tossed her blonde waves with a grin. "I heard you and Joan had quite the adventure."

Priscilla tucked her hat in her coat pocket, then hung the garment on the back of an empty chair and sat. "I see you filled them in, Joan."

"No, this beat her to the punch." Gail stuck a folded edition of the local paper under Priscilla's nose. "Take a look."

Joan rolled her eyes. "Our fifteen minutes of fame, apparently. The reporter wanted to get a picture of me by the tree, but I said no."

"'Skeleton Revealed by Record-breaking Storm,'" Priscilla read out loud. "Oh my. I had no idea the story hit the papers already." She scanned the article further. *Island residents Joan Abernathy and Priscilla Grant made the grisly discovery.* Nice. They weren't calling her a new arrival to the island anymore.

Uncle Hugh peered at Priscilla from under bushy brows. "I always wondered when Bitsy Parker's body was going to turn up."

Gail regarded her father with astonishment. "Pop, I never knew you had a theory about her disappearance."

"You never asked." Hugh's expression was smug, but Priscilla could tell something was wrong by the way he was sitting, more hunched over than usual, both hands wrapped around his mug.

"Are you feeling okay, Uncle Hugh?" she asked. He suffered from arthritis, and cold weather didn't do that any favors.

Before he could answer, Harper, one of the cooks and servers, appeared at the table. "Anyone want a refill?" She went around the table and filled mugs.

"I'm not ready for a refill yet," Priscilla told Harper. "But I do want to know more about the pastry Gail is eating. I haven't seen it here before." Since joining the bakery, Harper had introduced several new recipes, at owner Candy's invitation.

Gail popped a strand of fruit-studded cake into her mouth and chewed. "It's called panettone. It literally melts in your mouth."

"I learned the recipe from an Italian baker," Harper said. "It's not easy but, wow, is it worth it. We're selling a lot of them online too." Harper had set up a website so customers could buy from their favorite island bakery between visits. Sales had beaten projections.

"I'll try it." Priscilla took a closer look. "I see there are cranberries in it."

Harper smiled. "Local, from Sheila's farm. We wouldn't have it any other way." She hurried off to another table.

Gail nodded in approval. "Got to try new things. Keeps you young, right, Pop?"

Hugh's reply was a grunt. Priscilla took a close look at his face, noticing new frown lines etching his forehead. "What's going on, Uncle Hugh?"

He grunted again. "I'm concerned about an investment I made, that's all." He forced a laugh. "It's only money, right? As long as you've got your health..."

Priscilla gave Gail a puzzled look, and as she hoped, she was a bit more forthcoming than her father.

"Pop and a few of his friends have a little investment club. You know Chowder and Chowder Jr., right?"

How could Priscilla forget those colorful men? "I sure do."

Gail went on. "They're two of the guys. Anyway, they invested some money with a Boston firm, and Pop didn't get his quarterly statement. So he's in a tizzy."

"I don't blame him," Trudy said. "Have you called them, Uncle Hugh?"

He muttered something. Gail said, "I'm going to make him do it later."

The front door opened with a jingle of bells, and boot heels clacked across the wooden floor. Priscilla turned to see Jordan Parker cutting a swath through the room. She headed for the counter, her piercing eyes sweeping the room.

Priscilla crouched down a little, not wanting to be the target of the woman's wrath for the second day in a row. But after ordering and paying for a medium skim latte with no foam to go, the young woman headed right for their table.

"Help," Joan said. "And hide that newspaper."

Gail tucked it on her lap, out of sight. "Hello, Jordan," she said. "Nice to see you."

Jordan's eyes didn't quite convey the same message as they roamed over Priscilla and Joan. But she took a sip of her latte and focused on Gail. "I wanted you to know that I've had the flyers made for the cranberry sauce contest. Are you still on to pass them around town?"

"Of course," Gail said. "I can do it today, since I'm off."

"Great." Jordan handed Gail her cup and began to paw through her oversized handbag, slung over one shoulder. She pulled out a manila folder. "Here they are. Fifty copies. Plaster the town with them."

Gail regarded the folder dubiously. "I hope I can find fifty places."

Jordan took back her cup. "Sure you can. Go door-to-door down this street." She pivoted on her heel and marched toward the door, tossing a goodbye over her shoulder.

"That young lady is large and in charge," Uncle Hugh said with admiration.

Gail laughed ruefully. "If it weren't for a good cause..." Her voice trailed off, and she popped more cake into her mouth.

"I'm entering the contest," Priscilla said. Joan and Trudy echoed agreement. "So you have three entries already."

"Do your best, Gail," Trudy said. "We'll help you get the word out."

As Jordan exited, Mildred Pearson entered. Mildred was the caretaker of the East Shore Historical Museum, and she took her position seriously. So seriously that she dressed the part while working. Today she wore a houndstooth cloak over a flowing navy blue skirt, buttoned boots on her feet, and a bonnet on her head.

"Doesn't Mildred look a treat?" Trudy said. "I get such a kick out of her outfits."

"Me too." Priscilla smiled and waved at Mildred, who had become a good friend. They both shared a love of history.

Mildred sauntered up to the table, skirts swinging. "How are you all? How's the lighthouse museum, Priscilla?" Her advice had been invaluable in helping Priscilla set up several exhibits for lighthouse visitors. A local tour company brought people around.

"The museum is buttoned up until spring," Priscilla said. "They don't do tours in the winter."

Mildred cocked her head. "You have time for a special project, then."

The cousins hooted. "You got her, Mildred," Trudy crowed.

Uncle Hugh gave a throaty chuckle. "She's good at that."

Priscilla sighed, then laughed. She wasn't going to win this fight, so she might as well give in gracefully. "Okay. I'll bite. What do you want me to do?"

Mildred moved a little closer, lowering her voice. "Sheila Weller is donating her mother's papers and photographs to the museum for an exhibit on island farms I'm planning. Apparently she's got tons, well, I hope not literally tons, but a lot." She leaned forward. "And get this. A bunch of them came from the Parker estate. They sold many of their belongings before they tore down the old house."

Priscilla looked at Joan. "Are you thinking what I'm thinking?" Then she looked up at Mildred. "I'd be happy to go through the papers for you. I'll inventory them and you can decide which ones to keep."

Mildred patted Priscilla on the shoulder. "Maybe while helping me with the Weller Farm exhibit, you'll find some clues about that skeleton. Kill two birds with one stone." She spotted someone across the room and waved her hand in greeting, then flitted off.

"That was neatly done," Joan said. She smiled at Priscilla. "I think you'll be spending quite a bit of time at the cranberry farm."

"Let us know if we can help," Trudy said.

"Thanks, I'm sure it will be fine. I enjoy research." Trudy's offer was nice but Priscilla knew that all three of her cousins were busy, especially with the approach of the holiday season.

The bells on the entrance door jingled again. "Hopping place," Trudy said, swiveling in her chair to check on the newcomer. She reached out and grabbed Priscilla's forearm. "You'll never believe who just walked in."

Priscilla looked up. Professor Franklin Mayweather stood in the doorway, every inch the proud intellectual deigning to mingle with mere mortals.

CHAPTER FOUR

As Franklin gazed around the room, Priscilla shrank down in her seat again, with a soft groan. Quite frankly, she didn't like the man, and he had a habit of getting under her skin. His unshakeable belief that he knew best about almost any topic, his condescension, the way he dominated a group . . . even worse, there was the little matter of his unauthorized search for gold on the lighthouse property. That was putting it nicely. The man had literally broken into her house and ripped up her living room floor looking for gold coins. Forgiving and forgetting were two different things.

"Don't look now," Trudy whispered, "but he's coming this way."

Priscilla sank lower in her seat, groaning again when Trudy gave Franklin a friendly little wave. "Did you have to encourage him?"

"He's not so bad," Trudy said with a shrug.

Franklin strode directly toward their table, carrying a mug and a plate. In concession to the weather, he wasn't sporting one of his usual Hawaiian shirts. Today he wore a wool sweater under a tweed jacket with, of course, leather elbow patches. A truly hideous blue, green, and red striped scarf was wound around his neck.

"Good morning, ladies. And gentleman." Franklin nodded at the group. He had the local paper tucked under one arm so he set that and his meal down then reached for a spare chair and swung it around. "Do you mind?" Without waiting for an answer, he pulled up to their table.

"What brings you to the island?" Uncle Hugh asked. He didn't much care for Franklin either, considering him pretentious to the greatest degree. "Shouldn't you be teaching?" He was referring to Franklin's position teaching history at the University of Massachusetts.

Franklin shifted in his seat, making a big deal of unfolding his newspaper. "Yes, well, I have an assistant covering for me until after the Thanksgiving break." He stabbed a finger at the paper. "When I saw this, I had to come home to the island immediately." He scanned their faces with eyes gleaming under lowering brows. "You do realize this is Bitsy Parker."

Although that was Priscilla's theory too, Franklin brought out the contrary in her. "How do you know? The medical examiner hasn't even ruled whether it's a man's or a woman's skeleton."

Franklin scoffed. "Elementary, my dear Priscilla."

Joan gave Priscilla a slight shake of her head while touching her ring finger. This told Priscilla that while they might pump Franklin, they weren't going to reveal anything they suspected—or mention the ring.

"Do tell." Priscilla picked up her mug, gazing at Franklin with wide eyes. "It's so nice to have an expert around."

Gail choked, then pretended to cough. As for Uncle Hugh, he almost fell off his chair.

Franklin cleared his throat. "As I was saying, it's really quite simple. Elizabeth 'Bitsy' Parker vanished in 1932. She was never heard from again, which is really strange, considering she had many friends on the island. Even if she ran away with a paramour, surely she would have written to someone."

"Good point," Trudy said. "No one ever heard a peep?"

"Not a whisper." Franklin shook his head. "I've written several monographs on the Vineyard's prominent families, including the Parkers. Looking at the property records, I realized that where you live, Joan, once belonged to their estate."

"You're right," Joan said. "About half a dozen houses were built on a piece of land they sold before building the new house."

"So, putting two and two together, I've deduced that the skeleton has a very good chance of being Bitsy." He pursed his lips. "I do hope they discover evidence that can date the skeleton."

Priscilla bit her lip hard to prevent herself blurting out about the ring. Joan was also struggling, she could tell. When she could trust herself to speak, she asked, "So you're going to dig into the case based on that assumption?"

Franklin flapped open a paper napkin and laid it on his knee. He took a sip of tea and pronounced it satisfactory. "Not bad for an outpost like this. Back to you, Priscilla. Yes, that's right. I'm going to launch my own investigation into Bitsy's disappearance and death. Then I'll write a book." His eyes glowed with fervor.

"I can see the cover now. *Dr. Franklin Mayweather, best-selling author.*"

Franklin's optimistic assertion rang in Priscilla's head the entire way to the cranberry farm, which was located on the Atlantic side of the island. She couldn't fault him for wanting recognition. Didn't professors have to publish or perish, as the saying went? In addition, he was another experienced voice supporting her and Joan's theory about Bitsy.

But still, it rankled. She was digging into the story from a more altruistic motive, that of laying a victim to rest, not seeking fame or fortune. Though sheer curiosity was also a factor, she admitted.

She enjoyed piecing together the truth from scraps of information, using her intuition and knowledge of people. She didn't want Franklin to interfere, to get there first.

There. She admitted the truth, unbecoming as it was. *Lord, forgive me for my pride…*

A painted wooden sign and an Open flag hanging from a post marked the entrance to the farm. Priscilla drove through fields lined with stone walls. Some had rows of stubble, marking where crops had grown, while other were obviously hay fields. The glitter of water in the distance told her where the cranberry bog lay.

Until she'd moved to New England, Priscilla imagined that cranberries grew in water, but she'd quickly learned the truth. The bogs were flooded at harvest time to make picking easier, since cranberries floated.

The gray, shingled farmhouse and barns were set in a cluster of tall oaks and maples. A parking area near the big barn was filled with vehicles. Customers, no doubt, who had come to buy cranberries for Thanksgiving.

Priscilla found a place at the end, next to a small sedan she recognized. Anne Edwards had arrived safely at the farm, then. Maybe Priscilla would see her today and could check on how she was doing.

Inside the barn, bins of cranberries, winter squash, onions, and potatoes stood on long tables. Racks and shelves held other items, including reproduction cranberry crates, cookbooks, jars of provisions, and themed kitchen gear.

An oven mitt with a cranberry print caught Priscilla's eye. As she took it off the hanger, she reflected on how smart Sheila was to offer gifts in addition to the berries.

"Hi, Priscilla." As though summoned by her thought, Sheila appeared at her side. The short, wiry farmer brought the scent of fresh air and an aura of industry with her. "You talk to Mildred?"

Priscilla held on to the mitt, planning to buy it along with a few pounds of the tart berries. "I ran into her at the bakery this morning, and she told me about your project."

"Good." Sheila, never one to stand still, began rearranging goods on a nearby shelf. "You going to be able to help us out?"

"I'm looking forward to it." Priscilla laughed. "I guess Mildred has figured out I like to do research."

"That's dangerous." Sheila's nod was wise. "Once people know you're good at something, watch out."

Priscilla waved the mitt. "After I do a little shopping in here, I thought I'd start today, if that's convenient for you."

Sheila leaned closer. "Any time is good for me. I'm looking forward to finally fulfilling Mom's wishes. With the farm and all, it's hard to find time."

A middle-aged woman held up a box with wood tines on the bottom. "What's this thing?" she called to Sheila.

"That's a reproduction of a cranberry harvester." Sheila demonstrated the scooping motion needed to use the device. "From when they used to pick the berries by hand."

Priscilla pictured teams of pickers wading through knee-deep water, scooping berries. What backbreaking work.

"You don't do that now?" The woman looked appalled.

"No, we use equipment to pick the berries. Very gently, of course. But we're still much smaller than those big, fully automated operations." Sheila wandered off to help the woman, who had questions about a lot of things.

Priscilla selected a few bags of fresh cranberries, figuring she could freeze the ones she didn't use for sauce. After paying for the fruit and her mitt, she looked around the barn for Sheila. She was almost ready to ask someone, figuring Sheila might be back in the field, when she spotted her—standing at the rear of the barn, talking to Franklin Mayweather.

Her pulse leaped in dismay. *Did he follow me here?* Had he gotten wind of the possible clues hidden among Sheila's family papers? Before she could stop herself, she marched across the barn and interrupted their conversation.

"Hello, again, Franklin," she said. "Twice in one day. I can hardly believe my good fortune."

Both Sheila and Franklin gave her an odd look, probably picking up on her sarcastic tone and wondering why she was on the warpath. Franklin recovered first, drawing himself up to his full height. "I consider myself the fortunate one." He chuckled. "If I didn't know better, I'd think you had followed me here." At her puzzlement, he added, "I'm renting one of Miss Weller's cabins."

Priscilla took a step back in surprise, feeling ashamed of her presumption. *Lord, I really need help with this attitude.* "But...I thought you usually stayed at your uncle's place." The Mayweather mansion was a gorgeous historic home, set on a rise overlooking the Wellers' cranberry bog and the ocean beyond.

Franklin nodded sadly. "I do. But there's a problem with the heating system, so they had to drain the pipes. Hopefully I'll be able to move back there soon, but until then..." He gestured, encompassing the barn and beyond.

"Our cabins are nice," Sheila said. "Cozy. And we'll never say no to winter renters. In summer, we don't have a problem filling them."

"Many places are closed for the season right now," Franklin said. "So staying here is a perfect win-win."

Priscilla felt the tension drain from her shoulders. Franklin's presence was only one of those strange coincidences in life. On such a small island, they were bound to happen more often than, say, in Boston.

"Do you need anything else from me right now?" Sheila asked Franklin.

He patted his pocket. "I've got the key so I should be all set. Good day, ladies." He pivoted on his heel and set off at a brisk pace.

"He's a real gentleman," Sheila said. "I'm glad to have him renting. You should see some of the people we've dealt with." She rolled her eyes.

"I'll bet," Priscilla murmured. She hoisted her bag. "I'm finished shopping, so if you want to get started, I'm ready."

Sheila glanced at her watch. "How do you feel about a tour of the property first? I need to check on the boys right now."

"I'd love that," Priscilla said. "Let me just put this bag in my car first."

A few minutes later they set off on Sheila's all-terrain vehicle. "This property is so big, it'd take me all day to walk around," Sheila shouted over the wind noise.

"Good idea," Priscilla shouted back. She held on tight, hoping she wouldn't get thrown off when they hit bumps. The dirt lane was rutted, with quite a few potholes, and Sheila drove it at high speed.

She slowed by a field where workers were pushing machines across a field of berry plants. "They're dry harvesting, for our fresh berries."

"I didn't know there was more than one method," Priscilla said.

"Two. Wet and dry." Sheila hit the gas and they sped up again.

The next bog had been flooded and was now a sea of red. Bumpers had gathered the berries into an oval area, and three workers wearing waders were pushing them with rakes toward intake equipment. Priscilla recognized two of them, Chowder and Chowder Jr., Uncle Hugh's good friends.

Sheila halted beside the men. "How's it going?" she asked. To Priscilla, she said, "We had a little trouble with the intake pump this morning."

"Not too shabby." A man with gray stubble pushed his hat back, then adjusted it more firmly on his head. "I got it going, as you can see."

Sheila hopped off and examined the machine, a frown on her face. "It still doesn't sound right, Gilbert." Hands on hips, she surveyed the sea of red. "I sure hope we can get these all harvested before it dies on us."

As the former owner of a farm herself, Priscilla could sympathize. How many harvests in Kansas had involved a race against time or weather? Equipment had the unfortunate tendency to act up at the absolute worst times.

Sheila introduced Priscilla to Gilbert Jenks, then continued talking to him about the equipment. Priscilla moved aside and said hello to Chowder and Chowder Jr. "I just saw Uncle Hugh this morning," she said, "at the bakery."

The two men regarded her with identical pale-blue eyes. They were similar in appearance. Both were stocky and strong with gray hair, although Chowder Jr.'s was more salt-and-pepper. "How is the old coot?" Chowder asked. "He had a bee in his bonnet last time I talked to him."

"That's because he's worried about our money, Dad," Chowder Jr. said. "I don't blame him. I read something on a blog about Parker & Warren having some issues."

Priscilla didn't know what startled her more, learning that the old salt Chowder Jr. read blogs, or that the venerable investment firm was experiencing difficulty.

"Gail said that you two are in the investment club with Uncle Hugh?"

"That's right," Chowder said. "He talked us into it. Said it was better to invest than leave all our money in the bank. Banks don't pay much interest nowadays."

"We didn't put in a whole lot," Chowder Jr. said. "For a while we were making money hand over fist, returns were so good."

"Shoulda taken our money out then," Chowder said. "Get while the getting is good, I always say."

Now Priscilla understood Uncle Hugh's distress. He probably felt responsible for his friends' money being at risk.

Sheila made some tweaks to the equipment with a wrench and it began to run more smoothly.

"That's what I'm talking about," Gilbert said with a hoot. "Come on, boys, let's get these berries in the barn."

Sheila watched the men work for a minute, then waved to Priscilla to climb into the all-terrain vehicle. "Sorry about the delay," she said. "But we're at a critical point right now. With things being so tight, we can't afford to lose any of the harvest."

"I hear you," Priscilla said. As they drove back along the track at a slow speed, she told Sheila about the farm she had owned in Kansas with her husband.

"So you know how hard it can be." Sheila stopped the vehicle on a little rise with a good view of the farm's buildings and fields. "But living here is worth it. I love this land."

"It's beautiful," Priscilla said. "Has it been in the family long?"

Sheila smiled. "Only about three hundred years or so. The first Wellers had cows and sheep. Then cranberries started getting popular, so we diversified. Now they're most of what we do."

"Thanks for the tour," Priscilla said. "I'll appreciate the berries even more."

"Any time." With a smile, Sheila pointed the vehicle down the hill.

After parking, they went inside the farmhouse, a colonial furnished in a simple, lived-in style. Sheila showed her around the first floor briefly, allowing Priscilla time to admire family portraits, an antique spinning wheel—from the days of sheep—and the chrome-trimmed cookstove in the kitchen.

"I still use this beast," Sheila said. "We get the wood from our own property, and I never have to worry about the power going out. Plus it heats this part of the house."

"I can tell." Priscilla held her hands out to the warmth radiating from the banked stove. A kettle on top simmered, releasing faint steam. "What a beauty."

"Thanks. I feel connected to my mother and grandmother when I use it." Sheila moved the kettle to a warmer spot. "Want some tea? I've got homemade cranberry peppermint." After Priscilla agreed, she said, "Mom's office is this way."

Sheila led Priscilla toward a room adjoining the kitchen. "I've moved my office upstairs, where my computer is." Her voice became muffled when she went into the room and fumbled for a light string.

After she tugged it to turn the light on, Priscilla gasped. Not at viewing the lovely rolltop desk standing in the middle of the room, but in shock at the sheer volume of boxes, cartons, and crates lining the walls.

Sheila laughed. "What can I say? Mom was a bit of a pack rat." She sauntered over to a crate, picked up a vintage island tourist brochure, then let it fall. "I feel a little bad about this. Maybe I should take the time to go through it myself."

"No, Sheila. You're far too busy right now." Priscilla eyed the collection. "How about setting up a folding table in here? I can sort and repack the items by category as a first step." If it turned out to be overwhelming, she'd call in reinforcements.

"Okay, if you're sure." Sheila waited for Priscilla's nod then went to find a table. Together they set it up in front of the double windows, which overlooked the field behind the barn. At the edge of the trees, Priscilla spotted three small cabins set at a distance from each other.

"Those are the tourist camps, as my parents called them," Sheila said. "It's kind of a nice view from this room, isn't it? Even with the leaves down."

"I think so." Priscilla studied the stacks, trying to decide where to begin. A thrill of anticipation danced through her veins. Who knew what treasures awaited her in this dusty trove?

Sheila moved toward the door. "I'll bring you a pot of tea and cookies. You take cream or sugar?"

"Just a little milk, please," Priscilla said. She hefted the first crate to the table, the one holding the brochure Sheila found. Old tourism publications were one of her favorite browsing pleasures. She loved glimpses of the island's romantic, storied past.

Then she remembered Bitsy Parker, her real reason for being here. If their theory was correct, that story was a tragedy. A beautiful young wife, whose life was cut short in her prime.

Sheila brought a tray and perched it on the other end of the table. "I'll check on you in a little while. Have fun," she added as she slipped out.

The crate contained a hodgepodge, eclectic in content but all from the 1970s. With frequent breaks to sip the comforting yet zippy tea, Priscilla found more brochures, a few town reports, advertising proofs for the farm, letters from customers placing large orders—one Boston store ordered a literal ton of cranberries— and an envelope of family photos. She glanced through this last, smiling at the photo showing a young Sheila with cropped bangs and a toothless grin perched on a tractor with her father. She set that aside to show Sheila, along with the ad that called the cabins, "Cranberry Camps." How delightful. Maybe Sheila could incorporate some of these quaint ideas in her marketing.

To make organizing easier, she created piles containing island materials, farm paperwork, family papers, and miscellaneous. These all went in separate boxes, with Priscilla making lists as she went. She starred the items she thought Mildred might find especially interesting for the museum.

After making it through three or four boxes in good order, once she stopped reading things, she found something promising.

A musty crate held loose papers, several bound record books, and letters. She unfolded a piece of paper on top. A Boston millinery company's logo and address was at the top. The bill was addressed to Mr. Vernon Parker.

She'd found the Parker papers, or at least part of them. Her pulse quickened with excitement as she lifted the crate to the table. She loved the thrill of the chase, but nothing beat the euphoria of the find.

Pausing to gather her thoughts and calm her nerves, she stared out at the bucolic scene beyond the windows.

Smoke was billowing from one of the cabins.

CHAPTER FIVE

Priscilla abandoned the intriguing crate and ran outside, yelling "Fire, fire!" She waved her arms back and forth, attracting attention from startled customers.

"Where's the fire truck?" a little boy with blond curls asked his mother.

Good question. How long would that take? Maybe the farm had other arrangements. She sure hoped so. She and Gary had hundreds of feet of hose and a good strong pump to draw water out of the well fast. They'd needed all that, being miles outside town. There was nothing a farmer dreaded more than a barn fire, which could claim hundreds of thousands of dollars in building, equipment, and livestock.

Sheila burst out of the barn, her short legs churning like pistons. "Fire? Someone say there's a fire?" She looked at the house.

"Not in there," Priscilla said. "In one of the cabins."

"Come on." Sheila jumped into the all-terrain vehicle and started it up. Priscilla barely had time to join her before Sheila set off. "Which one was it?" Sheila shouted.

"The one on the end." After they circuited the barn, Priscilla pointed it out. Smoke was still streaming from the building, but she didn't see any flames. A slender figure was running across the field, her blonde hair gleaming in the sun.

Sheila pressed the gas, making the cart rocket ahead. When they drew closer to the running woman, Priscilla recognized her. It was Anne Edwards, sans wig. And she had a full head of hair. *So why the cover-up?* It didn't make sense.

Anne waved her arms frantically, as if they couldn't see her all alone in the field. When they got close, Sheila braked so hard, Priscilla swore the rear wheels lifted a bit.

"What's on fire?" Sheila barked. Her eyes darted to the cabin. No doubt her approach would depend on the fire's cause. "Did you use the fire extinguisher, like I told you?"

Anne shook her head. "No. I wasn't cooking or anything. It's the woodstove. I was starting a fire and smoke came pouring out."

Understanding dawned. "You didn't open the damper," Priscilla said. The damper let air flow out of the stove and up the chimney. Otherwise it went the other way, into the room. She'd made that mistake herself, back in the day.

"Damper? I didn't know anything about that." Anne chewed at her lower lip. "I'm so sorry."

Sheila laughed. "I'm not. I'm tremendously relieved." She dramatically wiped her forehead. "Whew! Hop on, lady. Let's go fix your fire."

Anne climbed onto the rear seat and they set off, a bit more sedately this time.

By the time they reached the cabin, Franklin Mayweather was standing outside, staring at the smoke. He'd shed the scarf and his jacket and was in his shirtsleeves. "Can I be of assistance?" he asked Sheila.

Sheila looked him up and down with a slight smirk. "Not dressed like that. You'll get all smoky-smelling. Wait here." She trotted toward the house and disappeared inside.

Franklin stared after her in consternation. He started following. "It's not safe—" he called.

"It's all right, Franklin." Priscilla evaded a billow of smoke pushed her way by the breeze. "There isn't a fire. Anne forgot to open the damper."

Franklin turned his attention to Anne. "My, that must have been disconcerting," he said. He stuck out his hand. "I'm Professor Franklin Mayweather. I'm staying in cabin three."

"I'm Anne Edwards." As she shook Franklin's hand, Anne slid her eyes to Priscilla. "And I'm in this one, as you can see."

Something about that glance and Anne's demeanor struck Priscilla as odd, and her habit of wearing a wig over perfectly lovely hair seemed strange as well. But she shrugged off her curiosity, telling herself it was none of her business.

The smoke began to drift out of the chimney and the windows thumped up, one by one. Sheila trotted back outside. "We'll need to let the place air out. Why don't you come back to the house and hang out for a while? Then I'll teach you how to make a fire."

"Thanks again, Sheila," Anne said. "I'm sorry to put you to all this trouble."

"I can show you, Anne," Franklin said. "I'm an expert." He straightened his shirt collar. "In my travels around the world, I learned how to start a fire in the wilderness without a match." He and Anne began to stroll toward the house, while Franklin regaled her with his adventures.

"Hop on," Sheila told Priscilla, shaking her head. "I'll put on the kettle again."

If Priscilla had been forced to listen to Franklin's tales about how brilliant and worldly-wise he was, her blood was what would be boiling. But thankfully she could escape on the buggy with Sheila.

At the house, Priscilla went to the back room while Sheila puttered in the kitchen. Now that the crisis was over, she couldn't wait to look through the crate from the Parker estate.

With laser-like focus, she lifted each item out and examined it. Invoices went in a pile. Normally it would be fun to read about the clothing, shoes, and accessories Bitsy had purchased, or to study the grocery list to see what she'd served for dinner.

Today Priscilla was on a mission to learn what she could about Bitsy's activities in 1932. As she sorted through to the bottom of the box she found several soft leather-covered journals. She struck gold when she opened a navy blue one to discover Bitsy's social calendar for that year.

She sucked in a deep breath, almost afraid she'd misread the date. No, the first entry was dated January 1, 1932. According to the penned entry, Bitsy and her husband had dined, "with the Stevensons, Helen served that chicken dish I like. I asked for the recipe."

What was the final entry? Curious, she skipped ahead and saw that the entries stopped on August 20, 1932, a Saturday, when there had been a dinner party at the Parker house. Priscilla wasn't sure, but she thought a woman might pack her social diary when she ran away. Or maybe not. Perhaps she'd left it behind as a relic belonging to her old life.

Perhaps she'd never left the island at all, and August 20th had been her last day on this earth.

Priscilla hugged the book to her chest, feeling a spark of connection to a woman who had lived almost ninety years ago. She prayed they'd find something in these pages to lead them to the truth about Bitsy, no matter how hard it was to hear.

"Hi," said a voice in the doorway. "I hope I'm not interrupting."

She turned to see Anne leaning against the jamb holding a mug of tea, a tentative smile on her face. "Come in," Priscilla said. "I'm just about done for the day." She set the journal on the table. Perhaps Sheila would let her take it home, where she could study it at leisure. She couldn't wait to show Joan.

Anne drifted closer. "What are you doing?" she asked.

Priscilla began to pack the Parker papers into the crate. "I'm inventorying historical papers for the museum in town. Sheila is donating them."

"Huh. Historical research isn't my forte." She picked up a farm brochure illustrated with cute cartoon cranberries and smiled. "But it looks like it might be fun."

"It can be," Priscilla said. "You learn a lot about how life used to be. Since I moved to the island, I've enjoyed researching my family history."

Anne leaned against the desk. "I take it they've been here a while."

Priscilla smiled. "You could say that." Never one to brag about her venerable family history, she deflected the discussion. "Sheila's family has been on this farm since the 1700s. Hopefully we'll find some really great original documents in those boxes."

Anne eyed the stacks with a laugh. "Happy hunting. That looks like three hundred years' worth of stuff right there."

"No kidding." Priscilla picked up the crate and placed it by itself on the floor, to signal that it concerned the Parker family, not the Wellers. She'd go through the boxes and crates next time and find the rest of the Parker items.

Anne cleared her throat. "Um, Priscilla? I want to apologize for something."

Priscilla let go of the crate and straightened. "For what?" She honestly couldn't figure out what Anne was talking about.

Anne sipped her tea, her eyes not meeting Priscilla's gaze. "For taking off that way the other night. It was rude." She twisted her lips in a grimace. "But I was nervous about getting here. I thought I'd better get going before they shut the roads down or something."

"We didn't think a thing of it. That was a smart move on your part. I was stranded at Joan's all night." Priscilla didn't mention the skeleton, not wanting to get into it unless Anne asked. She hadn't seen her leave, so she didn't know if Anne had witnessed the discovery.

Anne sighed. "Great. I'm glad you're not mad." She paced around the room, peering at the out-of-date calendars on the wall. "There is another thing."

Priscilla could guess what was coming next. She put up a hand. "You don't owe me an explanation."

"But I want to tell you." Anne's expression was pleading. "I'm running away from...from my husband. I wore a disguise so no one would recognize me."

Alarm tingled down Priscilla's spine. "He's from the island? Or does he have friends or relatives here?" She was afraid for Anne's safety. She knew how dangerous some spouses could be.

Biting her lip, Anne shook her head, her loose hair swaying. "No to both questions, thank goodness. I needed it on the mainland and ferry."

Questions rose in Priscilla's mind but she held them back, telling herself that Anne's marital woes were none of her business. But she did wonder why she'd come to the island. Maybe her husband didn't have a connection here, but did she?

"I'm glad you're okay," Priscilla finally said. "And if you need any help, any time of the day or night, please call me." She wrote down her numbers on a scrap of paper and handed it to Anne. "Of course you can always rely on Sheila too."

"I'm sure I can. She's a peach." Anne tucked the paper into her pocket. "And there's Franklin too, don't forget."

Priscilla coughed to cover her exclamation of disbelief. Well, she supposed the view changed depending on one's vantage point. "I suppose I'd better get going," she said, peering out the window. "It's getting dark already." She gathered her bag and the social diary, planning to ask Sheila if she could take it.

"Yes, the days are short this time of year." Anne stood near the window, looking out over the field, hazy with twilight. "Oh, how I long for spring. And winter hasn't even begun."

The young woman accompanied Priscilla into the kitchen, where they parted ways. Priscilla headed out into the chilly evening. The barn parking lot was empty, but bright lights still shone inside. She found Sheila tidying up the merchandise with a brown and tan basset hound at her heels, tags jingling with every movement.

Priscilla bent to pet his silky head. "What a lovely dog." In response, he gazed up at her with big, droopy eyes.

"That's Bosco," Sheila said. "I'm taking care of him for a friend. She just dropped him off." She moved to the cash register. "Done for the day?"

"I am," Priscilla said. "But I made some good progress." She showed Sheila the journal. "I'd like to borrow this, if I may. I want to study the entries more closely."

Sheila, busy punching buttons on the register, shrugged. "Fine with me. I know you'll take good care of it." She stopped working and gazed into the distance. Then she darted off, returning with a box of the tea Priscilla had been drinking. She pushed it into Priscilla's hand. "Please, take this. It's not much, but you're such a great help."

Priscilla gladly popped the tea into her bag. "Thanks. It's really excellent. I'll enjoy it while I'm reading the journal."

Bosco put his head back and howled, making the women jump.

Sheila put a hand to her chest. "That always startles me, every time I hear it."

The dog trotted toward the open barn door, focused on something they couldn't see. Outside, he uttered a few deep barks.

"Is something out there?" Priscilla asked. "A deer or another wild animal?"

"Maybe." Sheila's face creased with a frown. "I'd better go check. We've had some problems with raccoons getting into the trash."

Priscilla went outside with Sheila. Bosco stood on the fringe of the woods, still barking. A man's figure moved through the trees, and despite the shadows, Priscilla saw that he was dressed in hunter's cap and vest and carried a rifle.

"No hunting on this land," Sheila shouted. "Didn't you see the signs? We're posted, no hunting."

In answer, he gave her a quick salute and kept walking. Within minutes, he melted into the trees. The three of them watched him go.

All the way home, the blue journal taunted Priscilla from its seat on the passenger side. Did it hold the answers to Bitsy Parker's disappearance? Priscilla was almost afraid to find out.

It might not tell them anything at all.

Priscilla was walking into the house, Jake going ballistic at her return, when the landline rang. Joan. "Hey there, cousin," Priscilla said, slipping out of her coat. "I was going to call you. I have news."

"That was my line," Joan said with a laugh. "You first."

"Let me feed Jake, and then we'll get down to business." They made chitchat while Priscilla filled a bowl with kibble. Then while Jake crunched away, content, Priscilla sank into a chair at the kitchen table. From here, she could watch the sweep of the lighthouse beam across the night bay.

"You said me first?" Priscilla asked. "Well, I went to the farm today to start sorting those papers. And I found a crate of stuff from the Parkers, including Bitsy's social diary for 1932."

Joan gasped with delight. "That is awesome. Have you looked through it yet?"

"No, I haven't had a chance." Priscilla had an idea. "And I'm not going to do it without you. Why don't you come over tonight? I've got beef stew and biscuits." She got up and checked the slow cooker, where the stew was simmering.

"That sounds like a plan. I'll bring dessert."

"So what's your news?" Priscilla fished a spoon out of a drawer and tasted the gravy. *Needs a little more salt.* She salted the stew and stirred with the ladle.

"I got a call from the medical examiner's office," Joan said. "They were kind enough to tell me that the skeleton is a female, aged between twenty and thirty years." Joan gulped audibly and her voice thickened. "Oh, Priscilla. It has to be her. Poor Bitsy, lying under my tree all these years."

Priscilla blinked back tears, marveling that she and her cousin could feel grief for a woman they'd never known. "We'll find out what happened, Joan. It's something we can do for her."

"And we'll repair her reputation," Joan said. "We'll spread the news far and wide that Bitsy Parker was not an adulterous woman."

"Amen to that," Priscilla said. "Now get in your car and drive over. This stew is just about done." She said goodbye and pulled out a mixing bowl. The biscuits would be out of the oven and piping hot when Joan arrived.

Joan's timing was perfect, and Priscilla was putting the biscuits in a cloth-lined basket when she knocked on the door. "Come in," Priscilla called.

Joan entered, giving Jake his due, and shed her outwear. She noticed the table set up in front of the fireplace. Candlelight flickered on the pottery bowls and glasses placed on the dark green tablecloth.

"Oh, this is nice." Holding her hands out to the flames, Joan smiled at Priscilla. "I'll have to come over more often."

"Anytime," Priscilla said. She set a covered bowl of stew on the table along with the basket of biscuits. A pitcher of ice water and butter waited. "Have a seat."

Joan took the other chair, and after they settled in, Priscilla said grace. Then she pulled the lid off the tureen and turned the ladle over to Joan. "Help yourself."

The clock on the mantel struck the hour. In the middle of buttering a biscuit, Joan glanced up. "Maybe we should turn on the news. There might be a story about Bitsy."

Priscilla turned on the television, keeping the volume muted so they could eat in peace.

The headline story caught her eye. "Local investment firm Parker & Warren under investigation," read text on the screen. She turned it up. "Look, Joan. Chowder Jr. told me today this is the firm Uncle Hugh and the others invested with."

"Uh-oh." Joan swiveled in her chair. "That's the company Jordan works for."

The pair spooned up stew while learning about the joint Federal Bureau of Investigation and Securities and Exchange Commission investigation into possible improprieties at the well-established company.

The news gave Priscilla pause, but it was the video they ran with the story that truly surprised her. It showed a couple, an older man and a young woman, walking down granite steps. "Partner Dale Parker was one of those questioned," the newscaster said. She didn't recognize Dale, but the woman beside him, labeled as his niece Whitney Parker, looked awfully familiar. Priscilla knew her as Anne Edwards.

CHAPTER SIX

That's her," Priscilla shouted. "Anne Edwards is Whitney Parker." The truth came crashing in like the tide. Whitney Parker had come to Martha's Vineyard in disguise, hoping to elude the press and whoever else wanted to talk to her. No doubt the story of an abusive husband was pure fiction.

Priscilla was angry. She didn't care to be lied to, no matter what the reason was. Although she couldn't blame Whitney for not telling her she was under investigation by the Feds. That would be a tough thing to admit.

All this flashed through her head in the time it took for Joan to set down her spoon and say, "What are you talking about?" The television program had moved on, and a car advertisement blared.

Priscilla muted it, then turned it off all together. "Remember the young woman who came to your house during the storm?"

"Of course. Anne." Joan looked totally puzzled.

"No, she told us Anne was her name. She's actually Whitney Parker." Priscilla pointed at the blank television set. "She was in that video at the end of that story about Parker & Warren."

"So that's what you meant. But it didn't make sense then and it doesn't now." Joan picked up a biscuit and split it in half. She picked up her knife and cut into the butter.

Priscilla was all worked up. She knew she was right, but how could she convince Joan? She pulled out her phone and searched online for a picture of Whitney Parker. "Take a good look. See her hairstyle? I saw Anne without her wig at the farm, and she looked just like that."

Joan studied the picture while chewing on the biscuit. She handed the phone back. "I didn't notice Anne wearing a wig. But I'll take your word for it."

Priscilla set the phone on the tablecloth. "Good. I noticed it that night. But I thought she had cancer or something. Then today I saw she has long blonde hair. She tried to tell me she was running away from her husband, hence the wig."

"Okay. Say you're right. What are you going to do?" Joan dipped her spoon into the stew. "This is so good, I want seconds."

"Thanks. Mom's recipe." Priscilla considered Joan's question. What should she do? She could call the FBI, but that seemed a little harsh. She didn't even know Anne's, er, Whitney's side of the story. Although she wasn't exactly honest, and she might well deny the truth. "When I go out to the farm tomorrow, I'll talk to her. Then I'll go from there."

"Sounds good." Joan reached for the ladle, holding up her bowl. "So tell me, what did you find at the farm? You were pretty excited on the phone."

"After we finish, I'll show you." Priscilla absently ate the rest of her dinner, more out of duty than pleasure. Her mind was consumed with questions about Whitney Parker.

After they cleared the dishes and Joan helped Priscilla load the dishwasher, they sat down at the table again to look at the journal. Priscilla let Joan browse through it, the way she had. Naturally she leafed through and stopped at the last entry.

"Hmm. It says they had a dinner party. The guests included Ambrose, Lulu, Roger, and Helen. Do you think she was killed that night?"

"Maybe," Priscilla said. "She might have made the note before she was killed and then the party never happened."

"They had a menu of 'cold meats, salads, and broiled seafood,'" Joan said. "I know we're on a mission in looking through this, but it's fascinating. Like a time machine."

"I know," Priscilla said. "That's why I love research. It's a window to the past, which often seems romantic and colorful from this viewpoint."

Joan unfolded a piece of newsprint tucked into the book. "Well, the clothes were prettier, no doubt about it."

The yellowed paper depicted "summer frocks on sale" at one of the island boutiques. Priscilla sighed. "Sometimes I wish women still dressed like this." She pictured herself swishing around in an eyelet lace dress that grazed her knees.

Joan gently leafed through the book. "I see a lot of A's in here. Without any notation, which I think is very telling." She showed Priscilla a week's worth of entries. "See? This says 'lunch at the club, Edith' and 'golf with Vernon,' but this just says 'A.'"

Priscilla's heart sank. Had Bitsy been having an affair after all? "And look, it's during the week."

"What difference does that make?" Joan tilted her head.

"Because I'll bet Vernon was in Boston at the firm. Husbands used to come out only on the weekends, most of the summer. I remember reading about that in a history of the island. Most summer resorts were like that. Newport, Bar Harbor."

"Do you think A is Ambrose?" Joan asked. "That would be pretty bold, having your lover come to a dinner party your husband was hosting."

"Arthur, Alfred, Albert, Amos..." Priscilla listed all the old-fashioned names beginning with *A* that she could think of off the top of her head. "He could be one of those."

Joan laughed. "Fashions in names sure have changed. I couldn't imagine choosing one of those nowadays for a baby boy."

"Ambrose is the most old-fashioned of all." Priscilla traced a finger on the wood grain of the table, head propped on her hand. "We're going to have to do a lot more digging. Hopefully the boxes at the farm will have more of Bitsy's papers. Otherwise we'll have to widen our search."

"What's the first information you want to look for?" Joan asked.

Priscilla thought about it for a minute. "I think a list of the people closest to her, with their full names. Friends, relatives, even the employees in the house. Then we can track their lives. If Ambrose ended up dying at eighty in Boston, then he probably didn't run away with Bitsy. Not that she ran away, but you see where I'm going with this."

"I do see. Point me in the right direction, and I'll help," Joan said. "I feel a responsibility to learn the truth."

"So do I." Priscilla thought of something that made her smile. "Maybe you can help me figure out how to keep Franklin at bay. You'll never believe it. He's staying at the farm, in one of the cabins. His uncle's house is being renovated, apparently."

Joan gasped. "You're kidding. Does he know about this?" She tapped the journal.

"Not yet. And I sure hope he doesn't get wind of the fact that Sheila has Parker papers at her house. Otherwise he'll beat us to the punch for sure."

The next morning Priscilla experimented with cranberry sauce recipes before heading over to the farm. The cookbook she'd borrowed from Joan had a slew of concoctions to choose from— whole berry, jelly, with additives or without. Spiced, plain, the options were endless.

She selected two recipes, a sauce with blueberries and one with jalapeño peppers. That sounded really different. While she was slicing berries, one by one, her cell phone rang. Gerald.

"Hello, stranger," she said, a lilt in her voice. She hadn't seen him since he'd stopped by Joan's house after the storm. They usually ran into each other at the bakery.

"I know, I know," he said. "The aftermath of the storm has been keeping me busy. I've been volunteering with tree cleanup crews after working full shifts with the Guard."

What a nice man Gerald is. "I love that about the island," she said, holding the phone against her ear with her shoulder while she continued to chop. "Everyone is so neighborly, pitching in to help out."

"True, that. Anyway, I'm going to be driving past your place in a few minutes. I thought I might pop in, if that's okay."

"Sure thing. You can be my cranberry sauce tester."

"Sounds good. See you in a few. I have muffins."

Smiling, Priscilla put on a fresh pot of coffee. She so enjoyed having Gerald in her life. Their relationship had the perfect blend of friendship and that little something extra, not that she was ready to fan any embers into big flames yet.

A few minutes later, Gerald knocked on the door. Jake barked, racing Priscilla to be the first to greet him. "It's a beauty of a day but a bit nippy," he said, handing Priscilla the bag of muffins and sliding out of his coat. His nose and ears were pink with cold. He gave Jake a good neck and head rub, making the dog's tags jingle.

"Except for letting Jake out for his business, I've been enjoying it from in here," Priscilla said, waiting for him to hang up his coat. "Come on in. Coffee's ready."

Gerald was comfortable enough that he found a mug and poured coffee for himself. He carried the cup over to the table and watched her work while he enjoyed the warm drink. Jake slid under the table and lay down to supervise from there.

"Entries for the contest?" Gerald guessed.

"Yes." Priscilla divided the sliced berries into two pots. "And if I like one in particular, I'll make it for Thanksgiving too." She added the other ingredients to both and set them on the stove to cook. Then she poured a fresh cup of coffee and put the muffins on a plate.

They sat at the kitchen table, eating and gazing out into a chilly blue-sky day. The waves racing toward shore were crested with white, an indication of the high wind.

"Did you hear the news about the skeleton?" Priscilla asked. "It's a woman, between twenty and thirty years old."

Gerald's hazel eyes shone green in the brilliant sunlight. "So it's Bitsy, then."

"There's nothing conclusive yet, but it looks that way." Priscilla broke off a piece of muffin. How thoughtful of Gerald to bring her favorite: Candy's cranberry-orange. "Joan and I are determined to figure out what happened to her."

"That's a real challenge," Gerald said, admiration in his voice. "How are you going about it?"

Priscilla showed him the social diary. "We're hoping there are more clues in the papers at the farm. The ring was our first big clue, and of course there's the cuff link too."

"Oh yes, the cuff link." Gerald appeared fascinated.

Priscilla had taken a picture on her phone, and she showed it to him to refresh his memory. "It looks like the right period."

He studied the photograph. "It reminds me of cuff links my grandfather had, so I'd say yes. Kind of art deco."

Priscilla took her phone back. "I wonder if anything else is out there. Or if we'll reach a dead end."

"Finding her papers is a great step," Gerald said. "Perhaps you can piece together her final days."

The cranberries were bubbling and releasing delicious aromas, so Priscilla got up to stir them. "I hope so. We may never be able to prove who killed her, but we'll give it a shot." She lowered the heat on both burners. "Hopefully Franklin won't get in the way too much."

Gerald cocked a brow. "Franklin Mayweather? What's he doing here?" Gerald was well aware of Priscilla's uncomfortable history with the professor.

Priscilla grabbed the carafe and refilled both coffee mugs. "I'm not sure why he's here in general, since school isn't out yet, but he's on Bitsy's trail. He thinks he can get a book out of it." She snorted. "And guess what? He's staying at the farm."

Gerald paused in the middle of raising his cup to his lips. "Really? Does he know about the papers?"

"I hope not. He said his uncle's house was being renovated. And Sheila rents her cabins all year round."

"Coincidence, then." He set his cup down and picked up his muffin. "Back to Bitsy. Her story does seem like a good topic for a book. True crime is big."

"Sure, I can understand the appeal, but I don't want him taking over. He'll probably take all the credit for our hard work." Priscilla knew her pride was getting the better of her again. It just didn't seem fair for him to swoop in and scoop them. She sighed. "I'm sorry, I know that's not the nicest thing to say."

"Well, like they say, keep your friends close—"

"And your enemies closer." Priscilla nodded glumly. She had a sinking feeling her enemy was going to be clinging a little too close for comfort.

Later that day, the truth of Priscilla's own words became apparent much sooner than she wished. She and Gerald had tasted the cranberry sauces, both agreeing that the one with blueberry was the stronger contender. The spicy one was good, but a little unusual for the staunchly traditional judges. After he left, Priscilla had packed her tote and drove over to the cranberry farm.

In the office, everything was as she left it. With a leap of her heart, she unpacked the Parker papers again, eager to spend some time carefully going through them. Perhaps she would find additional materials relevant to Bitsy's case. At the bottom of the crate, a small, square, thick book underneath the journals attracted her attention.

It was a photo album. She sank into the chair behind the rolltop desk and began to look through the thick black paper pages. The photographs were black-and-white, of course, held to the pages with little black triangles. Priscilla's own baby pictures had been secured in an album the same way.

The first photograph was of the Parker cottage, a massive shingled and turreted affair. Lawns and flower gardens surrounded it. Priscilla recognized hollyhocks, which looked charming against the old-fashioned building.

The next photograph was a formal portrait of Bitsy and Vernon. Bitsy was seated, dressed in a frothy, square-necked frock. The famous ring adorned her hand, clasped with the other in her lap. Vernon stood behind her, resting his right hand on her shoulder. Cuff links shone in his white shirt cuffs.

Were they like the one Joan had found? Priscilla brought the picture closer to her eyes, wishing for a magnifying glass—

"Hi there. Find anything interesting?" An all-too-familiar voice made Priscilla jump.

Oh no. Franklin. Instinctively Priscilla closed the book and folded both hands over it. "Hi, Franklin. This is only my second day." Could he hear the shrillness in her voice? She always sounded like that when she was evading a question.

Franklin went to the table, where Bitsy's papers were laid out. He reached down and picked one up. "What's this we have here?"

She shot up out of the chair. Then she remembered the photo album. She covertly popped it into her tote before joining him.

"Please don't touch anything." At his start of surprise, she added, "Yet. Mildred has entrusted me with cataloguing these papers, so I'd like a chance to do that first."

Still holding the bill from a jewelry store—oh did she want to study that—he straightened, giving her what she privately called his pompous face. "I assure you, dear lady, I'm an expert in handling rare papers. I'd be glad to help you with your task." He gestured at the room full of potential archival material. "There's far too much here for one person to handle without exhaustion."

Priscilla had thought that very thing herself, but she wasn't about to admit it. "Oh, I'm fine. I'll be making a list of everything that's here. And then Mildred will determine what's valuable or of interest."

He bent his head and read the paper. "One pair of gold cuff links, with onyx and diamond inlay..." He held it up to the light and squinted at it. "They were quite pricey, especially for the day. Useful for determining provenance and potential value." He gave her a sly grin. "You just proved my point, you know. Everything here is probably of value to someone."

The man was incredibly and totally infuriating. Priscilla inwardly huffed in frustration, knowing she'd only succeeded in making him more eager to barge into her project.

"Did I tell you my theory about Bitsy Parker?" he asked. "You did hear they determined the skeleton was a woman of her age? Of course, you would have, she was found on Joan's property, after all." Franklin paused for a quick breath. "I think Ambrose Allen killed her. That's the theory I'm building my book around."

Ambrose has a last name. Thank you, Franklin. That was her first thought. The second was, *What on earth is he talking about?* "You think Ambrose killed her? Don't you think Vernon is the more likely candidate? They say it's usually someone close to the victim."

He gave her that sly smile again. "Who's to say Ambrose wasn't close to her? After all, the rumor was that Ambrose and Bitsy ran away together."

CHAPTER SEVEN

His words hit Priscilla square in the chest, and for a moment she couldn't utter a word. She had been so certain the villain was Bitsy's husband, due to the cuff link and because, quite frankly, she didn't like his face. He didn't look nice, and he was far too self-satisfied. Of course, she hadn't seen Ambrose yet, to compare.

Priscilla attempted a laugh, which sounded as false to her ears as her evasion had earlier. "I'm sure that's as likely an explanation as any other right now, Franklin." She moved toward the table, forcing him to step back. Then, remembering her conversation with Joan about the possibility of an affair between Ambrose and Bitsy, her conscience smote her. Shouldn't she tell Franklin he might not be too far off the mark?

But before she could choke out the first words, his phone rang. He pulled it out of his pocket. "I'd better take this." He sidled out of the room, phone already to his ear.

Humming under her breath and excited to begin, Priscilla retrieved the photo album from her bag and opened it to the page where she left off.

The next photograph was of a group lounging on the Parker mansion porch. Priscilla foraged in the desk drawer and found a magnifying glass to study the tiny faces. Bitsy, or whoever had put the album together, had thoughtfully labeled the people.

Ambrose Allen was tall and dignified, with handsome, regular features. He leaned against the porch railing next to a pretty blonde woman. Her name was Mabel Higgins. Vernon's second wife, maybe? Her name had been Mabel, Priscilla remembered from Joan's history book. The final couple on the porch was Helen and Roger Stephenson, most likely the guests of the dinner party Bitsy mentioned in her diary. Helen was short and somewhat stout, as was her husband.

Priscilla set the magnifying glass down, her thoughts captured by this glimpse into the past. Now when she read the diary, she would be able to imagine Bitsy and her friends.

The house was beautiful too, a classic so-called summer cottage. It naturally required a full roster of employees, like the man working in the flower bed below the porch, and the woman holding a tray in the doorway. Had the photographer meant to capture her or had she stepped out, only to realize she was intruding?

Priscilla picked up the magnifying glass again and examined the woman's face. She squinted. She resembled Sheila—something about her broad cheekbones and pert nose.

She flipped back to the picture she was looking at when Franklin interrupted her, and used the magnifying glass to examine Vernon's cuff links. Although the enlarged image was fuzzy, she was almost certain that the cuff links he was wearing matched the one Joan had found.

Sheila popped her head into the room, Bosco behind her. "I just put a pot of coffee on, if you want a cup."

"I'd love one," Priscilla said. She gestured for Sheila to come over. "Look at the photo album I found. It's fascinating." She turned back to the beginning and leafed through.

"Wow," Sheila said. "I can see why you like doing research. It's fun to see the clothes and hairstyles from a different era."

Priscilla pointed to the maid. "You know what's strange? That woman looks like you."

Sheila smiled. "That's because it's my grandmother, Gladys. She used to work for the Parkers. I think that's why Mother was so interested in the estate sale."

"That makes sense." Priscilla pushed her chair back and stood. She would grab a cup of coffee and keep going.

The fragrant hot beverage close to hand and Bosco resting at her feet, Priscilla sorted through the rest of the Parker papers from the crate. She found a number of bills, running the gamut from groceries to home furnishings to lengths of cloth. A brown book appeared to be a ledger, with monthly expenditures logged and totaled.

How fascinating to a student of household history. She put the ledger in her bag, planning to take it home for further study, as well as the photo album. Perhaps she could make copies of relevant photographs and papers, sort of like creating her own murder book. She chuckled to herself at the idea.

Her shoulders were aching from bending over, so Priscilla took a break. Picking up her coffee, she walked to the window and gazed out at the field.

Whitney Parker, formerly known as Anne Edwards, was striding across the field toward her cabin. She wore a red sweater, a pair of jeans, and leather boots. The unflattering wig was back on her head.

Without conscious thought, Priscilla set her coffee on the windowsill. She slipped on her jacket and left the house. She was going to have a little talk with the runaway financial planner. Bosco came along for the journey, ears flopping and tags clinking.

She caught up with the young woman at the front door, where she was digging out her key. "Good morning, Miss Edwards. Or should I say, Miss Parker?"

Stark fear flashed over Whitney's features, and for a moment Priscilla regretted her flippancy. Something was very wrong here, she had no doubt.

Whitney finally managed to turn the key in the lock. "You'd better come in," she said, leading the way.

The cabin was warm and cozy. Whitney checked the stove, then stood, arms folded across her chest. "How did you find out?"

"I saw you on the news," Priscilla said. "After seeing you without that wig, I recognized you."

Whitney turned her back and stared out the picture window overlooking the woods. "That's what I was afraid of, after that day when the stove was smoking. I've been really careful to wear it every time I go out in public." Her laugh was bitter. "It only took one mistake."

"One emergency, you mean," Priscilla said. "Don't beat yourself up over it." She lowered her voice, trying to reassure the frightened young woman. "I haven't told anyone. Well, except Joan. You remember her. She won't tell anyone either."

Whitney spun around, deep fear etching her features again. "Do you promise?" She stepped toward Priscilla, a hand extended in entreaty. "It's a matter of life and death."

"Life and death?" Priscilla couldn't hold back a laugh. "You mean some angry investors might try to kill you?" She was trying to inject a little levity into the tense situation but her joke fell horribly flat.

"I'm serious," Whitney said. She rubbed her arms. "I'm in big trouble."

Priscilla perched on the arm of the sofa. "I know. Maybe you should turn yourself in. It will go better for you if you do." She was no legal expert, but even she knew that cooperation often meant more lenient sentences.

Whitney shook her head. "You don't get it. I can't go to the Feds. Dalton Rogers, one of the investigators, is corrupt, and others might be too."

Priscilla considered this. "You can't turn him in to higher-ups?"

"No. He's threatened my life if I try that." She shuddered. "Why do you suppose I'm hiding here?" In a sudden movement, she darted to her handbag and turned the contents out onto the sofa. She picked up a cell phone and swiped at the screen, putting it on speaker mode. "Listen to this."

Priscilla was listening to a voice mail, she realized. The sound was bad, the male voice crackling yet robotic. "You won't get away from me, Whitney." He laughed. "I'll find you...you can count on it." His voice was an eerie singsong.

"That was creepy." Priscilla's stomach was churning with fear. "What does he want from you?"

Whitney pulled a chain out from under her sweater. Attached to it was an oblong object. "I have data from the firm. He wants it."

"What's in the files?" Priscilla asked.

"Proof of criminal activity." Whitney's expression was bleak. "But if I can't trust a federal investigator with it, who *can* I trust?"

Priscilla didn't have a good answer for Whitney. Maybe A.J. could help, although she didn't want to risk Whitney's life by making a rash move.

The young woman put a hand on Priscilla's arm, her expression pleading. "Please keep my secret. Don't tell anyone I'm here, okay?"

"I won't." Then Priscilla remembered. "Anyone else, that is. Remember, I did mention you to Joan."

Whitney considered this. "I trust Joan. It's only fair she know the truth, since I barged in on you the other night. You both were so kind and helpful."

"We try." Priscilla glanced toward the farmhouse. "I really better get back to work."

"Do you need help?" At Priscilla's surprised glance, Whitney said, "I saw the heap of papers in that room. I don't have much to do right now besides worry, so you'll be doing me a favor." When Priscilla didn't reply, she added, "I'm really good at organizing."

"In that case," Priscilla said with a laugh, "help away. There is one condition, though. I'm working on a secret project." *Involving*

Whitney's family. It was probably past time to get her involved in the search for the truth.

The next morning, Priscilla was a few minutes late arriving at Faith Fellowship Church, and she had to squeeze into a space between two pickup trucks, one already sporting a plow. A grumble almost escaped, but then she remembered to be grateful that so many people were making the effort to attend worship services.

Everyone was already inside instead of lingering on the veranda, with its stately white columns, to chat. Priscilla quietly opened the tall door, careful not to let it bang shut. In the tiny vestibule, she saw that the service was starting.

To the strains of organ music, she slipped inside, scanning the pews for a seat. Gerald was seated in the last row, and he turned to give her a smile of welcome. He patted the pew next to him, so she hurried to slide in.

They smiled at each other in greeting, then Priscilla reached for the bulletin to look up the day's verses. She liked to read along.

The chosen Bible reading struck her with its truth. Daniel 2:22: "He reveals deep and hidden things; he knows what lies in darkness, and light dwells with him." Goose bumps rose on Priscilla's arms. Oh, how she loved it when God spoke to her so clearly. This verse applied perfectly to both situations she was facing. She said a quick prayer that the truth of Bitsy's death and Whitney's situation would both be revealed, in the proper way and with God's perfect timing.

She set the bulletin aside and rose to sing, her voice mingling with Gerald's as they proclaimed their joy in dwelling in the Lord's house.

After the service, they lingered to talk. As she and Gerald walked down the church steps afterwards, Priscilla told Gerald a little about her progress on the Bitsy project. By then, Gail and Uncle Hugh had made their way outside and joined them.

"Did you hear about Franklin's talk this afternoon?" Gail asked.

"No, I didn't. What's it about?" But Priscilla had a sinking feeling that she knew. Franklin had thankfully made himself scarce since their encounter in the farmhouse, but she should have known he was up to something. No news was definitely not good news when it came to the crafty professor.

"He's outlining his theory about Bitsy's murder," Gail said. "Two p.m. at the library. Want to have lunch at my house first? Then we can all go together." She looked at Gerald, still standing there. "You too, Gerald. You're welcome to come along."

"I appreciate the offer, but I'm having Sunday dinner with my daughter and her family." He looked at his watch. "And I'd better get going. Good day, all."

The trio called goodbyes. "We're having tomato soup and grilled cheese sandwiches, if that's any incentive," Uncle Hugh told Priscilla. "My favorite lunch."

"One of mine too," Priscilla said with a laugh. Uncle Hugh was so endearing, almost childlike at times. "Sure, I appreciate the offer. And I can't wait to hear what Franklin has to say."

Priscilla followed Gail and Uncle Hugh in her own vehicle. Naturally her thoughts were consumed with Franklin's latest stunt for the entire drive. He was obviously trying to build buzz for his book before he'd written it. They didn't have official confirmation that the skeleton was Bitsy. Oh my, would he have egg on his face if it turned out to be someone else.

But in her heart, Priscilla knew he was right. The bones belonged to the socialite.

Gail and Uncle Hugh lived in a cozy cottage on a quiet side street. Priscilla pulled into the driveway and parked beside Gail's car, then got out and followed them through the breezeway between the garage and kitchen. Uncle Hugh was a little slow, of course, but he finally achieved the two steps and entered the house.

"Make yourself at home," Gail said, slipping off her coat and shoes. Priscilla did the same. After shedding outerwear, Uncle Hugh moved straight to his recliner, where he put a sports channel on, keeping the volume low.

"What can I do to help?" Priscilla asked. She peeked out the window overlooking the porch and backyard. Gail had lots of feeders up, and birds were darting in to feed, joined by squirrels foraging on the ground. "You have a lot of squirrels," she commented.

"Tell me about it." Gail opened the refrigerator. "I've given up on trying to keep them out of the feeders. Did I tell you about the guaranteed squirrel-proof one?"

While Priscilla put together sandwiches and Gail opened two cans of soup, Gail regaled Priscilla with the story. A wily little red squirrel had managed to get the supposedly tamper-proof lid off and was inside the feeder headfirst, eating the seeds.

"That is too funny," Priscilla said. "Where there's a will, there's a way." She cut a knob of butter and dropped it onto the hot pan.

Gail nudged her out of the way. "I'll take over here. Want to put on a pot of coffee?"

Priscilla did that, then set the table by the window, laying out plates, bowls, and mugs. She kept an amused eye on the squirrels exhibiting acrobatic ability as they leaped toward the feeders. They had trouble staying on, but their antics resulted in seeds falling to the ground. Those little creatures could teach humans a lesson about persistence and ingenuity.

Uncle Hugh shuffled into the kitchen, lured by the aroma of melting cheese and butter. "Lunch ready?"

"Almost," Gail said, flipping the golden-brown sandwiches. "Why don't you have a seat?"

He lowered himself to his usual seat with a sigh, causing Priscilla to look over in concern. "Are you feeling okay, Uncle Hugh?"

His answer was a snort. "Did you happen to see the news the other night? They're investigating my investment firm." He added sugar to the cup of coffee Priscilla poured him and stirred vigorously. "We won't be getting anything out of them."

Priscilla's heart sank. "Your particular fund is in trouble?" She wasn't quite sure how the financial world worked, but she'd been holding out hope that Uncle Hugh would be okay.

"Yep. Just about everything at Parker & Warren is messed up." His brows drew into a scowl. "I didn't put tons into it, but I feel really bad for my friends. Chowder and Chowder Jr. invested 'cause of what I told them. Gilbert Jenks too."

Gail put a platter of sandwiches on the table, then filled the bowls with soup. "Eat while it's hot," she said. "Priscilla, want to say grace?"

"Sure." Priscilla settled in a chair and unfolded a napkin on her lap. Once Gail and Uncle Hugh were ready, she said a short, simple prayer of thanks for the meal and the company. Then she included an addendum. "Lord, we ask that You would restore what the locust has eaten to Uncle Hugh and his friends. Amen." As she dipped into the creamy soup, Priscilla thanked God that they could bring all their needs to Him.

Cars were pulling up and parking when Priscilla arrived at the library, Gail and Uncle Hugh in the vehicle behind her. How many people were coming to hear Franklin's talk? That had to be why they were here, since the library didn't have regular hours on Sunday.

Priscilla found a spot, then waited on the sidewalk for Gail and Uncle Hugh to catch up. The day was raw and damp, with clouds moving in. Hopefully they weren't in for another storm.

The library was toasty warm. People were milling about, hanging up coats in the cloakroom off the vestibule while chatting.

Mildred came up to greet them. "Glad you could make it, Priscilla," she said. "I'm excited to hear what Franklin has to say."

"Me too," Priscilla replied. "Although he did share some of his theories with me the other day out at the Weller farm."

"How is everything going over there?" Mildred asked. "I haven't seen you to catch up."

"It's going well." Priscilla glanced around at the crowd. This wasn't the time or place to get into what she'd discovered. "Let's get together at the museum this week."

"Sounds like a plan." Mildred patted Priscilla's shoulder. "I'll see you then."

As she and her companions strolled toward the meeting room, Priscilla realized that what really mattered to her was learning what happened to Bitsy. That meant that no matter how much she wanted to be the one to find the truth, she should welcome anything that Franklin uncovered that might help.

The small meeting room was set up with a slide projector and podium in front of rows of folding chairs. Wearing a professorial-looking tweed jacket and baggy corduroys, Franklin was up front, peering at his laptop over a pair of reading glasses. So many people had shown up that volunteers were unfolding more chairs.

While waiting for a spot, Priscilla studied the event flyer tacked on a stand. Franklin had enticed people with a presentation he was calling "Cold Case: Martha's Vineyard Edition. Who Killed Beautiful Bitsy Parker?" The flyer also included a lovely head shot of Bitsy. No wonder people were flocking to his talk. She had to give him kudos for sparking interest in his project.

Mildred was up front welcoming Franklin when Priscilla finally slid into a seat in the last row, Uncle Hugh and Gail beside her. "Now I'll hand you over to Dr. Franklin Mayweather's capable hands. Please welcome the professor." Everyone clapped.

Franklin nodded and smiled, bobbing his head several times. Then he held up a hand. The room quieted. "Thank you everyone, for coming out tonight. I know it was short notice—"

I'll say, Priscilla thought. It was only by chance that she'd learned about it.

"But I was so excited to discover new developments about the mysterious disappearance of Bitsy Parker."

Franklin touched a button on his laptop, bringing a projected image on the wall to life. "This presentation will summarize what I've learned so far. My goal is to complete the investigation this winter and publish a book later in the year." He tapped a key, which showed the same information as the flyer. "Let us begin."

The first slide showed a shot of the downed tree in Joan's yard. "This venerable, ancient maple, which for many years provided welcome shade to those passing by, has hidden a secret for almost ninety years." He paused dramatically. "Bitsy Parker's poor body lay in darkness under these spreading limbs until a terrible storm struck."

Priscilla thought his style was excessively flowery and verbose, but the rest of the audience appeared enthralled. Not a sound was heard in the room while he spoke, taking them through a history of the Parker family. They made their initial fortune in whaling. Then he talked about Bitsy's childhood and youth—she was debutante of the year in 1923.

Thinking some of the information might be useful, Priscilla jotted notes in the small pad she carried in her handbag. By now the audience was getting restive, with coughing here and there and shifting in seats, but they became riveted again when Franklin brought up a photograph of Ambrose Allen.

"This is the man responsible for Bitsy's untimely death," he announced. Showman that he was, he paused to let the audience take that in. Gail turned puzzled eyes on Priscilla. "You don't believe that, do you?" she whispered. Priscilla shook her head. Though she suspected Ambrose of something, she didn't have enough evidence to accuse him of anything.

A shrill yet commanding feminine voice broke the fraught silence. "Don't believe a word he says." As one, the onlookers turned to the doorway.

Jordan Parker stood there, elegant in a fur-trimmed long coat and knee-high leather boots. She swung her glossy locks and said, "That skeleton is not Bitsy Parker, despite Dr. Mayweather's assertions. It is that of Evangeline Jenks, Mrs. Parker's maid."

CHAPTER EIGHT

The room erupted in an uproar of voices, everyone trying to be heard over their neighbors. Priscilla winced at the din, regretting that they were all so tightly packed in. Some people had stood up, blocking her view of Franklin. She was dying to know how he was taking this challenge to his knowledge and authority.

She didn't have long to wait to find out. A piercing whistle sliced through the racket, and almost immediately everyone quieted. Those standing plopped back down into their seats.

"You can tell he's been a teacher a long time," Gail whispered to Priscilla.

Franklin's piercing gaze raked the crowd. "Thank you." He lifted his eyes and focused on Jordan. "Miss Parker, I presume?" She nodded. "I'm so glad you could join us today and provide your refreshing take on this case. At another time, I'd love to talk to you in more detail. But today—" He reached down and pushed a button. "I will show you why I believe this is Bitsy." A picture of Bitsy wearing the ring appeared on the screen.

How did he figure that out? She and Joan had kept quiet about the ring, pending the medical examiner's ruling.

"A source told me the skeleton was wearing the same ring," Franklin said with a smug smile. "The entire medical examiner's report will soon be listed on a public site for missing and unidentified persons. However, I hope to help law enforcement close this case." He left the picture of Bitsy up while he asked, "Are there any questions?"

People had a few, but Priscilla didn't stay to listen. "I need to get home," she whispered to Gail. "Jake." She didn't need to say more.

As she was exiting the room, she heard Franklin say, "If any of you have information related to the case, please feel free to contact me. Check those attics, folks, you never know what's up there."

Franklin already knew she had papers from the Parker house. How long did she have before he'd demand to see them?

Once she arrived at home, Priscilla bundled up and took Jake for a walk by the water. The threatening clouds were now producing light snow, which wafted down to the steely waves like tiny pieces of floating lace.

Jake snuffled in the dunes and among the rocks, undeterred by the cold that surely dampened most odors. Hands in her pockets, Priscilla trudged along the still, cold November beach, noticing how different it was from the height of vibrant summer.

But it was beautiful, this time of dormant waiting. Winter would give way to new life, and spring would come again. "'For, lo, the winter is past, the rain is over and gone,'" she whispered to herself. Sometime, not too far in the future, those words would prove true.

Priscilla stood at the water's edge and studied the lighthouse and the cottage, hunkered on the bluff as they had been for over one hundred years. Not much was certain in human affairs, but the sight of the shore's ever-present guardian was comforting. Smoke drifted from the cottage chimney, a sign that all was warm and toasty inside.

When she got back to the cottage she'd brew another pot of coffee and read through Bitsy's journals. Maybe she'd find something of interest. Priscilla whistled to Jake, who bolted along the sand, tongue hanging out. "Let's go, boy. You deserve a treat. And a nap by the fire."

Once they got back inside and settled in, the roaring flames provided not only warmth, but cozy comfort too. Priscilla made a cup of coffee and settled in her favorite chair with the social diary and household ledger, Jake sprawled at her feet. Through the windows she noticed the snow had intensified. Fortunately it wasn't really accumulating as it danced and swirled its way to the ground.

Priscilla sipped coffee and worked her way back in the social diary. A note on the 14th of August startled her. "Eva left," it said. "Need to place ad. Perhaps talk to Helen for recommendations."

With the abbreviation, Priscilla was pretty sure Bitsy was talking about Evangeline Jenks, the maid Jordan mentioned.

Where had she gone? The surname Jenks rang a bell. Then she remembered that Uncle Hugh's friend Gilbert was a Jenks. Maybe he was also the Gilbert who worked at the cranberry farm. Probably, since he was there with Chowder and Chowder Jr.

Why had Evangeline left? And what evidence could there possibly be to convince Jordan she was murdered? Priscilla made a note to ask Gilbert about the maid. Maybe they were related, and if so, he might know something.

Sheila's grandmother had also worked as a maid for the Parkers. What was it like, having numerous household employees? Priscilla had never even paid for a cleaning service, although she'd been tempted many a time. But she'd always talked herself out of it, figuring that it was self-indulgent and lazy, especially since she'd never worked outside the home.

Priscilla set the diary aside and picked up the photo album. Maybe there was a picture of Evangeline in there. Near the end she found a photograph that looked promising. A row of servants stood in front of the Parker's house, men and women both. Several men were in overalls, a clue they were gardeners. There were two maids, identified by black uniforms and white aprons. One she recognized as Sheila's grandmother, the other was dark-haired with narrow features. Maybe that was Evangeline. A plump woman wearing a bib apron and a man in a suit were most likely the cook and chauffeur.

What a quaint custom to take pictures of "the help." Perhaps she should have Ida Lee Jones and Beau Ortmann pose in front of the cottage, she thought with an ironic smile. Ida did her gardening, and Beau, who was also Candy Lane's fiancé, was her go-to handyman and carpenter.

The phone rang. Ready for a break, Priscilla readily answered. "I heard I missed something exciting this afternoon at the library," Joan said. "I wasn't feeling well this morning so I stayed home." She laughed. "That'll teach me."

"I noticed that you weren't in church. I'm sorry. I should have called to check on you. And I'm sorry to hear that you're under the weather. A touch of flu?"

"Maybe. I've learned the hard way to spend a day in bed when I first feel it coming on. I hated to miss church, but I didn't want to spread my germs either."

"Probably a good call. If you're up to talking right now, I'll tell you all about Franklin's presentation."

Joan sighed. "I sure am. Bored doesn't even begin to describe what I feel. Bring it on."

"Let me go refill my coffee." Priscilla topped off her cup and, after settling by the fire again, she took Joan through Franklin's presentation and Jordan's interruption. "I also found a picture of the mysterious Evangeline in Bitsy's album."

"Hmm. This is all so fascinating. Guess what? Sam is interested in doing a story about the skeleton." Joan's son was a television producer in Boston.

"Really? Don't let Franklin find out." The professor was a publicity hound.

"Mum's the word. I told Sam I wanted to wait until we figured out more of the story."

"That's exciting, but I'm not sure I want to be on television. I'll let you do it."

"Maybe." Joan laughed. "When are you going back out to the farm? I'd like to tag along."

"I'd love your help," Priscilla said, thinking of the remaining papers waiting for her to inventory. "Maybe tomorrow, if you feel better. Or I can wait until later in the week."

"Let's plan on tomorrow, after I get out of work at noon. I'm going to get over this thing even if it kills me." With that dramatic pronouncement, Joan signed off.

Priscilla picked up the household accounts book next. It was fascinating to see the purchases made weekly and the cost of things in 1932. Bread was seven cents a loaf, the soup she'd eaten with Gail and Hugh, seven cents a can. Oranges were twenty-five cents a dozen and eggs, fifteen cents.

As with the diary, the entries ended in August. Who had managed household costs after Bitsy was gone? Priscilla kept leafing through, hoping she might discover something more.

On the next to last page, she was rewarded—but confused. In the same handwriting as the rest of the book was a column of letters followed by several columns of numbers. Abbreviated dates headed the number columns. Priscilla closed the book. At the moment, she had no idea what Bitsy had been recording—or why.

A while later, Priscilla was sliding a casserole into the oven when Rachel called. "I bought my tickets, Mom," she said. "Only a few more days."

"I can't wait to see you." Priscilla leaned against the kitchen counter, her heart warming at the idea of being with her precious daughter again. "I'm going to make my famous roasted potatoes for you."

Rachel laughed. "Yum. Can we have it with a rack of ribs?" Kansas was known for its barbecue, and Priscilla had a special dry rub recipe she used.

"Definitely." Priscilla grabbed a piece of scrap paper and a pen and jotted a grocery list. "Want some real New England fish chowder while you're here?" She pronounced the words with a regional accent, making Rachel laugh.

"You're turning into a real islander, Mom."

"I sure am, ayuh." Priscilla giggled. "I sound like Chowder and Chowder Jr."

"What?" Rachel squawked. "Are those real people?"

"They sure are." Priscilla described the gentlemen. "Friends of Uncle Hugh's." That reminded her about their possible lost investments and, by extension, Whitney Parker and her troubles. It was on the tip of her tongue to say something to Rachel about A.J.'s possible assistance. With effort she suppressed that thought. "I can't wait to see A.J. too. How is he?"

"Fine. I guess," Rachel snapped with one of the lightning changes of mood she was known for. Her laugh was a trifle frustrated. "He's been hung up on some case, so I haven't spoken to him for days."

And that worries her, both for his sake and for their relationship. Priscilla turned over various responses in her mind. She didn't want to sound patronizing or dismissive either. "I'm sorry to hear that," she finally settled on.

"Me too." Rachel sighed. "We'll see how it goes when I come East." Her voice wavered then broke. "Oh, Mom. What if I'm making a huge mistake? What if he doesn't care for me—"

The way I care for him. Priscilla finished the sentence. Her heart swelled with love and empathy. "Oh, darling. Has he done or said anything to indicate he's changed his mind?" She'd heard of people pulling back when things got serious, and she prayed that wasn't happening to Rachel.

A sniffle. "No. He sent flowers to my office on Friday. Said he was counting the days until he sees me."

That was encouraging. Although it had been a while, Priscilla still remembered the tender vulnerability of being in love, of hoping and praying it wasn't a mirage that would vanish, leaving only heartbreak.

"These feelings are normal," she said, hoping to bolster Rachel with common sense. "I remember feeling exactly like that the day before your daddy proposed. I had myself convinced he was going to ditch me."

Rachel laughed. "Ditch you? Dad worshipped you."

He had. Priscilla allowed the tangled, bittersweet emotions of love and loss to reign in her heart for just a moment. She was fortunate to have had the love of a good man, and she prayed fervently that Rachel would too.

"Thanks, Mom. You always make me feel better," Rachel said with another sniff. "I guess I'd better go. I've got an early meeting tomorrow."

"Talk to you soon. Love you." As Priscilla disconnected the call, she breathed a prayer of gratitude for the loving relationship she shared with her adult daughter. In today's world that was far from a given, and she was incredibly blessed.

By the next day, Joan had recovered from her brief illness, so Priscilla picked her up at work. The plan was to have lunch at the Colonial Inn and Restaurant then head over to the farm.

"Good afternoon, ladies." Owner Tilly Snyder greeted them when they walked in. Once in a while Tilly worked as hostess, when she was short-staffed. Otherwise she preferred to float around the dining room and talk to customers. "Two for lunch?" She gathered two tall leather menus and indicated for Joan and Priscilla to follow her.

As they followed Tilly to a table, Priscilla saw that the restaurant was fairly full. The place was a favorite eatery all year round. Her gaze went to the booth where Gerald usually sat, but he wasn't there today. She tried to ignore the pang of disappointment.

"Do you have shrimp sandwiches today?" Priscilla asked as she slid into a booth seat. Those were her hands-down favorite here.

Tilly set the menus down, lining them up exactly with the place mat and silverware. "Of course. You can have the winter version, a shrimp melt if you want. It's broiled open-face with cheese."

Priscilla and Joan exchanged looks. "Yum. I'll have that," Joan said. She opened the menu. "With a cup of clam chowder."

"Your server will be right over to take your orders," Tilly said. She turned to go, then paused. "Franklin Mayweather is wrong. Bitsy Parker did not run off with Ambrose Allen." She began to bustle away.

"Tilly." Joan slapped her hand on the table. "You can't say something like that and run off on us."

"Please, Tilly. Don't torture us," Priscilla added.

Tilly stopped, pivoting on her heel with a sigh. "All right. I suppose I have a minute." She glanced at the hostess station. "But if someone comes in, I'll have to go."

"We understand." Joan propped her chin on her hand, smiling up at Tilly.

Tilly crossed her arms. "Ambrose Allen courted a distant cousin of mine, Hazel Snyder. Her father was an attorney here on the island."

Joan raised her eyebrows at Priscilla. "Very interesting."

Priscilla agreed. "Do you have anything of Hazel's related to that courtship? A photograph? A diary entry?"

"Maybe." Tilly cocked her head. "Is there a reason I should give it to you and not Franklin? I was so tempted to set him straight yesterday, I couldn't sit still."

"You were at the library?" Priscilla hadn't seen her, but the room had been packed.

"I was." Tilly glanced over her shoulder at a party of four who had just come in. She moved restlessly, obviously eager to get going.

"Give us the information, Tilly," Joan said. "My son is producing a television feature on Bitsy's story. He'll probably want to interview you."

"Really?" Tilly's eyes widened, and she patted her hair. "All right. I'll give you a call after I dig through Hazel's things. Now please excuse me." She beetled away.

"We'll make sure Franklin gets the information," Priscilla called. To Joan, she said, "Eventually. It's the right thing to do."

After enjoying the shrimp sandwiches and chowder, they bundled up again and drove to the farm. "I really should buy some cranberries today," Joan said. "I need to practice my sauce for the contest." She threw Priscilla a teasing glance. "Especially if I'm going to beat you."

Priscilla laughed. "I think it's the other way around. Did I tell you about the recipes I tried?" As she navigated the now familiar road, she described the two recipes. "Gerald agreed the blueberry one was the keeper."

"Oh, you have your own private tester?" Joan kept up the teasing. "I should get me one of those."

"How about Franklin?" Priscilla suggested. "He's very discerning, don't you know. Or so he tells me."

They burst into laughter. "Poor Franklin," Joan said. "If only he knew how often he's the subject of our mockery."

"Couldn't happen to a nicer guy," Priscilla muttered. Then she felt guilty. "I'm sorry, Joan. I know it's wrong to talk about someone behind his back, especially when it's mean. I'm trying to do better. It's just so hard for me to get past what he did when I first got here."

Joan studied the passing landscape. "If it wasn't so hard sometimes, attempting to be righteous wouldn't mean much, would it?"

After a moment, she added, "He does have a way of getting under one's skin. But maybe it's because he's so socially inept."

"You could be right." Maybe what Priscilla interpreted as self-absorption and pride was merely awkwardness. She knew from experience that sometimes the most insecure people were the most boastful.

As they approached the farm entrance, Priscilla slowed the vehicle. "On another topic, I'm really enjoying coming out here. Sheila gave me a tour. You should take one too."

"Let's." Joan's expression was eager. "I've always wanted to see cranberries in the wild."

"They're pretty cool, the way they float." Priscilla slowed to let a car coming from the other direction pass on the narrow lane. Franklin was at the wheel. Despite her earlier remorse, her heart lifted. She wouldn't have to fend him off today.

To make up for her unbecoming relief, she waved and smiled. Startled, he waved back, a grin lighting up his face. Now she really felt crummy.

The parking lot was half full, with patrons buying cranberries and other items from the barn store. "Can we shop first?" Joan asked, halfway out her door.

"I have no problem with that," Priscilla said. She needed more berries anyway, to make more batches of cranberry sauce. She was also thinking about making a cranberry sour cream coffee cake for breakfast Thanksgiving weekend.

Inside the store, Sheila and Bosco sauntered over to greet them. "I understand there's all kinds of excitement about Bitsy

Parker," she said. "It's kind of fun to be part of it." Bosco immediately made friends with Joan, who oohed and aahed over the friendly mutt as she gave him a thorough ear rubbing.

"Your mother's collection is really helping us," Priscilla said. "We'll fill you in when you have a chance."

Sheila hooked her thumbs into her belt, gazing around at the busy store. "It will be a couple of weeks yet. Got to make hay while the sun shines. Or should I say, sell those berries."

"That's part of why we're here," Joan said. "I need to stock up on berries for the sauce contest and Thanksgiving."

"Thank the Lord for Thanksgiving," Sheila said. "Without that holiday, a lot of people would never even taste a cranberry."

Priscilla considered Sheila's words. She was no doubt correct, although cranberries were tasty in baked goods, and a lot of people drank the juice. But for many, the traditional sauce was probably their first taste of the tart fruit.

"Are you doing tours today?" Joan asked. "I know you're busy, but if you are..." Her tone was wistful.

"For you, yes," Sheila said. "Let's wait until closing time at four. How's that?"

Joan looked at Priscilla, who nodded. "That's perfect. We'll get a lot done on the inventory between now and then."

After they made their purchases and stowed them in the car, they went into the farmhouse. Sheila had urged them to make themselves at home. "Put the kettle on or brew a pot of coffee," she called. "And help yourself to vanilla-orange-cranberry cookies." She winked. "A new recipe I'm testing."

"What a wonderful woman," Joan said as they entered the cozy kitchen, warmed by the cookstove. Something savory bubbled in a slow cooker on the counter. "I can't believe I've never really gotten to know her."

"She's great," Priscilla agreed. "I consider her a new friend. Once the cranberry season winds down, let's invite her over for a meal at your place or mine." After conferring with Joan, Priscilla set a kettle to boil. Then she gave her the grand tour of the office.

"Oh my word," Joan said when she saw the stacks of boxes and crates. "I had no idea you were dealing with all this alone."

Priscilla shrugged. "I'm taking it one box at a time. Whitney has offered to help too." She pulled out her phone. "I'll let her know we're here and see if she wants to come over."

Whitney didn't respond to the text but as Priscilla was pouring hot water into mugs, she burst into the kitchen, bringing a gust of cold, fresh air with her. "Priscilla. I'm so glad you're here," she cried, panting for breath. She waved a piece of paper. "Someone left me a threatening letter."

CHAPTER NINE

Whitney held the letter out to Priscilla, who put her hands up. "Careful. There might be prints on it."

The young woman frowned. "Oh. I should have thought of that." She set the paper on the table so they all could read it. "I know who you are," it said, scrawled in black marker.

"That's not from the FBI agent," Priscilla said, earning an astonished look from Joan. "Sorry, Joan. I meant to tell you. Whitney is hiding from a corrupt investigator looking into her family's firm. He's searching for her and that's why she's here, on the island." She found a plastic bag and slid the note gently inside using a dish towel holding one corner, careful not to touch it with her fingers.

Joan eyed Whitney. "Want to take it from the top?"

Whitney bit her bottom lip. "Sure. But let's go in the other room, in case Sheila comes back."

They carried mugs of tea and a plate of cookies into the office, along with the letter in its envelope. Joan shut the door behind them. "All right, you two. Tell me everything."

Between Priscilla and Whitney, the story was told to Joan's satisfaction. "Hearing all that makes me think someone else knows who you are," she said. "Dalton Rogers doesn't need to send you a note. He'd just show up, right?"

Put that way, Whitney's situation seemed dire. She sank into the desk chair and covered her face. "I'm so scared. And confused."

Once again Priscilla realized she needed to confide in A.J. The sooner Whitney and her information were in the right hands, the safer she would be. "Whitney, you need to go to someone with this. My daughter's boyfriend, A.J., is with the FBI. He can help you."

"It's too risky," Whitney said. "He might be friends with Dalton." She reached out a hand and clutched Priscilla's sweater sleeve. "How can I know he's honest?"

Priscilla chuckled. "I sure hope he is, since he's serious about my daughter."

"He's a good guy," Joan said. She pointed at the note. "What should we do about that?" The missive glared up at them.

"I don't think we can do anything," Priscilla said. "Telling the police will only bring attention to Whitney. And we don't want that."

Whitney sat bolt upright in her chair, pointing to the driveway. "Speaking of which, there's my cousin." She jumped up, scanning the room as though seeking escape.

Priscilla looked out the window overlooking the barn and drive. Jordan Parker was climbing out of her vehicle. Instead of heading to the barn, she bustled toward the kitchen entrance. "I take it you want to avoid her?"

"Yes." Whitney wrung her hands. "She doesn't know I'm here."

Was Jordan involved with the firm's financial problems? Obviously Whitney didn't trust her enough to stay with her, instead of here on the farm.

But there was no time for Priscilla to ruminate. Jordan was knocking on the kitchen door, loud enough to be heard from the office. Priscilla spotted a door in the corner and opened it, finding a closet pretty well packed. "How about in here? I think there's room."

With a sob of relief, Whitney ran to the closet. "I'll make myself fit." She squeezed inside, and Priscilla shut the door.

"Let's go see what Jordan wants," Priscilla said.

"And I'll hide the note." Joan opened the desk drawer and popped it inside.

Priscilla exited the office and crossed the kitchen to the back door. "Hello, Jordan. How are you?"

Jordan took a step back. "Priscilla? What are you doing here?"

Since Whitney was hiding in the office, Priscilla certainly didn't want to get Jordan interested in the contents of the office. "I'm inventorying papers that belong to the Weller farm." She moved away from the door. "Do you want to come in?"

"I'm actually looking for Sheila." As Jordan entered the kitchen, Priscilla saw that she was clutching a flyer for the cranberry sauce event. "I want to list the farm as the main cranberry supplier for the contest."

That would be a nice promotion. "She's out in the barn," Priscilla said, hoping to send Jordan that way. Then she saw Sheila charging across the drive. "Oops. No, here she comes."

Joan joined them in the kitchen at the same time Sheila burst in. "Hey, Jordan. Thanks for coming out." She surveyed Priscilla and Joan. "How's it going in there with those papers?"

"We're just getting started. The kettle's hot, if you'd like tea, Jordan."

Some people were good at discerning a topic others would rather avoid, and apparently Jordan was one of them. "Did you find anything good yet? Mildred mentioned the farm display to me."

"Yes, a few things." Priscilla pointed a listless finger toward the office, hoping she would drop the subject.

Jordan set the flyer on the table and bustled toward the half-open door. "I just want to take a peek. History is another of my hobbies."

Priscilla and Joan exchanged looks then followed Jordan, moving at double time.

"I'll heat up the water," Sheila said, turning on the stove. "I've already seen those papers more than enough times."

Inside the office, Jordan was looking around and peeking into boxes. Joan quickly stationed herself in front of the closet door.

Priscilla followed Jordan, doing her best to distract her. "It's a huge collection, isn't it? I've barely gotten started. But there's all kinds of good stuff." She grabbed an antique calendar at random and displayed the pictures of vintage automobiles. "All of this is so fascinating."

"As you can tell," Priscilla said, "we've got a long way to go in here." Her gaze fell on the third mug of tea. Uh-oh. While Jordan was opening a file drawer, she picked it up and set on the window-sill behind the curtain.

Jordan slammed the drawer shut and cast a critical eye over the mess. "Yes, I can see that." The kettle whistled in the kitchen. "Good luck."

Priscilla left the door open a crack behind Jordan, and a few minutes later, once Sheila and her guest left the house, she said, "It's safe to come out now, Whitney."

Joan opened the closet door. Whitney practically fell out. She straightened with a wince, rubbing her legs. "I was getting cramps in there," she said. She pointed at a steamer trunk studded with hobnails. "And that thing was digging into my skin."

"I wonder what's in there." Priscilla took a closer look at the trunk.

"Does it matter?" Joan asked. "We've already got too much to look at."

Priscilla picked up the leather tag looped through a handle. "Elizabeth Parker," it read. Wasn't Bitsy's full name Elizabeth? "Um, I think it might be important. Come on, give me a hand."

It took the three of them to tug the trunk out into the room. Priscilla pushed on the latch, thankful it wasn't locked. When she raised the lid, a faint, floral perfume rose from the contents.

Heaps of folded clothing lay inside. When Priscilla picked up the first garment, she saw that it was a pink summer dress of 1930s vintage. She shook it out and held it up to herself. Whoever it belonged to was petite. "I think we just found Bitsy Parker's clothes."

"What does that mean?" Whitney asked. She reached out and touched the wrinkled crepe fabric.

"I think it means that Bitsy did not run away," Priscilla said. "Surely she would have taken these garments with her."

"Have you heard Bitsy's story?" Joan asked. "She disappeared in 1932 from Martha's Vineyard."

Whitney sat on the edge of the desk. "I might have. Was she my great-grandfather's first wife? There was some kind of scandal about her, I vaguely remember."

"If he was Vernon Parker, then yes," Priscilla said. "Joan and I found a woman's skeleton during the storm, and we think it might be Bitsy. The medical examiner said it was the right age and gender."

Whitney's eyes widened. "A skeleton? Are you talking about the storm when I stopped by your house, Joan?" She swallowed. "I guess I missed that. When that officer waved at me, I panicked and left. I didn't even say goodbye to you two, which wasn't nice."

"You were in a crisis. We understand that." Priscilla continued to gently remove the clothing from the trunk, shake them and lay them on the desk. "Anyway, I was the one who spotted the skeleton under the tree. Talk about a shock."

"And you think it might be Bitsy?" Whitney asked. "Why is that?"

Priscilla filled her in about the ring and the proximity to the Parker property. "It was also there a long time. That was a huge tree."

Joan drank the last of her tea. "Does anyone want another cup? I could use one."

Whitney hunted around. "I didn't even finish my first cup. Where did it go?"

Priscilla retrieved the mug from behind the curtain. "I hid it back here so Jordan wouldn't see it."

"That's got to be freezing." Joan reached for the mug. "I'll get you a fresh one."

Whitney watched while Priscilla continued emptying the trunk. "They don't make clothes like that anymore, do they?"

"They sure don't." Priscilla held up a gossamer gown in pale-green silk shot with silver threads. It had both beading and embroidery. She showed Whitney the tiny stitches. "Look at this delicate work. This dress was handmade."

Carrying a tray with three steaming mugs, Joan pushed the door open with one elbow. "I have an idea," she said. "I think Whitney needs to see the photographs you found."

Whitney picked up her mug. "Hold on. You have pictures? Where did they come from?"

Priscilla picked up her own cup and blew on the hot tea. "Sheila's mother bought a lot of things from the Parker mansion before it was torn down. We've been finding Bitsy's belongings among them and setting them aside. One thing I found was a photo album of her last summer."

"We're trying to piece together her final days on the island," Joan said. "Maybe we can figure out if the skeleton really is Bitsy and if so, what happened to her."

Whitney regarded them with wide, admiring eyes. "What are you, detectives?"

Joan and Priscilla laughed. "Inadvertently," Joan said. "Somehow the mysteries come to us." She patted Priscilla's shoulder. "Mostly to this lady right here."

Priscilla pulled a velvet evening cloak lined with white satin out of the trunk. "In this case, I feel a sense of responsibility, since I'm the one who found her."

Whitney tipped her head, thinking. "Is Franklin also looking into the skeleton? He invited me to a talk he was giving yesterday. I told him I didn't feel like going. But you know the real reason. I'm keeping a low profile."

"That's a good idea," Priscilla said. "But we've got to work on a plan to solve your situation." Again, she felt an urgency to call A.J., but until Whitney gave her permission to do so, it was out of her hands.

"Unfortunately, I'm fresh out of ideas," Whitney said. "But I suppose I better figure out something fast." She glanced around. "Where's the note I got? It was on the desk."

Joan pulled the desk drawer open. "I put it in here so Jordan wouldn't see it."

"Good thinking." Whitney sank into the office chair, staring at the letter. "Priscilla, are you sure you didn't tell anyone I'm here?"

Priscilla opened the clasp of a small velvet evening purse. "Not a soul, except Joan. And that's only because she already met you." She dug her hand inside, feeling among the velvet folds, finding a gold lipstick and compact. She opened the lipstick and twisted it. Dark red. The compact held a pale powder and a puff.

Her throat thickened with unexpected emotion at touching another woman's personal things decades after her death. Bitsy Parker was suddenly very real to her. Blinking back tears, she put the makeup back into the purse and snapped it shut.

Whitney rocked vigorously, making the chair protest. "I'm sorry, Priscilla. I know I can trust you. But who could have left this?" She jabbed a finger at the mocking letter.

Joan put a comforting arm around Whitney's shoulders and squeezed. "You can always stay with me if you want."

"Or me," Priscilla said. "Door's open anytime."

"I can't put either of you in danger." Whitney bit her lip and shook her head. "No, I've got to stick this out on my own."

"Well, if you change your mind, please call either of us, okay?" Priscilla began to put the clothing back into the trunk. She wanted to take it home and go through it more thoroughly there. She said as much to the others. "Now let's get busy. Or else Sheila is going to think we're slackers."

They worked in the office for the next couple of hours. "How's it going, ladies?" Sheila asked when she came to check on them. "You still want that tour, Joan?"

"I'd love one." Joan stood up, dusting off her hands. She'd been sitting cross-legged on the floor sorting a box of Weller family photographs. "You've got some great old photos in there, Sheila. You could make reproductions of some and sell them in the shop."

Sheila scratched her head. "Really? I've never thought of that."

Joan showed her some of the best farm scenes, including ones that depicted using horses to hay the fields, a wagon, and a proud and handsome Mr. Weller displaying a basket of cranberries, a pipe held in his grinning mouth.

"That's my pop," Sheila said. "He was a good egg."

"I think that picture would also be great on your website," Whitney commented. "He's so happy, he makes me want to smile."

"Smiling is good," Sheila said. She glanced out the window. "We'd better get going before it starts getting dark. Are you coming along, Priscilla?"

"We rode here together so it's either wait here or go," Priscilla said. She looked at the trunk. Maybe she could take another look inside while they were touring. She'd still like to take the clothing home, to show Mildred. "I'll stay. Make sure you hang on tight, Joan."

"Now what's that supposed to mean?" Sheila said in mock anger, hands on her hips. "Are you accusing me of being a reckless driver?"

Everyone laughed. "No, just a speedy one," Priscilla said.

After the other three left, Priscilla opened the trunk, her heart rate ticking upward. What might she discover inside? Maybe nothing, but she would keep looking until she learned the truth about Bitsy. She knew herself well enough to say that.

She pulled the clothing out and placed it on the desk. She searched all the pockets and found only a folded handkerchief, the creases no doubt permanent by now. The inside of the trunk was lined with faded floral fabric. She knelt down and peered inside, hoping for a pocket or compartment.

There was nothing like that, but she felt a small, hard object under a flap of the lining on the bottom. She pulled the cloth back only far enough to see what it was.

The object glimmered softly gold in the light of the overhead bulb. She picked it up and set it in her palm.

A cuff link, exactly like the one Joan had found. But how did Vernon's cuff link end up in the trunk? Unbidden, an image of Vernon packing Bitsy's clothing in a hurry came to mind. Perhaps it had fallen off and he hadn't noticed.

Priscilla found an unused envelope and put the cuff link inside. A moment later, the ATV roared into the yard and sputtered to a stop beside the barn. Shortly after, Joan came in, bringing the scent of fresh air with her. She brushed at her windblown hair with a laugh. "You're right about Sheila. It was a pretty exciting ride." Her gaze fell on the envelope. "What do you have there?"

"Vernon's other cuff link." Priscilla showed it to her, then set the envelope down and pointed to where she'd found it. "I want to take this one to April tomorrow, along with the picture I found of Vernon wearing them."

Joan stared into the empty trunk with a frown. "So one cuff link was lost outside and the other in the trunk? I don't like the sound of that."

"Me neither," Priscilla said. "They weren't exactly cheap, so he must have had bigger things on his mind, or else he wouldn't have been so careless." She began to put the clothing back into the trunk.

Sheila popped into the room. "I have chicken pot pie in the slow cooker. Would you two like to eat with me?"

"My mouth's been watering over that all afternoon," Priscilla said with a laugh. "I'd love to stay. Joan?"

"Me too," Joan said. "I had no idea what I was going to make tonight. That's the downside of cooking for one, no motivation. I often make do with a bowl of cereal."

Priscilla recalled a few nights when she'd done that too. But she made an effort to eat a balanced diet. She felt much better when she did, and had more energy too.

"Working outside always gives me an appetite," Sheila declared. "So I eat like a horse, quite frankly." She noticed the open trunk. "What's in there?"

Priscilla explained, and showed Sheila the cuff link. "I'd like to take the clothes with me, for the museum, if you're agreeable."

Sheila shrugged. "I'll be glad to get them out of here." She reached out and touched the velvet cloak. "But that sure is lovely fabric."

"Isn't it? Genuine silk velvet." Priscilla turned it over so Sheila could see the satin lining. "They don't make clothes like this nowadays."

"No they don't," Sheila agreed. "Now please excuse me. I'm going to pop a tray of biscuits into the oven."

Joan followed her. "I'd be happy to help."

Sheila's voice drifted in from the kitchen. "How about setting the table?"

Priscilla stowed the rest of the clothing in the trunk and closed the lid. She'd need some help getting it into the SUV. The wooden trunk was both heavy and bulky. Then she set the rest of the room in order for their next visit.

A few minutes later, she washed her hands in the powder room and joined Sheila and Joan in the kitchen. "Anything I can do?"

Sheila pulled out a chair at the kitchen table. "Sit and eat." She whirled over to the oven, where she pulled out a pan of golden brown biscuits. These went into a basket. Then the busy cook ladled out big pottery bowls of chicken pot pie.

Joan said grace at Sheila's invitation, and the trio dug in. "Everything except the meat is from my own garden," Sheila said. "But I buy that from another farmer on the island."

Priscilla spooned up bite-sized chunks of potatoes, carrots, and peas in golden gravy. They were delicious, as was the tender meat. "You have time for a garden?"

"I make time," Sheila said. "Nothing like home-grown veggies."

Joan murmured agreement. "Some years I only do tomatoes in containers, but they're a treat I look forward to all year."

"You can't beat a tomato right off the vine," Sheila said. "Store bought doesn't compare. Like cardboard, they are." She passed the basket. "Another biscuit?"

Priscilla took one and buttered it, admiring how flaky it was. "Maybe I should do a small vegetable garden next year," she said. "I used to have a big one on the farm. I canned and froze vegetables and berries."

They spent the rest of the meal chatting about vegetable gardens and swapping favorite foods and recipes. Priscilla's cell phone rang while Sheila was serving cranberry-apple crisp made with fruit from the farm.

"Go ahead and answer it," Sheila said. "We don't mind." She pointed the spoon at Joan. "Can you please get the ice cream out of the freezer?"

While Joan obeyed, Priscilla pulled her phone out of her handbag. Tilly Snyder was calling. Without a greeting, she said, "I found Hazel's things. Want to come over and see them tomorrow?"

CHAPTER TEN

Priscilla rose early the next day. Somehow she'd ended up with a full schedule. As she slipped into her robe and padded out to the kitchen, she mentally reviewed everything she had to do that day.

This morning she had a meeting at the food pantry with Gail and several other people, since she was now on the committee running the cranberry sauce contest. How that had happened, she wasn't quite sure. But how could she say no to Gail after she admitted she didn't want to face Jordan Parker's wrath alone? Whatever that meant. She'd find out at nine.

Jake bumped her knee while she was making coffee. "Hang on. You're next." Priscilla opened the pantry door to fill Jake's bowl with dog food. Late morning, she was going over to the Colonial Inn and Restaurant to see what Tilly had found.

She poured the kibble into Jake's dish, and he crunched away. The coffee was ready, so she poured a cup. At three, she was meeting with the cousins at the bakery to discuss Thanksgiving. Hopefully before that, there would be time to dash to the police station to show April the cuff link.

With a sigh, she sank into a chair at the kitchen table, tired already. Sipping her coffee, she took a moment to enjoy how pretty the rising sun looked touching waves rippling toward the shore. What a beautiful world.

Priscilla reached for her Bible and began reading her daily devotional. Days always went better when she took the time to read Scripture and pray. Today's reading featured Psalm 30. There it was again, the theme of gratitude. "'Sing the praises of the Lord, you his faithful people; praise his holy name.'"

The words lifted Priscilla's spirits. Watching the sunshine strengthen, she turned them over in her mind, allowing them to take root in her heart.

Her cell phone rang. Gerald. With a laugh, she snatched it up. "Good morning."

Silence for a second. "Hi, Priscilla," he said. "You startled me. I thought for sure I was going to get your voice mail."

"Who calls hoping to get voice mail?" she teased.

"Someone who thinks they're calling too early." He cleared his throat. "I wanted to ask if I could cook you dinner tomorrow night."

Priscilla absorbed his invitation. "Now that's an offer I can't refuse," she finally said with another laugh. "Thank you, I accept. What are we having?"

"I've made some modifications to my stuffing recipe, and I want you to be my tester. I thought I'd bake a chicken."

Priscilla liked his idea. "Perfect. We can also test my sauce with a full meal."

"Exactly." His chuckle was a throaty rumble. "I want you to be the star of that contest."

"Not much chance of that, but thank you." They set a time for Wednesday evening, then wished each other a good day.

She was staring at the view, mulling over the dinner plans, when Jake trotted over and nuzzled her knee. It took a few tries before she tuned in to what he was doing. "I'm sorry, boy. I was daydreaming. Let me get dressed, and we'll go for a walk."

At nine on the dot, Priscilla pulled up in front of the food pantry, located in a nondescript brick building that also held a thrift store. Its presence was a reminder that on this beautiful island, many were in danger of going hungry. A sobering thought, especially this time of year.

A bell jingled above the glass door when she walked inside. An elderly woman was arranging canned goods on the shelves that lined the room. She turned to look at Priscilla, a can of baked beans in each hand. "Can I help you?" she asked.

"I'm here for the cranberry sauce meeting," Priscilla said. Besides the canned goods, a variety of packaged foods were available. A couple of chest freezers and several glass-fronted refrigerators rounded out the selection. Bins held a slim selection of fresh fruits and vegetables.

The woman used one of the cans to point. "They're in the back room."

Priscilla noticed an open door at the rear and heard the murmur of voices drifting out. "Thanks. I'm Priscilla Grant."

"I'm Effie Blair," the woman said with a sweet smile. She placed the cans on the shelf and bent for two more.

Priscilla walked to the back room and found four people sitting around a table. The small space was barely large enough for the long table and folding chairs that were crammed inside.

Gail looked at Priscilla with relief. "Good. You made it." She patted the empty chair beside her.

As Priscilla squeezed inside, she noticed Jordan Parker sitting at the head of the table. On the other side were Harper Jenson and Ida Lee Jones.

"Grab a coffee if you want," Jordan said, tipping her chin toward the carafe sitting on a side table. "Does everyone know Priscilla Grant?"

"I sure do," Harper said. The young woman had cropped dark hair and a mischievous grin. "And I know you love cranberry muffins."

"Is that how you categorize people?" Priscilla asked with a laugh. "By their bakery orders?" She dispensed coffee into a Styrofoam cup and added milk.

"Yes, ma'am," Harper said. She ran a hand through her hair, making it stand on end. "People love when I remember their favorites."

"I know Priscilla too," Ida Lee said. "She's one of my gardening clients."

Jordan's fine brows drew together. "I guess I shouldn't be surprised. It is a small world out here, isn't it?"

Since Whitney was also on the island, only a few miles away, Priscilla wondered if Jordan knew just how small. But she took her seat with a smile and said, "Hi everyone. It's good to be here."

Jordan allowed her thirty seconds to get settled. "Gail was just about to give her report on the flyers. Take it away."

Gail shifted in her seat, looking miserable. "I hate to say this, but I only got rid of twenty. So many businesses aren't open this time of year, and a lot of the ones that are open don't let you post flyers."

Jordan made a note. "So there are thirty more to go?"

"That's right," Gail said, squirming like a reprimanded child. "More or less."

When Jordan leveled a chilly, disapproving stare at Gail, Priscilla understood why Gail had asked her to come along.

"Maybe flyers aren't the way to go," Priscilla said. "How effective are they, anyway?"

Gail shot her a grateful look. "That's what I've been saying."

Jordan bristled. "But we've always used flyers for this contest. It's the way my mother set it up." She tapped her hand on a battered binder, the manual on the cranberry contest no doubt.

"I hate to say this," Ida Lee put in. "But our numbers have been steadily going down each year. It's time for something new. The pantry needs our best."

Jordan's frown was dour, and a lesser person than Ida Lee would have quailed under the force of her glare.

Harper put up a hand. "I know I'm new here but I have an idea. Let's put it out on social media." When Jordan started to protest, she waved her hand. "Hold on. Let me explain." She went on to share the customer reach and increased business the bakery had enjoyed since she'd started using social media. "You have one of those flyers?" she asked Gail.

Gail pulled one out and slid it across the table. Harper held it up. "We'll use this as our ad on the social media pages. Then when people do see it around town, it will be familiar. People need to see something several times before it sinks in."

"I know I do," Gail said. The tension around the table had broken, and she appeared almost giddy. "Maybe we can run it in the church bulletin too."

Jordan at least had the grace to admit when she was outnumbered. "All right, Harper. We'll give it shot. But Gail, keep those flyers handy. You never know when you'll spot an opportunity to post one."

"That is so true," Priscilla said. "Why don't we all take a few copies?" The other two women agreed so she took the folder from Gail and divided them up, giving Jordan an equal share.

Jordan's glacial stare was now bestowed upon Priscilla, but she didn't object. "Moving on. Let's talk about day-of logistics. We'll need more volunteers that day. Any thoughts?"

When the meeting broke up half an hour later, Gail leaned close to Priscilla. "I knew you'd be a good choice for the committee." She winked.

Priscilla took her leave and drove over to see Tilly. This time of day, before the restaurant opened for lunch, spots along the street were abundant. She chose one and parked.

Tilly was in the lobby, talking to a young woman wearing a bib apron and pushing a vacuum cleaner. She spotted Priscilla and waved. "I'll be right with you." After the young woman pushed the vacuum into the dining room, Tilly crossed the carpet to where Priscilla was waiting. "Let's go into my office."

Located down a short hallway, this enclave was a pleasant room with floral wallpaper and a view of the harbor. "Have a seat," Tilly said, indicating a round table with four chairs in the bay window. The other furnishings included a polished antique desk and a pair of velvet armchairs for visitors.

Priscilla noticed an array of objects lined up on the table. These must have belonged to Tilly's aunt Hazel. "Thanks for taking the time to meet with me, Tilly. I know you're busy."

Tilly waved that off. "I don't mind. If I can help solve the mystery of that skeleton, all the better." She poked through the items, then handed Priscilla a photograph.

Priscilla studied the small black-and-white square, which was a head-and-shoulders shot of a young, pretty woman with bobbed hair. "This is Hazel?"

"Yes. She was a beauty." Tilly opened a photo album to a group shot. This showed several young people on the deck of a sailboat, Hazel among them. Ambrose Allen was standing next to her, jaunty in a V-neck sweater and white trousers.

"What good-looking young people," Priscilla said. In this photograph, Hazel wore a cute sailor-inspired frock.

Tilly slid a piece of paper in front of her, a handwritten letter. "Read this."

Priscilla read aloud. "'Dearest Hazel, Leaving for Boston this morning on the ferry was positively tragic. I stood at the rail and watched the Vineyard recede into the distance, tempted to jump overboard and swim back. Only the rumors of whales and the press of business prevented me from drenching my best suit.'" Priscilla paused the reading to say, "He sounds like a hoot."

"Doesn't he?" Tilly said. "I would have liked to know him."

"Me too," Priscilla said. She began reading again. "'I'm counting the days until I return to the island, which of course is Friday. You'll need to put on your best dress so we can go dancing at one of the hotels. Your job is to discover which one has the best band. Until then, know that I love you, sweet girl. Hugs and kisses, your Ambrose.'"

"Look at the date," Tilly said.

Priscilla checked. "It's the week before Bitsy disappeared."

"That's right." Tilly smiled in satisfaction. "Does that letter sound like a man who is about to run off with a married woman?"

Priscilla shook her head. This new information strongly implied that the rumors about Bitsy and Ambrose were pure lies. Convenient lies, to cover a murder.

But where did Ambrose go?

Tilly was flipping through a small, navy-blue book. "This is Hazel's diary. Take a gander at this entry." She set the book in front of Priscilla.

Again, Priscilla read to Tilly. "'Dear diary, How do I begin? I'm a mess, a massive snarl of pain, grief, and fear. And the worst thing is, no one believes me. The whole town is whispering that my darling Ambrose ran off with Bitsy Parker. That is impossible. He was very good friends with Bitsy, of course. Who wasn't? She's a delightful person, although her husband is a cad. Imagine spreading those kinds of salacious rumors instead of searching for your wife? And dear Ambrose. Something terrible happened to him, I know it in my heart. Oh, Ambrose, I will always love you.'"

Priscilla set the book down, her heart touched by the young woman's grief. "Oh my, this is so sad. Did Hazel ever get over him?"

"I guess so. A few years later, she married her father's partner and had three kids. She lived here on the island the rest of her life." Tilly rummaged around and found another photograph, this one of a good-looking family. Priscilla recognized an older but still lovely Hazel.

"I'm glad she went on to find happiness," she said. The couple looked happy anyway, standing close together and beaming with pride at their children.

Tilly gathered the memorabilia, stacking it neatly on the table. "If you want to take another look, let me know. I'm glad you're working on this mystery. Maybe you can find out what happened to Ambrose. I'd like to know."

"Me too," Priscilla said. "I have a feeling it all revolves around that weekend at the Parker house."

When Priscilla left the inn, it wasn't even noon. Fired up by what she'd read, she decided to go by the police station and see if April was in. Then she'd go home for a while before her meeting with the cousins at three.

Like so many of the buildings on the island, the police station was a small, white clapboard structure. Priscilla entered the small lobby and crossed to the front desk, where Officer Teddy Holmes was on duty.

"Is Officer Brown in?" she asked. She patted her handbag. "I have something to give her regarding the Parker case."

Teddy's eyebrows rose. "That's right. You found the skeleton, didn't you?" He pursed his lips. "Wish I'd caught that call. Talk about a cold case."

"It wasn't that much fun, believe me," Priscilla said dryly. "Anyway, is she here?"

He nodded and stood. "I'll go get her."

A moment later, April gestured from the doorway to the back. By the aroma that clung to the officer and the half-eaten sandwich in her hand, Priscilla guessed she'd been eating lunch.

"I'm sorry to bother you," Priscilla said. "It could have waited."

"No, that's fine." April led the way to her desk, her shoulder-length hair swaying. She set the sandwich down and pushed aside a mug of soup. She sat and folded her hands on the blotter. "What do you have for me?"

"Remember that cuff link Joan found on her property?" Priscilla opened the envelope. "I found its match in a trunk of Bitsy Parker's clothes." She tipped the envelope so the piece of jewelry fell onto the middle of the blotter.

April picked it up and studied it, turning it this way and that. "It does look similar." She reached for a file, flipped it open, and compared the cuff link to a photograph. "Yes, it's from the same pair."

"I think this proves Vernon killed Bitsy," Priscilla said. She foraged in her purse for the second thing she'd brought.

The officer rocked back in her chair. "Now that's a bold statement."

"I know. But it makes sense." Priscilla placed a copy of Vernon's photograph in front of April along with the magnifying glass from Sheila's desk. "See, he's wearing those cuff links."

Again, April compared the items. "Looks like it. But how does that..."

Priscilla tapped the desk to emphasize her points. "All right. Let's assume he was wearing the cuff links that night. He lost one in the garden when he buried her. Then later, when he was packing up her clothes so he could claim she ran away, he lost the other." She sucked in a breath. "Under normal conditions, he would have looked for them. They were pricey." She put out the third piece of evidence, the bill for the cuff links Franklin had spotted.

April considered all this. "Tell me more about the trunk."

"We found it at Sheila Weller's. Her mother bought a lot of Bitsy Parker's things before they tore the old house down. The trunk said 'Elizabeth Parker' on an attached tag, and the clothing looked like it came from the right time. We're convinced the clothes are hers."

"We?" April's brows went up. A smile teased at her lips. "Who is playing detective with you?"

Priscilla sighed, regretting that she'd revealed so much. "Me and Joan, basically. We're just doing some research, that's all."

To her surprise, April nodded. "You might as well. To be honest, we don't have the resources to devote to this case. Think about it. Whoever killed Bitsy, if that skeleton is indeed her, has got to be dead. And there's no family outcry to learn the truth, which would be another reason to pursue it."

"I understand." Priscilla could appreciate the officer's pragmatism. But the fact they couldn't bring a killer to justice didn't dent her resolve. She was committed to learning the truth, and so was Joan. That would have to be enough.

CHAPTER ELEVEN

At three on the dot, Priscilla entered the bakery. This time of the afternoon, there weren't a lot of people there, only a couple of writers tapping away in the corners and a group of friends having coffee.

Despite this lack of crowding, Trudy gave a piercing whistle and waved her arm when Priscilla walked in. Everyone naturally turned to look, including one writer who glared then slapped on headphones. Trudy shrugged and smiled. Joan and Gail waved a greeting.

"Hey," Priscilla said. Glancing at the table, she saw that everyone had their drinks and baked goods. "I'll go up and order." She took off her coat and left it on the chair.

Harper was working behind the counter. "Hello again," she said. "What can I get you?"

"I'm not sure." Priscilla pondered the bakery case. "I feel like having something different."

Harper ducked to check the case. "How about molasses cranberry cookies?" Priscilla's expression must have been dubious, because she said, "Here, try one."

Priscilla tasted the cookie and was pleasantly surprised at the mix of tart, spicy, and sweet flavors. "Not bad. I'll take another along with a cup of decaf, please."

Harper reached into the case and put another cookie on a plate. She set it on the counter and went to pour Priscilla a mug of coffee. She was placing the drink on the counter when the bells chimed on the door. She glanced over Priscilla's shoulder with a groan.

"What is it?" Priscilla asked, turning to look. She saw a tall, well-groomed man entering the bakery. She didn't recognize him.

"That gentleman was here earlier, pestering the customers." Harper pressed her lips together in annoyance. She rang up the sale, only charging for one cookie and the coffee. She brushed off Priscilla's protest. "You're a great customer. You get free samples once in a while."

Priscilla thanked her and carried her snack to the table. "I'm trying something new," she announced. "Molasses-cranberry cookies." She noticed that the tall man was speaking to two ladies on the other side of the room.

Seated next to her, Gail peered over and examined the cookies. "Huh. I think I'll stick with the tried and true."

Now the man had walked to the next table and was speaking to the writer who was not wearing headphones. Was he a salesman or something? Maybe that's why he annoyed Harper, coming in here and bothering customers.

"If they're good, tell Sheila," Joan said. "She's always looking for ways to sell more cranberries."

"How's it going at the Weller farm?" Trudy asked. "I haven't even seen you to catch up."

Priscilla's eyes met Joan's. "The short of it is, a lot has happened," Priscilla said. "If you really want to hear about it, I'm happy to share."

Trudy glanced at the clock. "How long will it take? I wanted to talk about Thanksgiving. It's coming up really fast, you know."

"Holidays always do," Joan said. "They zoom up and then zip, they're gone. Why can't Thanksgiving and Christmas last more than one day?"

"That would be nice," Gail said. "I love both."

Trudy's eyes widened, and she elbowed Joan. "Here he comes." Priscilla turned to see the tall man making his way toward them. The sociable Trudy patted her hair and shifted in her seat. Gail hunched her shoulders while Joan watched over the rim of her mug, bemused.

Priscilla smiled to herself, enjoying the varied personalities of her cousins. What was her reaction? Curious but ready to be annoyed. She did not like sales pitches of any sort.

"Good afternoon, ladies," the man said, bestowing a toothy grin around the table. "How are you today?" They chorused hellos, then fell silent, waiting for him to reveal what he wanted. He reached into his jacket and pulled out a wallet, then flipped it open. "I'm Geoff Sanders, from the FBI."

Trudy gasped, and the others exchanged alarmed glances. Joan gave Priscilla a tiny, significant nod, but when Geoff glanced at Joan, her face was totally neutral.

"So what is the FBI doing here on the island?" Trudy flipped her hair back with a smile. She picked up her mug, cradling it in both hands. "Big case?"

"You could say that, ma'am. We're looking for someone." His face became grave, and he appeared to blink back worry. "We think this person may be in danger."

Priscilla felt a chill go up her spine. She could guess who he was talking about, but was he actually one of the good guys? She darted a glance at Joan, hoping for a cue.

"Who is it?" Joan asked, her voice calm. "Maybe we can help you."

"Glad to hear that, ma'am. We couldn't do our jobs without caring, concerned citizens like you all." He favored each woman with an intent, seemingly earnest stare. Then he pulled out a picture and handed it to Gail.

Gail shook her head. "No idea." She passed it to Trudy, who pursed her lips and also denied knowledge. Now Joan had it. By a subtle start she gave, Priscilla guessed it was a picture of Whitney.

Finally it came to her, and that's who it was. The square photograph appeared to be a duplicate of Whitney's driver's license photo. It had that bug-eyed, solemn expression and of course didn't do her justice.

Priscilla glanced at it long enough to be convincing, then gave it to Geoff. "Well, if I see her, I'll be sure to let her know you're looking for her." She tipped her head. "But if I—we—happen to, is there a way to reach you?"

"I'm sorry, I'm out of business cards." He rattled off a phone number while tucking away the photograph. Priscilla did her best to write it down.

After Geoff wandered off to the next table, she excused herself to go to the restroom. But on the way, she covertly took a picture of the federal agent. She'd show it to Whitney and see if Geoff was actually Dalton Rogers.

By the time she returned to the table, the agent had left. "Joan was telling us about all the cool things you've been finding," Trudy said. She twisted her lips in a grimace. "Besides a skeleton. I'm so glad it wasn't me who found it."

"Yes, I'm the fortunate one all right," Priscilla said dryly. "But I guess it made me feel a connection to Bitsy."

"I feel the same way," Joan said. "How did it go with Tilly this morning?" Joan had to work, so she couldn't go along to the inn, to her dismay.

"I learned a lot." Priscilla told the others about Hazel's relationship with Ambrose. Then she relayed her lack of progress at the police station. "April took the cuff link into evidence but I think that's where it will stay. She doesn't think they'll be able to solve the mystery. They just don't have the resources or time."

Trudy patted Priscilla's hand. "Then you'll have to do it. I have total faith in you."

Priscilla laughed. "Thanks. I'm glad someone does."

"You were a big help this morning," Gail said. "Jordan called me on the carpet about those flyers. But now we're headed in a different direction, thanks to Priscilla."

"And Harper." Priscilla nodded at the young woman behind the counter. She was chatting and laughing with a customer. "She works wonders with social media."

They chatted about the contest for a few minutes, then Trudy said, "Now let's talk about why I asked you here." She grinned. "Thanksgiving plans."

"Dad and I are doing the mashed potatoes," Gail said. "I'll cook about ten pounds in my lobster pot, and Dad will whip them with a mixer."

"That's a lot of potatoes," Priscilla said.

"Hers are the best," Joan said. "Lots of milk and butter." She sipped her coffee. "I'll make sweet potato casserole and green bean casserole."

"We're doing two turkeys," Trudy said. "So everyone will have leftovers to take home."

"Yum. I love leftovers," Gail said. "Turkey sandwiches with mayo, stuffing, and cranberry sauce are my favorite." The others chimed in on how to make the perfect turkey sandwich.

"How many people are coming?" Priscilla asked. She was planning to make her cranberry sauce, but she wanted to bring another side dish. Maybe pearled onions.

Trudy counted on her fingers. "Probably between twenty and twenty-five. What are you thinking of bringing, Priscilla?"

She mentioned her ideas. "I can do rolls too. And Rachel and A.J. will want to bring something."

"Have them bring cheese and crackers," Trudy said. "For appetizers. And pies, all of us do one pie each." They each called out a different pie—pumpkin, apple, and pecan so Priscilla offered to bring a crustless cranberry pie she'd come across.

"Good," Trudy said. "Something new and different. I'm sure it'll be great."

She'd better test the recipe. Maybe she'd take the pie to dinner at Gerald's. He would give her an honest opinion.

On the way home from the bakery, Priscilla drove out to the farm. She needed to talk to Whitney. The news that an FBI agent had been looking for her was not something to deliver over the phone.

By the time she arrived, the farm stand was closed, the big doors to the barn shut. Priscilla knocked on the house door to let Sheila know she was on the property, but she didn't answer. Leaving the car where it was, she walked across the field to Whitney's cabin.

She had almost reached the cabin when the door to Franklin's cabin opened. He emerged onto the porch and put his hands to his mouth. "Ahoy, Priscilla. Can you make a detour over here?"

Priscilla waved in response to indicate she would. Meanwhile her mind was whirring. What did Franklin want to talk to her about? Steeling herself, she forced a smile to her lips as she approached.

He bounded down the stairs to greet her. "I've just put the kettle on. Won't you join me for a cup of tea?"

She hesitated. "I was on my way to visit Anne."

"Come on. I'll only take a few minutes of your time. Besides, she's not here right now." He indicated the parking space beside her cabin, which was indeed empty.

Maybe talking to Franklin would be a way to kill time for a few minutes. Then she'd call Whitney and find out where she was.

He ushered her into the cabin. "This is much smaller than my usual digs," he said, reaching out for her coat. "But it's quite cozy, don't you think?"

Priscilla looked around the compact space. It was similar in style and furnishings to Whitney's, simple but attractive. "Yes, very nice." Priscilla took a seat at the table, in the chair with a view of Whitney's cabin. That way she could watch for her arrival.

Franklin busied himself in the small kitchen area. "Is black tea all right? I buy a special blend that is nice."

"That sounds fine," Priscilla said. She watched as he poured boiling water into a teapot, slid on a cozy, and placed it on a tray. Then he added two mugs, a pitcher of milk, and a sugar bowl. Something about his bustling movements and soft murmuring made her think he was happy to have a guest.

Is Franklin lonely? The unbidden thought caused her to shift in discomfort. Looking at a person through a different lens changed everything. Perhaps she should be more patient with the professor, more forgiving of his foibles.

"Here we are," he said, setting the tray carefully on the table. He poured a mug and handed it to her. He poured one for himself, then added milk and a spoonful of sugar. "I need it to sweeten me up," he said with a boyish grin.

Priscilla poured milk into her tea and stirred. She wasn't sure what to say, so she brought up the weather. "We're getting snow soon, I heard. Think we'll have a white Thanksgiving?"

Franklin sipped his tea. "Maybe so. It wouldn't be the first time." He set the cup down. "I have exciting news. And you're the first person I'm sharing it with."

Priscilla cringed. *Why her*? Because she happened to stop by? "I'm honored," she finally managed to choke out.

He tapped his hand on the table. "I've got a publisher interested in my book about Bitsy. I've just been on the phone with my editor. She is absolutely thrilled at the concept and thinks the book will be a best seller."

"That's fantastic news." Priscilla meant it. Then her heart sank at a realization. She couldn't allow him to keep going down the wrong path. That wouldn't be the right thing to do, at all. "I know you have your theories about Bitsy's death. But I've learned some things you might want to consider."

"And what are those, dear lady?" Franklin's eyebrow rose in a patronizing manner.

Priscilla felt her hackles rise but she managed to remain calm. "One of Tilly Snyder's relatives dated Ambrose. She has Hazel's diary, photographs, and a letter from Ambrose." She couldn't quite squash her glee when she added, "He was very much in love with Hazel."

Franklin was quiet for a moment, turning over the new information. Finally he smiled and said, "I'll have to take a look. But have you thought that Ambrose's alleged romance with Hazel might have been a cover? In those days, a relationship with a married woman might get you run out of town on a rail."

Or murdered. But Priscilla didn't believe that about Bitsy and Ambrose. Hazel's diary had the ring of truth. "Well, you'll have to take a look for yourself."

"I'll do that. Some things need to be left to the experts." Franklin nodded toward her cup. "More tea?"

Priscilla saw to her relief that Whitney was pulling in next door. She was ready to throw her resolution regarding Franklin out the window. "No, thanks. This was lovely but I'd better go. I need to speak to Anne about something."

Whitney was inside the cabin by the time Priscilla extracted herself from Franklin's clutches. He'd been reluctant to lose his audience, she figured. She rapped on the door. "Oh, hello, Priscilla," Whitney said. "I thought that was your SUV in the parking lot. I thought you were in the house."

"No, I was next door talking to Franklin." Priscilla left it at that. She pulled out her phone. "You might want to brace yourself. A man was looking for you today. I ran into him at Candy Lane Confectionery."

Whitney paled as she gasped. "A man? What did he look like?"

"I took a picture." Priscilla found the picture and handed Whitney the phone. "Sorry, it's a little blurry. I had to take it without him noticing."

"I'm not sure if it's Dalton." Whitney squinted at the screen, zooming in for a better look. "Too bad that lady is blocking his face." Priscilla had caught him leaning over a table.

"Well, he was tall, with short, dark hair. Not bad looking." Priscilla reflected. The agent hadn't had any unusual or outstanding features. Probably a good thing for a federal agent. That way he blended in, rather than stood out.

"Dalton is tall, with dark hair." Whitney studied the photo again. "I'm sorry, I just can't tell."

"He said his name was Geoff Sanders. Does that ring a bell?"

"No. I never met anyone with that name." Whitney handed her the phone. "But he was looking for me?"

Priscilla tucked her phone into her pocket. "He was. Whitney, you can't hide out here forever. You need to let me call A.J."

Whitney began to pace, wringing her hands. "I know. Every day I think, this is the day I go to the FBI. And then I have a panic attack, so I don't."

"Like I said before, A.J. is a really good guy," Priscilla said. "I can vouch for his integrity. Can I call him now?"

Whitney stopped pacing. "How do you know for sure he's honest?" Her mouth twisted. "I trusted Dalton at first."

Priscilla injected calm assurance into her tone, knowing that the young woman was in the grip of deep fear. "Because he's practically part of the family. I have a strong feeling he might be *the one*."

"You mean your daughter's going to marry him?" That surprised Whitney, and delight shone on her face.

"Perhaps. I hope so." Rachel wouldn't approve of this speculation about her love life, Priscilla knew. But if she ever found out, she'd probably forgive Priscilla. It was for a very good cause, after all. She was trying to help a vulnerable young woman get out of a terrible mess.

"All right." Whitney perched on the arm of the sofa. "Give him a call. But don't give him too many details, okay? Feel him out first."

Priscilla released a breath. "Fair enough." She thought of something. "Can you tell me a little more about what's on that flash drive?"

Whitney reached up to the chain around her neck. "It contains company records that prove there was a pyramid scheme. And I've got the money trail to offshore bank accounts."

"So the investment funds are still there?" Priscilla's heart leapt. Maybe Uncle Hugh and the others would get their money back.

"Most of it, yes. They've been funneling it overseas and stockpiling it in bank accounts." Whitney clasped the flash drive. "You can see why I'm frightened. A lot of money is involved. Millions."

When Priscilla got home, she looked up A.J.'s personal cell number on her phone and called. Rachel had given it to her once she was seeing the federal agent on a regular basis. She got voice mail, which didn't surprise her since A.J. had even been out of touch with Rachel. She left a message, asking him to call, too nervous to give many details. She'd try again first thing in the morning, she promised herself.

But morning brought its own problems. Jake woke her up by barking in her face. "What are you doing, boy?" Priscilla threw back the covers, annoyed. "This isn't like you." He usually waited patiently for her to get up and feed him. Then she'd let him out for his morning constitutional. It was their morning ritual.

She pushed her feet into her slippers and stood, so groggy she could barely stand. "Hang on," she muttered, reaching for her robe. "I'm going as fast as I can."

He preceded her to the kitchen, turning to bark every few steps. Maybe he was ill and needed to go out right away. But then her slipper sank into something cold and wet. She gave a tiny gasp, thinking at first that he had an accident.

Then she saw the puddle covering the kitchen floor. Jake didn't do that. No dog in the world could produce that puddle. Before she could stop him, Jake went splashing through the water, right to a closet. Then he barked again.

The water heater had sprung a leak. After staring at the problem in disbelief, Priscilla turned and squished away. The first step was to call Beau Ortmann, her go-to contractor. He was licensed to install water heaters, she'd heard.

Beau showed up right after Priscilla finished mopping the water from the kitchen floor, which had never been this clean. She put on a pot of coffee, finally fed poor Jake, and ran to answer the door.

"Have a little problem, do we?" Beau greeted her, a wide smile on his good-looking face.

"I'll say." Priscilla closed the door behind him. "I woke up to a puddle." She pointed to her wet slippers on the boot tray.

Familiar with every inch of the cottage, Beau carted his toolbox right to the closet. "These new-fangled water heaters do that once in a while. Some of my customers have stone-lined ones that were put in during the 1920s. Those never seem to leak."

"Newer is not always better, it seems." Priscilla reached for mugs. "Coffee?"

"Sure." Beau was checking over the heater. "Good job turning off the power and the water feed." He'd advised her how to do that over the phone. He hunkered down to examine the bottom. "I'm afraid you're going to need a new one."

"That's what I figured." Priscilla poured coffee and set milk and sugar on the table. "How much will it cost me?" She waited for his answer with a wince. The joys of homeownership.

While Beau went to get a water heater, Priscilla did her best to wash up with cold water. Then she took Jake for a walk. Tonight was her dinner with Gerald, and she planned to make a fresh batch of cranberry sauce and the crustless cranberry pie to take as her contribution.

The weather wasn't bad for November. Although thin clouds blocked most of the sun, the air was mild, a gentle onshore breeze carrying a briny aroma. She trudged down the rocky beach, pausing often to gaze at the pretty sights, like waves cresting on boulders or a pale-green tidal pool sprinkled with shells. She strolled along, saying her prayers.

Whitney Parker. The name flashed into her head. Oh yes, she'd been meaning to call A.J.

The noise of an engine made her look up, and she saw Beau's truck. Priscilla whistled for Jake and headed back up to the house.

Beau was already lugging the new tank inside. While he worked, she went ahead and made the cranberry sauce, cutting up cranberries then adding water, seasonings, and whole blueberries to the pot.

"Something smells good," Beau said when the concoction began simmering on the stove. "Reminds me of Thanksgiving."

"Good nose," she teased. "I'm testing a recipe for the cranberry sauce contest."

"Oh yeah. My mom's entering that too." Beau's mother, Katie Ortmann, ran a local grocery store. "It's for a great cause. Mom donates food from the store to the pantry."

"That's so generous of her." Without the donations of big-hearted store and restaurant owners, the hungry on the island would be sunk.

Beau nodded. "That's the way she is. Taught us to do the same from the time we were very young." He shook his head ruefully. "She also had us donate toys to the needy. They had to be good ones too."

Priscilla laughed. "That taught you a good lesson." Her already high opinion of Katie went up a notch. The islanders in general were good folk, especially those who lived here year round and saw the struggles.

By the time the hot water was ready for her shower, it was well into the afternoon. Priscilla headed into the bathroom, eager to test her new heater. Then she stopped.

A.J. She needed to call him again—now. With a sigh, she reversed direction and went to find her cell phone. Once again she got voice mail. She thought for a minute, then called Rachel.

Thankfully her daughter picked up, which didn't always happen when she was at work. "Hello, Mom. You caught me on a break."

"I'm glad." Priscilla hesitated. "I have a favor to ask. I need to contact A.J. regarding a situation here on the island."

Rachel laughed. "The FBI is required? Not for the skeleton, surely."

"No, it's to do with another case." She gave Rachel a brief rundown. "I've called A.J.'s cell but I've only gotten voice mail."

"That's what I was talking about before." Rachel's tone was resigned. "Sometimes he's working on cover operations, even undercover, and he can't do anything personal during that time. Or very limited stuff, anyway."

Priscilla absorbed that. "So what should I do?"

"Keep calling. He'll eventually call you back. And if I happen to talk to him first, I'll tell him to get in touch with you ASAP."

"Thanks, darling. Looking forward to seeing you." They chatted for a couple more minutes then Rachel had to go. Hopefully A.J. would call back soon. Whitney needed to know someone was on her side, besides a middle-aged widow.

CHAPTER TWELVE

Gerald lived outside Tisbury, in a neighborhood of older homes. Priscilla arrived at six on the dot, knowing that he would appreciate the promptness. And enough time to get ready. Gerald took his hosting duties very seriously.

Container of cranberry sauce, crustless cranberry pie, and bouquet of flowers in hand, Priscilla rang the doorbell. Like the other homes around it, Gerald's house was sided with weathered shingles. Other houses had green, white, and red shutters but Gerald's were a nice faded blue, perfect for a coastal cottage. The muted sound of surf drifted from a block away and stars winked in an inky sky.

Gerald answered the door right away, his old Irish setter Sammy hovering at his knees, panting. "Come on in," he said, his face bright with welcome. His gaze fell on the flowers. "For me?"

"Host gift," Priscilla said, handing over the cellophane-wrapped bundle. She laughed when Sammy pushed her head forward for a pat. "Aren't you a love?" She edged past the dog and gave Gerald the cranberry sauce. He set it down on the hall table with the flowers then held his hands out for her coat.

Such a gentleman. Priscilla slid off her boots while Gerald hung her coat in the closet. She'd be in her stocking feet all evening, like Gerald.

Gerald carried her offerings toward the back of the house, to the combination kitchen and dining area. To their left was the long, pleasant living room, decorated with pictures of sailing ships and the model ships Gerald either made or collected.

The kitchen had modern appliances, but Gerald had maintained the quaint charm of the older home, like the tall beadboard cabinets with their brass latches. Gerald foraged in one for a vase. "Want to do the honors?" He nodded at the flowers while sliding on oven mitts.

"Sure thing." Priscilla unwrapped the flowers and arranged them in the vase.

Gerald opened the oven to check on the chicken, releasing clouds of savory aroma. "We're just about there." He shut the door again. "I use the high heat method. Cooks poultry quickly while sealing in the juices."

Priscilla set the vase of flowers on the table set for two. "Tell me more. I've always cooked chicken low and slow."

He gave her the details while checking the boiling potatoes and setting fresh green beans to blanch. "I love to try new foods and methods, especially in the winter when I can't grill."

Gerald rose even higher in Priscilla's estimation. Many single men and women ate out of packages or lived on prepared food. Some, like Gerald, and to a lesser degree, Priscilla herself, rose to the challenge of cooking healthy and interesting meals for one.

"What can I do?" she asked.

He pointed to the fridge. "How about giving the salad a toss? I've got a selection of dressings in there too. Pick whatever you like."

The salad was lovely, fresh lettuce studded with tomatoes, green peppers, black olives, and cucumbers. Priscilla found wooden fingers and gave it a good mix. Then she set it next to the flowers on the table along with French, Italian, and Russian dressing. *International flavors*, she thought with a smile.

"This is going to be a feast," she said, finding a small glass bowl in the cupboard for her cranberry sauce. She'd serve it in that instead of the plastic container.

Gerald smiled and nodded, holding up one finger as he prepared to turn on a hand mixer to whip potatoes. He added plenty of milk and butter. The fluffy tower of potatoes went into one bowl, the green beans in another.

Lastly he carved the golden chicken, a work of art in itself. "White or dark meat?" he asked, fork and carving knife poised.

"Both," Priscilla said. "Please." He'd cooked his famous oyster stuffing separately, and she carried the hot pan to the table.

"You must be excited for Rachel to be here for Thanksgiving," Gerald said, sawing away at the meat.

Priscilla leaned against the counter. "I am." Then she felt her lips turn down. "She's coming early, but guess what? She's staying in Boston, not coming out here right away."

"Doesn't A.J. live there?"

"He does." She flapped a hand, annoyed at her childish attitude. "I know I sound like one of those clinging mothers. It just stung me, that's all."

"Understandable. She's your baby, and you miss her." Gerald used the fork and knife to convey slices of chicken onto the plate. "I think we're done here."

Gerald carried the platter to the table, and they sat. After they were settled, napkins on their knees, he said grace, giving God gratitude for the day, the company, and their families. He even asked for travel blessings for Rachel.

They loaded their plates and dug in.

"Oh my, this is good." Priscilla was amazed by the sweet yet salty flavor of the oyster stuffing. "I was worried I'd hate it." She put a hand to her mouth, mortified by her confession.

His eyes twinkled at her as he spooned her cranberry sauce on a slice of chicken breast. "Would you have told me?" He took a bite and nodded approval. "Perfect."

"Maybe not. I would have hid it under my napkin, like Rachel used to do." Priscilla recalled the days of picky eating. For a while, Rachel had liked only oat cereal, baked chicken, macaroni and cheese, and corn. Everything else was a battle.

"My son went through that too. His mother and I were worried he'd be stunted." Gerald laughed. "Then he grew taller than me."

"Rachel got over it, thank goodness." Priscilla put a little bit of everything on her fork. What a delicious combination. "Once she went to college, she tried all kinds of cuisine. Now she enjoys just about everything." She laughed. "Like her mom."

"I like a woman who eats." Gerald's eyes were warm. "A good appetite shows a zest for life."

Priscilla laughed again. What was it about this man? She felt so bubbly around him. "I've got you covered there, then."

Gerald took another few bites. "What's new with the skeleton mystery?"

"Oh, you won't believe what we've found." Priscilla took him through the recent discoveries of the clothing, the cuff link, and the items Tilly had shared.

"Your conclusions from all that?" Gerald inquired. He'd steadily worked his way through his plate while Priscilla was talking. Now he leaned back, hands folded across his trim middle in satisfaction.

Priscilla took another bite of chicken layered with stuffing and potato. "I think Vernon killed her, then packed her clothes to make it look like she'd left. The cuff link got caught on something and fell into the trunk." She chuckled. "Of course Franklin still thinks Ambrose Allen is guilty. Oh, and Jordan Parker doesn't believe the skeleton is Bitsy, either. She said it's one of the maids."

"You've got to follow the clues and keep an open mind," Gerald said. "Neither of them appears to be doing that." He leaned forward, tapping a finger on the tablecloth. "What I want to know is, where did Ambrose go?"

Gerald's question hovered in the back of Priscilla's mind the rest of the evening, during dessert and a few games of cribbage they played. Priscilla wasn't the expert cribbage player Gerald was, but she won two out of three anyway. "I've created a monster," he said with a laugh as he put the pegs and cards away.

"Let's do this again," Priscilla said. She blushed. How forward of her.

His eyes shone in the soft light. "I'd like that. Very much." Then he broke the tension by saying, "Your turn to cook."

Once at home that evening, she managed to put the mystery of Ambrose aside and get a good night's sleep. But the next morning, while driving out to the farm through a misty fall rain, it returned in full force.

If Ambrose was the killer, as Franklin asserted, then it made sense that he'd fled the island. She had to give Franklin credit for that logic. The same applied if Ambrose and Bitsy ran off together.

But they'd found Bitsy. At least she believed they had. Learning what had happened to Evangeline the maid rose in priority on her mental checklist.

The expense ledger. She could find out how long Evangeline worked for the Parkers by checking the payments to the employees. The ledger Bitsy used was at the cottage, with the other papers she'd found so far. Maybe she could find the next in the series at the farm, one Vernon used after Bitsy was gone.

The parking lot at the farm was empty and the barn door closed, not surprising in this weather. Not many customers would be venturing out, she guessed. Priscilla pulled up the hood of her raincoat before she got out and splashed to the house. At least it wasn't the horrendous downpour of several days ago. According to Gerald, parts of the island were still recovering from the storm.

All was warm and cozy inside the kitchen. The woodstove radiated heat, and a jovial group was seated around the kitchen table. "Come on in," Sheila called. "You know the guys, right?"

"I do." Priscilla shed her raincoat and hung it on a peg. "How are you all on this miserable day?"

Chowder, Chowder Jr., and Gilbert Jenks called greetings, interspersed with complaints. "Not much fun in the bog when it rains," Chowder Jr. said.

Gilbert scoffed. "You're already wet from the knees down on a good day. What's a little water up top?"

"I don't see you out there," Chowder said. He reached for a muffin. "Let me know when you're ready to give it a go."

"Want to join us?" Sheila asked Priscilla. "Grab a cup of coffee."

Priscilla filled a mug from the perking coffeepot on the stove. She took a seat next to Gilbert, across from Chowder Jr. Sheila and Chowder sat at the ends of the table. When Priscilla slid her feet under the table, she found Bosco underneath, snoring. She gently ran a stocking foot across his back.

"We've got cranberry-raspberry streusel muffins," Sheila said. "Help yourself."

"Don't mind if I do." Priscilla grabbed the smallest one, noticing that the men had shifted their discussion to hunting. The muffin was the perfect combination of tart and sweet.

"Dad and I are going out this Saturday," Chowder Jr. said. "We have our own special places. One of us gets a deer every year."

"Is that so?" Gilbert said. "I have a camp out in the swamp." He winked, a gesture that was more of a grimace on his weathered, tanned face. "The deer love it out there."

"So we've heard," Chowder said. "We gotta keep these places quiet. Don't want any outsiders interfering." He sat back in his chair with a grumble.

"Did I tell you about the hunter I ran into the other day?" Chowder Jr. asked. "He didn't seem to know which way was up, he was so dumb."

"Where was that?" Sheila asked. "Want to know so I can duck." Everyone laughed.

"Actually it was right out here. I asked him, 'Can't you read? The sign says no trespassing, no hunting.'"

Sheila clicked her tongue. "What is wrong with people? I have to run them off every year."

Priscilla was thankful she didn't have enough woods around her house to attract hunters. Otherwise she and Jake would have to wear orange. At least there wasn't much chance of a fatal accident from the fishermen who frequented the shore.

"Did you hear people have been poaching again?" Chowder asked. "I talked to the Game Warden, and he told me that they caught a hunter who didn't tag his deer."

"What does poaching involve?" Priscilla asked. She'd heard of the criminal act, of course, but wasn't clear on the details.

"Basically it's taking deer improperly," Chowder Jr. said. "Using bait. Hunting where it's prohibited. Messing with tags, either omitting them or using someone else's."

"It must be hard to detect," Priscilla said. "You'd have to catch them in the act, basically."

"Yeah, it can be. The Game Warden relies on the good hunters to keep an eye out for lawbreakers."

"Always a bad egg spoiling it for the rest of us," Gilbert grumbled.

Someone rapped at the kitchen door, then opened the door and Whitney entered. "Brr. It's freezing out there," she said. "The rain is turning to snow."

"No, you're kidding," Chowder said with a groan. In unison, they all looked out the window where snowflakes were now mixing with raindrops.

"I guess that settles it," Sheila said. "I'll have you boys work in the barn today. There's equipment to fix, plus berries to bag." She looked at Priscilla. "People have been cleaning us out, cooking for that contest."

"That's a lot of sauce," Gilbert said.

"They're not buying just for sauce," Sheila said. "They end up wanting to cook all kinds of cranberry dishes." She smiled. "It was my dad's dream to see the humble cranberry as popular as blueberries. Maybe we'll get there yet." She pushed her chair back and stood, a signal to the men that the break was over. Bosco got up from his nap, shaking his tags with a jingle.

The men bumbled to their feet with a scraping of chairs and filed out, exclaiming at the weather and joshing each other. Inviting Whitney to help herself to coffee and muffins, Sheila added more wood to the stove. Then she and Bosco followed the workers.

Whitney poured a cup of coffee and gave Priscilla's mug a warm-up. "You need help today, Priscilla?"

"That would be wonderful," Priscilla said.

"Great. I've been suffering from cabin fever, especially in this weather." She laughed. "Literally, since I'm staying in one."

"Have you seen Franklin?" Priscilla asked. He'd offered to help with the inventory but she had yet to see him come through, not that she wanted his assistance.

"He took off a while ago," Whitney said. "All dressed up." She took the seat beside Priscilla.

"We've got to make a serious dent today," Priscilla said, leaning her head on her hand. "Or else we'll be here all winter." She'd allowed the Bitsy Parker mystery to derail her efforts to inventory materials related to the farm exhibit.

"Like I said, I'm eager to help." Whitney's eyes were somber. "Did you call your friend for me?"

Priscilla sat up, reminded of her call to A.J. "I did. I had to leave a message, but I'm sure he'll call me back."

Whitney stared into her cup. "I hope so." Her shoulders hunched, and she wrapped one arm around her middle. "I feel like it's all closing in on me. I could leave...but I'm afraid to at the same time."

"Why did you come here?" Priscilla asked. She'd been wondering about that.

Whitney's lips curved in a wan smile. "It was a strange choice, wasn't it? When it all...went down, I had to pack and get out of town. I thought of flying somewhere but they track that now, you know? So I bought a ferry ticket instead, with cash." She grimaced. "I should have picked another island. I can't believe Jordan is hanging around Martha's Vineyard with all that's going on with the firm. When we were younger, you couldn't get her here after Labor Day."

"What's her role in the company?" Priscilla asked, curious.

Whitney set her mug down. "She's one of the investment counselors. I worked in the accounting department." She touched her necklace. "That's how I could access the records."

Priscilla didn't want to ask if Jordan was involved with the firm's financial misdeeds, but Whitney sensed the question.

"I don't know if she's involved," Whitney said. "But it's her dad, my uncle Dale, who authorized the money transfers." She gulped, her eyes glistening with fear. "I couldn't believe it when I found out what was going on"

Whitney couldn't hide forever. "Are you waiting for something in particular to happen before you come forward?"

"As you can tell, I ran away without a plan, after learning Dalton was a crook," Whitney admitted. "But now I'm hoping your friend can help me. I want to give the evidence to someone trustworthy. Or else that money is going to disappear, along with most of the case against the firm."

CHAPTER THIRTEEN

Priscilla and Whitney made good progress on the contents of the office. By noon, they had organized the farm's financial paperwork by chronological year. Anyone wanting to study the ledgers would be able to see associated bills and invoices. Priscilla had also found two more Parker ledgers. These went into her bag for later perusal at home.

"You two want a sandwich?" Sheila asked, putting her head around the doorjamb. "I've got turkey and roast beef."

Whitney looked at Priscilla. She had a cute smudge of dust on her nose. "I'm leaving it up to you."

Priscilla regarded the tidy folders of materials. "I think this is a great place to stop. I'm going to call Mildred after we eat and give her an update."

They washed up and joined Sheila in the kitchen, Whitney now minus the smudge. There were only three plates on the table.

"Where are the men?" Priscilla asked as she and Whitney took their places.

Sheila poured potato chips into a bowl. "They had to go get parts for a tractor. I think they're stopping for lunch somewhere." She set the bowl in the middle of the table.

"I need to catch up with Gilbert later," Priscilla said. "One of his relatives worked for the Parkers, and I want to ask him about her."

"Is that so?" Sheila sat and offered a short grace. Then, with a gesture, she invited them to start eating.

Priscilla took a bite of her sandwich. Turkey, cheese, and mayonnaise went perfectly with the crisp lettuce Sheila had added. "*Mmm.* This is good." She dabbed her mouth with a napkin. "A woman named Evangeline Jenks was a maid there at the same time as your grandmother."

Whitney softly gasped. When the other two looked over, she gave a weak smile. "Sorry. It's just that I always heard stories about Evangeline from my grandmother. There was some kind of scandal attached to her too, as well as Bitsy."

"I wouldn't mention that part to Gilbert," Sheila said. "He's kind of touchy."

Priscilla grabbed a handful of chips. "Don't worry, I'll be tactful. I know all about family pride." Many of the situations she'd encountered involved family histories. And on a long-settled place like Martha's Vineyard, people were protective of reputation.

Before she even asked Gilbert a thing, she would check the ledgers for a clue to Evangeline's tenure with the Parker family.

After finishing lunch, Sheila drove off in her truck with a promise to return soon, Bosco beside her. Priscilla called Mildred, as promised.

"Are you still at the farm?" Mildred asked.

"I am." Priscilla regarded the next task, organizing the farm's marketing materials. This would be a little more fun than the bookkeeping side. "I'll probably stay until around four." The sun would be very low in the sky by then and with the continuing snowfall, Priscilla wanted to get home before dark.

"I'll pop over," Mildred said. "See what you've been doing. Plus I need to buy some cranberries for that contest."

"That'd be great," Priscilla said. Sheila wasn't open today, but Priscilla knew she wouldn't turn Mildred away. No one ever did. "See you soon."

"I think I know Mildred," Whitney said, her eyes wide. "Is she that lady who always wears vintage clothing?"

"That's her. Although I've seen her in regular clothes a few times." Priscilla could count those times on one hand. She picked up an artistic poster displaying a man guiding berries in a bog. "Let's put the posters together. Mildred is going to love them."

Mildred arrived in a whirl of checked cloth cloak and snow-flakes. She brushed stray flakes of snow out of her hair while regarding the new collection. "All I can say is, wow. This is even more extensive than I imagined."

Priscilla rested her hands on her hips. "I know, right?" She reached out and opened the closet door. "And there's more."

"We already brought out one of the best things," Whitney said helpfully. "A trunk full of 1930s clothes."

Mildred, lover of all antique clothes, pursed her lips. "From the farm?"

"No, Bitsy Parker," Priscilla said. "They're gorgeous. And at my house."

"I'll want to see those," Mildred said. "Let me know when I can stop by."

Priscilla neatened a stack of postcards advertising the cranberry farm. Decades ago, most businesses did that, creating a colorful record.

Mildred leaned against the desk, supporting an elbow with one hand while the other hand rested on her cheek. She was silent for several moments, her eyes assessing the piles of ledgers, the posters, and the stacks of family photographs. "I'm going to be able to do a lot with this," she announced.

"There's fodder here for a dozen researchers," Priscilla said.

"Yes indeed." Mildred nodded. "I've got someone writing a book about Martha's Vineyard farms through history. They'll enjoy the ledgers. And I'd like to celebrate our farming heritage with a special exhibit of vintage posters, photos, and postcards. Tools, crates, and the like too."

"Not many people realize there are farms out here," Priscilla said. "And with the interest in local food, they're having a revival." Besides buying from Sheila, Priscilla made a point of purchasing fruits, vegetables, and flowers from local growers. Everything was much fresher, plus it was fun to visit farms.

"Exactly," Mildred said. "I've got the local farmer's market vendors involved, and some foodie chefs. We'll cross-promote and serve local food at an opening reception."

"I never knew research could be so much fun," Whitney said. "I always thought it was about dry and dusty history books."

Mildred smiled. "Oh, it's so much more than that, dear. It's stories about real people. At best it's like stepping into a time machine for a little while."

Priscilla thought about Mildred's observation while she and Whitney got back to work. If only she could step into a time machine and solve Bitsy's murder. How much easier it would be to solve cold cases that way. Instead she was stuck putting little pieces together bit by painstaking bit.

But she loved it. There was almost nothing she'd rather do.

They wrapped up just before four. Outside the big windows, snow was still coming down, but fortunately it hadn't accumulated much. "I'm going to head out in a few minutes," Priscilla said. "Thanks again for your help."

"I really enjoyed it," Whitney said, sliding into her coat. "It kept my mind off things. Let me know if you need me again."

Priscilla glanced around at all that remained. She laughed. "I think I might."

After Whitney left Priscilla proceeded to tidy up, making notes about what she would tackle next. An unexpected trove had held dozens of vintage tourism brochures and flyers for other businesses on the island. Sheila's mother's interests had certainly been far ranging.

Priscilla had even found several pictures of the lighthouse she'd like to add to her own small museum. Those she set aside to ask

Sheila about. The one featuring a group of Victorian ladies taking tea on the lawn was especially intriguing.

Priscilla was putting on her coat when the outer door slammed open and Whitney burst in, her face white. "Priscilla. Someone has been in my cabin."

Priscilla dropped one of her gloves. "What?" she asked, although she'd plainly heard the words. She bent to pick up the glove and put it on. "Show me."

They trotted across the field, leaving footprints in the thin snow cover. Whitney reached the cabin and thumped up the steps. She'd left the door partially open.

Franklin's car was parked next to his cabin. Maybe he'd seen something.

"Are you coming?" Whitney called from the porch.

Thinking of their own prints, Priscilla continued to scan the ground and in a moment, was rewarded. She could plainly see a set of larger prints approach then leave Whitney's cabin. "Hang on a second. Come see this."

She pulled out her phone and took a picture for future reference. The print had distinctive wavy treads, meaning it was probably a winter boot of some kind.

Whitney appeared at her side. "Do you think the intruder left those?"

"They're going in the right direction." Priscilla pointed to the line of prints coming out of the woods and heading toward the steps. They also circled to the back of the cabin. "I'll look inside the cabin in a minute. These prints aren't going to be here long in this snow.

It's melting already." She walked around the cabin, careful not to step on the impressions. She took several more pictures.

Then she noticed a window in a shed attached to the back of the cabin. It was wide open. That was probably how the intruder got in. Looking closer, she saw how the lock had been jimmied. She photographed that too. Another set of footprints went in the reverse direction and headed to the woods. And that was how the intruder left.

Priscilla went around to the front. "I figured out how the intruder got in," she told Whitney. "He came in through the shed window."

Whitney pressed her lips together. "I didn't go out there. When I saw the mess, I ran."

"Well, let's go take a look." Priscilla mounted the steps, bracing herself. It was never pleasant when someone broke into a person's home. It was both intrusive and frightening.

The place didn't look terrible, but it was evident someone had searched. Cushions were off the sofa and armchairs, and the bed had been stripped. Bureau drawers and kitchen cupboards were ajar.

"What do you think they were looking for?" Priscilla asked. She had a very good idea, of course. She used her phone to take more photographs.

Whitney touched the chain around her neck. "This. It's the only thing I have of value to them."

Priscilla checked the pictures she'd taken, making sure they were clear. "Shall we call the police? Or tell Sheila at least?" They needed to mention the broken lock, for sure.

Whitney sank down onto the arm of the sofa, her face miserable. "No to both. You know I can't go to the cops. And I don't want to upset Sheila. She's been so good to me. I feel bad for bringing trouble to her door."

Priscilla considered the young woman, her trepidation and concern growing. Someone was definitely on her trail. First a warning letter, and now someone had broken in during daylight hours.

Tears streaming down her face, Whitney began to pick up the cushions and put them in place. "This is all so horrible. Why is this happening to me?" She sniffed. "I'm just an accountant."

"Who is also incredibly observant and honest." Priscilla considered the options. There really was only one. "You're coming home with me." Priscilla knew she was sticking her neck out, but really, what choice did she have? Whitney couldn't stay here. And when A.J. called, he could talk directly to her.

Whitney stared at her, the tears still coming. "That's so generous of you, Priscilla."

Priscilla brushed her off. "Let's get this place straightened up. And then pack a bag. I've got someone I want you to meet. He has four legs and is very friendly."

That startled a laugh out of the young woman. "Should I follow you over, do you think?"

"No, let's go in my car. Let whoever it is think you're still here." Priscilla reached to switch on a table lamp. "We'll draw the curtains and leave a couple of lights on."

Between the two of them, the place was in good shape and Whitney was ready to go within fifteen minutes. She picked up a small duffel bag and her handbag. She also retrieved a package from the fridge. "I bought some fresh haddock earlier today," she said. "It'll be my contribution towards dinner. And I'll lock the door when I leave this time. Though I doubt he'll be back."

If he was, he'd probably want to talk to Whitney—or worse, Priscilla feared. That's why she was whisking her away. Let the intruder find an empty cabin. And if he caused enough of a ruckus, perhaps someone else would call the police.

They were making their way down the front steps, now also covered with snow, when Franklin's door opened. Priscilla braced herself, having hoped to escape unnoticed.

He emerged onto the front porch. "Where are you ladies off to?" he asked, his tone jovial.

"Oh, here and there," Priscilla said. "How are you?" She deftly turned the subject to Franklin's favorite topic, himself.

"I'm great, thank you." Rocking back and forth on his heels, he preened. "Popped over to the mainland. Had an excellent meeting with my editor."

"That's good to hear," Priscilla said. Hopefully he wouldn't submit a manuscript full of half-baked theories. That wouldn't help his reputation any.

Franklin continued to beam. "Let's get together soon and look at those little things you found." He pointed a finger. "Give me a call."

"Or you can call me." She smiled sweetly. Franklin liked to be in charge, to have people come to him.

"Yes, well." Franklin huffed a bit. "I'd better get inside. It's chilly out here." He reached for the door, then paused. "Did you see your visitor, Anne?"

For a second Priscilla didn't know who he was talking to. Then she remembered that Whitney was still traveling under her alias.

"Visitor?" Whitney darted a glance at Priscilla, her face blanching. "Did you see what he looked like? Or she?"

Franklin thrust out his bottom lip with a headshake. "No, not really. He was tall, wearing a winter coat and hat. Boots." He laughed. "Like everyone at this time of year."

"What time was he here?" Whitney asked. "I was over at the farmhouse all afternoon."

Franklin made a show of checking his watch. "Maybe thirty, forty minutes ago. Now if you'll excuse me." With a wave, he entered his cabin.

At least they'd learned when and that Whitney's visitor was indeed a man. Of course they still had no idea who, but from the description, it might well have been Dalton Rogers. That would mean Whitney's cover was blown. Priscilla peered into the woods, seeing only trees standing close together. Was he in there now, watching? The thought made her skin crawl.

With the same instinct, Whitney turned to look into the forest. "I'm so scared," she said, twisting her hands together. "I hope your friend calls soon."

"I'll call him again when we get to my house," Priscilla promised.

Back at the farmhouse, Priscilla gathered her bag and the ledgers she wanted to review. She took one last look around, and then she and Whitney went out to her car. The lights were on in the barn, but Priscilla didn't bother to track Sheila down. The more low-key they were about Whitney leaving with her, the better. She'd tell her about the lock on the shed window later.

The ride to the cottage was quiet, both women lost in their thoughts. Priscilla spent most of the time praying, knowing that it was all she could do. And it was the best thing she could do.

"I can't believe you live here," Whitney said when they pulled into the driveway. "It's a real lighthouse."

Priscilla laughed. "It sure is. The Coast Guard maintains it." While she parked in the garage and they made their way inside the house, she gave Whitney a brief history of her move to the island.

Whitney sighed. "What a wonderful story." She looked like she wanted to say more, but Jake's arrival cut her short. He leaped up despite Priscilla's scolding and licked Whitney's cheek, yipping and whining the whole time.

"I think you made a new friend," Priscilla said, grabbing the dog's collar and pulling him away. If Jake was any judge of character, Whitney Parker was okay.

"He's adorable." Crouching down, Whitney gave him a thorough neck rub. "I met you at Joan's, with your friend, Sister."

At the mention of Sister, Jake whined again. "And they say dogs don't understand what we say." Priscilla shook her head.

"Why don't you make yourself at home? I'm going to let him outside for a few minutes."

In the yard, Priscilla let Jake run around while she called A.J. and left another message. "It's really urgent," she said. "I know you are on another case but please, as soon as you can, call me." She wanted to say more but felt constrained by the need for secrecy.

When Priscilla and Jake returned from their excursion, they found Whitney in the living room in front of the fireplace. She stood up and gestured with pride. "Look what I did." The fire was small but growing, the flames licking at the bark of a birch log.

"Good job," Priscilla said. "It's a perfect night for a fire." With the arrival of snow, the temperatures had plummeted. The wind was up too, howling around the eaves.

Whitney gave the fire another stir. "There. That should do it." Tugging at the hem of her sweater, she asked, "What shall we do with the haddock?"

"Let's go figure that out." Priscilla led the way to the kitchen, taking a detour to show Whitney the small but comfortable guest room.

"I have a good chowder recipe," Whitney said. "It doesn't take long." She named the ingredients she'd need, and Priscilla had them all.

"It's settled, then," Priscilla said. "I'll make a batch of buttermilk biscuits to go with it." She fed Jake his dinner, then got out the fixings for the chowder and let Whitney get to work.

To the soft strains of classical music from the radio, they moved about the kitchen in pleasant harmony. Watching Whitney at the stove reminded Priscilla of Rachel, causing a sharp pang of longing in her heart. Most of the time she was fine, while at other times she missed her daughter fiercely. Why did they have to live so far apart?

Many families did that nowadays, she reminded herself. Hardly anyone she knew had grown children living on the island.

"This reminds me of cooking with my mom," Whitney said softly, her eyes somber. "One of my few memories. I lost her and my dad in a plane crash when I was really small."

Without even thinking about it, Priscilla crossed the kitchen and gave her a hug. "Sorry," she said. "I have flour all over my hands." She'd been rolling out the biscuits.

Whitney laughed. "I don't care. I smell like onions." She hugged Priscilla back. "What is your daughter like?"

Priscilla told her all about Rachel and even brought out a photograph—after washing her hands. "She's coming here for Thanksgiving, and I can hardly wait."

"I'll bet." Whitney continued to smile, but her eyes were sad again. "I usually celebrate with my aunt and uncle, Jordan's parents. They won't be doing much this year."

If Dale Parker was guilty of fraud, as the government thought, Priscilla couldn't muster much sympathy for him. But as with any crime, there was fallout, with innocent victims hurt. If only Dale Parker and his ilk would realize that. But perhaps for them greed and riches overrode anything else. Priscilla had never understood that, and she still didn't. The best things in life were free, as the old saying asserted.

"If you're still around," Priscilla said, "then you're welcome to join the Latham clan for Thanksgiving. It's at my cousin Trudy's house, and I know she won't mind." Priscilla knew that Trudy had a warm heart and would never turn away an orphan.

"That's such a nice offer." Whitney's face shone with happiness. "Thank you." She stirred the chowder again and set the spoon on the rest. "Point me to the dishes, and I'll set the table."

They ate at the kitchen table, chatting companionably about the lighthouse, Whitney's summers on the island as a child, and other innocuous topics. After dinner, they settled in the living room in front of the fire, sipping tea and reading. Whitney had brought a novel, although every time Priscilla looked up from her work, the young woman was staring into the fire.

Priscilla pulled out the Parker ledgers and went through them carefully. The live-in servants were paid once a month. Those who worked sporadically or lived elsewhere, like Sheila's grandmother, were paid weekly.

There was no entry for Evangeline in the ledgers after Bitsy's disappearance. Priscilla wished she knew what that meant. Had the woman quit? If she was close to Bitsy, that might have happened. But Whitney had said something about a scandal.

Whitney had set aside the book and was petting Jake, who naturally was eating up the attention.

"Whitney, can you remember anything your grandmother said about Evangeline or the scandal surrounding her?" Priscilla asked.

Whitney thought for a moment, running her hand across Jake's fuzzy head. "Not in any detail. Whenever Grandmother was discussing employees with her friends, she would bring her up. 'They're no more reliable than that Evangeline who used to work for Vernon.'" Whitney's face lit up. "Oh, and then she'd say sometimes, 'Let's hope they're not light-fingered like her too.' For a long time I had no idea what that meant. I thought Grandmother was talking about the size of her hands."

Considering that Mabel hadn't even been married to Vernon then, Priscilla found her keeping this grudge against the maid quite remarkable, but some people were like that. The spite was of use in this case. They knew Evangeline had been suspected of stealing.

"That's helpful," Priscilla said. "It gives us a little more information about Evangeline, although not why she left or exactly when." She tapped the book. "I do know it was right after Bitsy disappeared. There are no payments to her afterward."

"Why is Evangeline important?" Whitney asked. She gave Jake a final pat, and he collapsed onto her feet with a huge sigh.

"She's not to me, really. But your cousin is convinced that the skeleton is actually Evangeline. I'm trying to rule out that possibility."

Whitney snorted. "She probably doesn't want to believe it could be Granddad's first wife. She never wants any bad press about the business."

So that was why Jordan was so adamant the skeleton wasn't Bitsy. She was afraid it would reflect badly on Parker and Warren.

"But I suppose it could be possible Grandmother told her more details about Evangeline than she told me," Whitney added after a moment.

That was a thought. Priscilla could question Jordan. "I'll talk to her when I see her. She's in charge of the cranberry sauce contest. My cousin Gail roped me into serving on the committee."

"Be careful," Whitney warned with a smile. "Once they get you for one committee, you'll be asked to join all kinds of them."

"What's that they say? If you need something done, ask a busy person?" Priscilla pushed herself out of the far-too-comfortable chair. "Would you like more tea?"

"I'd love some."

Priscilla gathered their mugs and took them to the kitchen. While waiting for the water to boil, she looked out the window. The sweep of the lighthouse beam allowed her to check the weather. Snowflakes still danced, but although steady, they weren't heavy. They'd be getting a foot of flurries, as the old-timers said.

She pulled out two fresh tea bags, raspberry peach this time. She poured boiling water into the mugs, dunked the tea bags, and carried the drinks into the living room. She handed Whitney her cup, then moved the ledgers aside so she could set her mug safely down on a coaster. An idea popped into her mind.

"Whitney, I found something odd in the back of Bitsy's ledger." Priscilla lifted that book from the pile. "Can you take a look?" She leafed through to the final pages, then took the ledger to Whitney, since Whitney was trapped by Jake lying across her feet.

It only took the young woman a minute to reach a conclusion. "These are stock market notations. Bitsy was tracking certain companies." Her brow furrowed in a frown. "And by the way the prices are jumping around, I'd say someone was manipulating their value."

CHAPTER FOURTEEN

W hat does that mean?" Priscilla asked. She really didn't have more than a basic knowledge of the stock market and how it worked. She also lacked the deviousness required to figure out how someone could manipulate stock transactions to their own advantage.

"Criminal activity like this is why the Securities and Exchange Commission was created," Whitney said. "Crooked investors worked together to artificially inflate prices by making it look like the stock was in demand. Then once other people were jumping on board, they would dump the stocks and take their profits."

Priscilla mulled that over. "I've heard of insider trading. Isn't that when people know company secrets and use them to their own advantage?"

"Exactly," Whitney said. "The stock market, since it seeks investment from the public, is supposed to give all investors a level playing field. Insider traders circumvent that law to give themselves an unfair advantage."

"The question is," said Priscilla, "was Bitsy doing the manipulating, or was she on the trail of someone else doing it? Parker & Warren handled stocks back then, didn't they?"

Whitney laid her head against the chair back and sighed. "I believe so. I guess the apple doesn't fall far from the tree. They're still up to tricks." She stared into the crackling flames. "I think it's time for the tree to turn over a new leaf."

Priscilla regarded Whitney with admiration. This was one Parker who wasn't content to amass wealth through crooked means. A chill went down Priscilla's spine despite the fire's toasty warmth. She wasn't going to let anything happen to Whitney, not on her watch.

As though sensing her thoughts, Jake raised his head, growled, and gave a sharp bark. He remained with his head lifted and ears perked for a moment, then lay down again with a huge doggy sigh.

Priscilla and Whitney laughed.

"I guess he was dreaming," Priscilla said. But before they went to bed, she went around the cottage and made sure all the windows and doors were firmly locked.

First thing in the morning, Priscilla's phone rang. A.J. Taking a gulping breath of relief, she said, "A.J. Thank you for calling. It's about the—" The phone hissed and buzzed. "Can you hear me?" she asked. His reply was garbled, and then the phone disconnected. Dead silence. Priscilla bit back a groan.

Whitney entered the kitchen right after Priscilla hung up. "Good morning," she said. Her face was radiant in the early morning sunshine. "I slept great. And this guy kept me company." Jake was at her heels.

Priscilla tucked away her frustration and returned her guest's smile. "I wondered where he got to." Priscilla wasn't really surprised. Jake often slept in the guest room when she had visitors. "Ready for some breakfast?"

Jake wagged his tail. "Absolutely. I'm starved." Whitney headed for the coffee carafe. "Okay to pour a cup?"

"Of course." Priscilla thought about options while feeding Jake. "I can make french toast. I've got fresh farm eggs and maple syrup."

Whitney added a dash of milk to her coffee. "Yum. I love french toast."

"Bacon or sausage links?" Priscilla had both.

"Sausage links, please. Is there anything I can do to help?" Whitney stared out at the gilded bay and sipped. "Wow, what a view."

"Not a thing. Drink your coffee and relax." Then Priscilla had a thought. "Unless you'd like to take Jake out for his morning walk?"

Whitney readily agreed, so after Jake ate, she bundled up and took him down to the beach. Priscilla, meanwhile, cooked the sausage and mixed egg batter. She'd wait to make the french toast until Whitney returned.

Her phone rang and Priscilla snatched it up, hoping it was A.J. It was Joan. "Hello, cousin. Want to come over for lunch today? I've got seafood chowder in the slow cooker." By the background noise, Priscilla could tell Joan was at work.

"That sounds delicious," Priscilla said. "Is there enough for three? I brought Whitney home to stay with me."

"Of course." Joan laughed. "I make a huge batch, and it usually lasts me for days. If you two help me, I won't get so sick of it."

Priscilla couldn't imagine getting tired of seafood chowder. "I'll make a batch of cheddar biscuits if you want."

"Yes, I want. Excuse me a second." Joan muffled the receiver and spoke to someone. "Got to go. See you at one?"

"It's a plan." Priscilla reached for her mother's recipes, collected in a typical spiral-bound notebook. She enjoyed leafing through, seeing the notations in her mother's handwriting. The cheddar biscuits were a family favorite.

Whitney and Jake entered the kitchen, bringing the scent of fresh ocean air and snow with them. "That was fun," Whitney said. "I had to yell at him not to go in the water, though." She shrugged out of her coat and ran a hand through her hair.

Priscilla fed Jake a dog biscuit. "Tell me about it. He doesn't get that the water is only about forty degrees."

"*Brr.* That's cold." Whitney rubbed her arms at the thought. "I'm glad I stopped him."

"Yes, or we'd have a dog with hypothermia." Priscilla put the jar of dog treats away, to Jake's chagrin.

Whitney inhaled with appreciation. "*Mmm.* Something smells good."

"I made the sausage but waited to put on the french toast." Priscilla moved back to the stove and turned on the heat under a big frying pan. She dipped the first piece of bread. "We have a lunch date at Joan's."

"How nice." Whitney refilled her coffee mug and added some to Priscilla's mug on the counter. "That'll be fun."

A rapping sounded on the front door and then the bell rang. Priscilla thought of asking Whitney to get it but reconsidered. She handed her the spatula. "Can you watch these for me, please?"

Priscilla wiped her hands on her apron and went to answer. They weren't expecting anyone, so she had no idea who could be visiting this early.

Franklin stood on the front steps, she saw to her surprise. Perhaps her jab had hit home.

"I'm sorry to drop by, Priscilla," he said, "but I was in the neighborhood." He gestured vaguely, stamping from foot to foot to keep warm. More than cold, Franklin looked like he was agitated.

Priscilla sighed. She couldn't leave him on the steps. "Come on in."

He stepped inside and shed his coat and boots, unwinding his favorite striped scarf from around his neck. "I've interrupted your breakfast."

"Are you hungry? We can set another place."

His eyes brightened. "I'd love that. I haven't eaten yet." He put a hand on his midriff. "I couldn't previously, but your friendly face restored my appetite."

Catching a glimpse of her less-than-cheerful face in the hall mirror, Priscilla pasted on a smile. "We're having sausage and french toast."

"My favorite," he said, padding along behind her.

Priscilla halted, the meaning of his words sinking in. "Franklin, is something wrong?" she asked in a soft voice. "Did something happen?"

His nod was miserable. "Let's discuss it after breakfast, okay? That's why I came by."

"Okay. We can do that." If she was the best thing he had for a confidant, then he was indeed a lonely man.

Whitney regarded Franklin with surprise when they entered the kitchen. "Good morning, Professor."

Franklin dipped his head with a smile. "And good morning to you." He rubbed his hands together and turned to Priscilla. "Is there anything I can do?"

Priscilla thought of a task. "How about pouring glasses of juice?" She pointed him in the right direction.

Working together, the trio soon had breakfast on the table. "Would you like to say grace?" Priscilla asked Franklin.

He tugged at his collar and cleared his throat. "I'd be happy to," he finally said. He offered an eloquent, and for Franklin, brief, blessing on the meal.

Priscilla added butter and syrup to her french toast, then dredged a sausage link through the pool of maple goodness. This combination had to be one of the best ever. "Looks like a lovely day," she said to get the conversation going.

The other two took up the ball, making light chitchat while they ate. After they finished, Priscilla poured another round of coffee. "Wh—Anne, Franklin needs to discuss something with me. Will you be all right on your own for a few minutes?"

"Absolutely," Whitney said. "I'll clean up in here—no, I insist—then I'll go read some of my book in the guest room."

Franklin followed Priscilla to the living room, where she added kindling to the banked coals. "I've always thought this place is charming," he said. "You must find it pleasant living here."

"Oh, I do." Priscilla used the bellows to coax a flame. Once the kindling caught, she added several small pieces of wood. She sat in her armchair, keeping an eye on the fire and waiting for Franklin to speak.

He laced his fingers together and stretched them back and forth. "I want to thank you for your willingness to be a listening ear. At times it's hard to know to whom one can unburden oneself—"

"Franklin. I have a lunch date so please, go ahead and spill." Priscilla smiled to let him know she was teasing.

"Sorry." He coughed, putting a fist to his mouth. "It's just that I've made a decision, and I'm hoping it's the right one."

And he wants me to tell him so? Priscilla straightened in her chair. "Franklin, I have no idea what this is about, so I don't know if I can give you good input."

"I know that." For the first time, his eyes met hers. "I think I'm going to take a buyout at the university."

It took a second for Priscilla to process that. "You mean you're not going to teach anymore?"

"Well, I might do a bit of adjunct teaching now and then. Online courses and the like also. But I won't be a full-time professor anymore." He tore his eyes away and stared into the fire. "Things haven't gone well in the department under recent leadership changes so it's...time."

From friends, Priscilla knew enough about university life to understand that the ivory tower was often fraught with intrigue and politics.

"I'm sorry to hear that," she said. "But nothing lasts forever, right?"

He swung his head around to look at her. "That's right. I'm on to a new chapter." He rubbed his hands together, this time in glee. "And my book about Bitsy will give me an excellent boost."

Priscilla groaned inwardly. Now even more was riding on Franklin getting the story right. "Don't forget to visit Tilly, then. I'm sure she'd be happy to show you what she found among Hazel Snyder's things."

Now that he'd unburdened himself, Franklin appeared restored to his usual cocky, almost smug self. "I'll do that, dear lady. But I doubt I'll find anything to influence my theory there." He patted the arms of his chair before launching to his feet. "I'll let you get on with your day. Thank you again for breakfast, and for listening to an old fool."

Priscilla's rising irritation ratcheted down at his humble statement. "Of course, Franklin. Any time." She got up to show him to the door.

Once she shut the door behind him, she took a moment to reflect. It seemed like each encounter with Franklin was a test of her character. *What are You trying to show me, Lord?*

Priscilla and Whitney puttered around the cottage for most of the morning, then Priscilla made a batch of biscuits. Whitney watched closely and helped by grating the cheddar cheese. "I've never had these," she said.

"You haven't lived," Priscilla assured her. Once the biscuits were ready, Priscilla packed them in a cloth-lined basket. At the last minute, she let Jake come along for the visit.

Fresh snow still covered the roads since there hadn't been enough to plow. Lawns and fields glistened in the sunlight, and evergreens still wore a coating of white tracing their branches.

"I like this much snow," Whitney said. "Just enough to be decorative."

Priscilla drove slowly, not wanting the wheels to slip. "That's a good way of putting it. It doesn't look so pretty in March, when the snowbanks are brown and crusty."

They arrived at Joan's just after one. As they slowed to enter the yard, Priscilla noticed a crew of workmen working near Joan's stone wall. Some of the branches from the fallen tree had dislodged rocks, she remembered. She gave them a wave and a smile.

Joan greeted them at the door. "Come on in where it's nice and toasty." Jake pushed past her knees and she had to grip the doorknob for support. "He knows the way, obviously."

While Jake and Sister touched noses to say hello, Priscilla and Whitney shed their winter clothing. Joan held the still-warm basket of biscuits. She put her nose close and inhaled.

"These smell fabulous."

"That's what I thought," Whitney said. "But Priscilla said I couldn't taste them until we got here. Let's eat!"

"I've got a nice low-calorie lunch for you," Joan said, laughing. "Unless you count the brownies I picked up at the bakery." Accompanied by the dogs, they made their way to the kitchen.

The table was already set so after Joan served big bowls of chowder, they sat down and said grace. Priscilla spooned up a mouthful, spotting tiny shrimp, haddock, and clams. Chunks of potato and bits of onion and celery rounded out the flavors. A touch of fresh ground pepper added some spice.

"This is yummy." Priscilla gave her verdict. Whitney murmured appreciation.

"I'll have to cook a meal for everyone," Whitney said. "You've both been feeding me. And so has Sheila."

"What's your specialty?" Joan asked. She picked up a biscuit and split it, then spread it with butter. She rolled her eyes in delight after taking a bite. "Oh my, Priscilla, these are so good."

"Believe it or not, I make an excellent roast beef with Yorkshire pudding," Whitney said. "My nanny was English, and she gave me cooking lessons."

"What other recipes did she teach you?" Priscilla reached for a second biscuit, hesitating only briefly. A long walk in the cold air would help burn it off, as would the outerwear ritual required before and after. Boots weighed a lot more too.

Discussion of English dishes took them through the first bowls of chowder. They were deliberating about having seconds when someone knocked on the front door.

For a second, Priscilla felt a certain déjà vu. "I hope that's not Franklin," she joked. At Joan's questioning look, she said, "He popped in at breakfast. Probably not on purpose," she added. Then she bit her lip. She'd better be quiet about Franklin, or else she'd say something unkind and regret it.

Joan bustled to the front door, and they heard her conferring with a man, his rumbling tones clear if not the words he was saying.

A couple of minutes later, Joan ran back into the kitchen. "Come on, ladies. Let's get dressed. They've found something I need to look at."

Without question, Priscilla and Whitney abandoned their lunch and hurried to the hall. Then the trio tramped outside and across the snow-covered yard. Near the stone wall, two men stood, one still holding a crowbar. The small tractor they'd brought to move the larger stones stood idling, chains attached to its rear.

"Morning, Clem, Tom," Joan said. "What'd you find?"

One of the men pushed his hat back then settled it again, a gesture Priscilla recognized as signaling the beginning of a statement. "Tom and I were moving this large rock." He pointed to a slablike stone. "Since it really didn't belong here. It wasn't part of the wall, which was probably built a hundred fifty years ago."

Priscilla held back her frustration, wishing he would get to the point. By the anxious expression on Joan's face and her fidgeting gloved hands, she felt the same way. But Joan merely nodded, probably guessing that rushing the man would be futile and might even slow him down.

Clem crouched, pointing a work glove at the hole left after they'd shifted the rock. "So then we were looking down, and we saw this. Thought you should take a look."

The women crowded close. Holding her breath, Priscilla leaned forward and blinked to sharpen her vision. At first all she saw was white and brown, snow and dirt and—

"Is that what I think it is?" Whitney whispered. "Oh no."

Moving the rock had exposed another skeleton.

CHAPTER FIFTEEN

Priscilla turned away from the hole, dizziness sweeping over her. She bent and rested her hands on her knees, trying to take deep breaths, the way she'd been told. But she was having trouble getting air past her chest, which felt as if an iron band circled it.

Another skeleton. Located very close to where they had found Bitsy. Horror and sadness flooded her mind.

She felt a hand slip through her arm and gently tug her upright. Whitney. "Let's go inside, Priscilla," she said. As they trudged down the lawn, Priscilla saw that Joan was still conferring with the workers. They would have to leave that area alone for now.

The warm air inside the house enveloped them. Priscilla's cheeks stung from the cold. "I'm sorry," she said. "I don't know what came over me."

Whitney's eyes were dark with emotion. "It was a real shock. And you've already been through it once."

"You'd think I might get used to it." But Priscilla shuddered at the idea of ever becoming numb to such discoveries. "Let's put on a pot of coffee."

The busy work in the kitchen helped. By the time Joan walked in, the lunch dishes were cleared away, the coffee was ready, and a plate of brownies waited on the table.

"Just getting ready to pour coffee," Priscilla said. She reached for the first mug.

Joan sighed. "I could use a cup. I've got to call the police. And then of course the medical examiner will have to come."

Through the window, they saw the men driving posts and threading orange caution tape, to let people know not to trespass.

"Do they want coffee?" Priscilla asked, her hand poised to take more mugs out of the cupboard.

"I already invited them down. They'll be here in a minute." Joan picked up her cell phone and strolled into the living room to make the call.

Priscilla added several more mugs to the ones on the counter. The officers would probably appreciate a cup of something hot on such a chilly day.

Joan wandered back in and poured a cup of coffee. "They'll be right over. April Brown caught the call."

"That's good." While Priscilla liked all the Martha's Vineyard police officers, April was her favorite. She was intelligent and levelheaded, and best of all, she listened.

The trio settled at the table again, a much more somber mood settling over them. "Who do you think it is?" Joan asked.

Priscilla had a sinking feeling she knew. "I'll bet it's Ambrose. He disappeared at the same time as Bitsy. They didn't run away. They were murdered."

"But we don't know if that skeleton is male yet," Whitney pointed out. "It could be another woman."

Joan stared into her coffee. "Like who? Evangeline?"

Such a dreadful thought, that someone had killed two people. Despite a strong effort, Priscilla's mind whirled with theories. Maybe Evangeline witnessed Bitsy's murder and was killed as a result. Perhaps a serial killer stalking the island shores—she discarded that wild theory. There hadn't been any more deaths reported, and why would a serial killer stop at two? In fact, no deaths at all had been reported, which made this case all the more suspicious. Someone had gone to great lengths to cover up their misdeeds.

"Guess what Whitney figured out?" Priscilla said. "Bitsy was tracking the stock market."

"I guess a lot of people did that back then," Joan said. "That's what led to the crash, all the dabbling."

"No, we think it's a bit more sinister than that," Whitney said. "She was gathering information related to stock manipulation." Whitney broke off a bite of brownie. "A lot of people made fortunes that way, before the Securities and Exchange Commission got really ramped up to stop it."

Blue and white lights signaled the arrival of the police. A horrified thought flashed into Priscilla's mind. "Whitney, you can't let the police see you." Once the missing Whitney Parker was located, they might as well put a bull's-eye on her back.

Whitney dropped her brownie. "That's true. In all the excitement I forgot."

Joan jumped up. "Come with me."

"Of course." Whitney stood. "As soon as we hear from Priscilla's FBI friend, I'm coming out of hiding." Her mouth turned down. "I'm so tired of it."

"I'll bet," Joan said. "Let's go." A moment later, their footsteps sounded on the stairs.

That reminded Priscilla to check her phone. And yes, there was a missed call from an unfamiliar number. "I think he did call, and I didn't hear it ring." That happened sometimes on the island, with its often spotty coverage.

While Joan and Whitney were upstairs, Priscilla checked her voice mail. It had been A.J. "Hi, Priscilla. I just got your message. I'm sorry, I've been working a case and I'm out of touch a lot of the time. Call me back at..."

The police knocked at the door. Priscilla saved the message with a promise to herself to return the call as soon as the officers left.

Joan hurried down the stairs and greeted the officers. A moment later, the door closed again and Priscilla saw Joan walking with April Brown and Bill Denton up to the site. They stood around the hole, talking to the workmen. By the body language, she could tell that they were being asked to come to the house to make their statements.

After shutting off the tractor, the workmen headed down the hill in company with the others. Priscilla got ready to pour coffee, figuring they'd all like to warm up. In the couple of minutes she had before they reached the door, she said a prayer. The scripture from Daniel drifted into her mind: *"He reveals deep and hidden things."* And things lost to the mists of time. "Lord, help us figure out this mystery," she prayed. "Help us put these bones to rest."

The officers took statements from Tom and Clem in the living room first. Priscilla and Joan sat at the kitchen table, unable to resist staring out at the stone wall.

"I can't believe we found another one." Joan blinked back tears. "How many are there in my garden?" Her voice cracked.

No more, we hope. Priscilla didn't blame Joan for being upset. For decades she had lived in this house with no idea what was waiting to be discovered. Priscilla got up from the table and put an arm around Joan's shoulders. "It is disconcerting. But the good news is, those unfortunate souls will finally be laid to rest, once we discover the truth."

Joan blew her nose. "You think so? There's been nothing conclusive so far."

"That's true. But we'll know more once the medical examiner has had a chance to look at the bones." Perhaps the forensics team would find clues to the person's identity among the bones. At least they could determine gender and probable age.

"Did I tell you what I learned about Evangeline?" Priscilla asked, to change the subject.

That perked Joan up. "No, what? She was a maid for the Parkers, right?"

"Yes. And according to the Parker ledgers, she wasn't paid after Bitsy disappeared. As you know, Jordan thinks that was Evangeline out there, not Bitsy. So I have to find out if she quit, left town, or..." Priscilla allowed her words to trail off.

Joan hopped up and brought the coffee carafe over. She refilled their cups. "That sounds like something to sink our teeth into. Her fate could be another piece of the puzzle."

"Yes, or another tangent. But at least we're moving forward."

Tom and Clem came into the kitchen. "We'll have to come back another day," Tom said. "Can't do any more work until the police say so."

"I understand." Joan rose to her feet. "Send me a bill for what I owe you." She escorted the men out.

Priscilla heard voices in the hall, then the front door opened and shut. Joan went into the living room, then circled back to the kitchen. "They're ready to take our statements. But they want to talk to me alone first."

"Why?" Priscilla was so startled she got up from her seat. "That skeleton is ancient."

Joan's shoulders slumped. "I know that. But they have to be careful until the age is officially determined." She spotted her cup. "I'm going to take that with me."

Priscilla couldn't sit still while Joan was being questioned, so she made a fresh pot of coffee. While that was brewing, she found paper and pen and made notes about the case. What they knew and what they didn't.

She set her pen down in disgust. There were very few certainties at this point. Everything else was speculation and rumor.

As soon as the police were finished taking her statement, she'd head over to the farm and talk to Gilbert. Maybe Evangeline was a dead end. She'd probably gotten married and moved to the mainland. But there had to be some reason why Jordan thought the skeleton was hers.

Looking out the window, she witnessed the arrival of other officers. As they had with the first skeleton, they set up a white tent. At least the weather wasn't interfering with the ferry schedule this time. The medical examiner should be able to get to Martha's Vineyard right away, even today perhaps.

Priscilla looked up at the ceiling. Whitney might well be trapped for a while. She stared at her phone. The sooner she called A.J...But she couldn't do that here, while the officers were in the other room.

"It's your turn." Joan stood in the doorway, her lips set in a thin line.

"How was it?" Priscilla stood, ready to get her statement over with. It shouldn't take long.

The answer was a headshake. Joan stopped by the coffeepot. "Thanks for making fresh." She smiled when Priscilla detoured to give her another hug. "I'm glad you were here."

Priscilla was too. Finding a burial site in your backyard was not something to face alone. After a pat on Joan's back and a final encouraging word, she squared her shoulders and strode into the living room. "I understand you're ready for me?"

April looked up from her notes. The two officers were seated at a round table near the window. She gestured. "Have a seat."

"You really don't think Joan had anything to do with that skeleton, do you?" Priscilla blurted. She pulled out a chair and plopped down, annoyed at herself for being so blunt.

April lifted a brow. "It's protocol. We find a body in someone's yard, we question them." She put up a hand when Priscilla began to protest. "No matter how old we think it might be."

Priscilla shifted in the chair. "Fair enough." She sipped her coffee. "Go ahead, shoot." Unfortunate choice of words but she kept quiet rather than correct herself.

April reviewed her notes again. "Take us through what happened."

"We were having coffee when the workmen came to the house," Priscilla said. She went on to tell them what she had seen, which fortunately wasn't much.

"Do you have any idea who is out there?" Bill asked, his keen eyes fixed on her face.

Priscilla nodded. "Yes," she said, making the officer rock back a bit at this unexpected answer. "I think it's someone associated with the other skeleton we found. I think you'll discover it's of the same vintage. Another cold case."

"Could be," April said, making a note. "The medical examiner's office will tell us approximately how long it's been buried."

"Is Dr. Stanley arriving soon?" Priscilla asked, assuming they would send the same examiner. "I'm eager to find out the results." She might as well admit it.

The officers exchanged glances. "The state police boat will probably bring someone pretty fast this time, since the weather is cooperating," Bill said. "Until then, we're keeping the site secure. The forensics team is putting up a tent as we speak."

"I saw that." Priscilla was both gladdened and concerned by this update. Was Whitney going to have to hide until after the medical examiner arrived? He'd have to take away the skeleton after they excavated, which was a painstaking process.

She had to call A.J. right now. After the officers released her and she heard them leave the house, she slipped upstairs. First she checked on Whitney, who was reading her book in the guest room. Then she went into Joan's room and placed the call. She had to leave another voice mail. This time she gave him a hint that her call concerned financial crimes in Boston. If he was as intelligent as she'd observed, he'd understand her cryptic message.

Priscilla pressed the gas after she pulled out of Joan's driveway. Whitney laughed. "I feel like we're in a movie, making our escape." She glanced back over her shoulder. "Who are all those people?"

"I don't know, but it's a good thing they showed up." Priscilla moderated her speed, not wanting to get a ticket.

To Joan's dismay, the road in front of her house had become a circus that morning. Once word leaked out about the discovery of another skeleton, a steady stream of passing automobiles and dog walkers had appeared. They used every excuse to linger and chat and try to get a glimpse under the tent.

The officer in charge of guarding the bones had spent all his time shooing people away. But that distraction meant Priscilla, Whitney, and Jake, who of course was excited by all the activity, could sneak away from the house unobserved. Without appearing to hurry, they'd gone out to the SUV and climbed in. Pretending she hadn't a care in the world had taken more acting ability than Priscilla knew she possessed.

On the way to the farm, they passed a steady stream of traffic headed the other way. "My goodness, this is a big event," Whitney said.

"I can't blame them for being curious," Priscilla said. "Otherwise it's a fairly dull November day." What wouldn't she give to be bored right now? She wasn't sure her nerves could take much more.

Sheila emerged from the barn right when they pulled into the parking lot. She waited for them to get out of the SUV, hands on her hips. "What's all this I hear about another skeleton showing up? At Joan's house, right?"

Priscilla sighed to herself. *Get used to it*. For a few days at least, everyone would be questioning her. Besides, Sheila was her friend. "That's right. Some workmen were fixing the stone wall when they found the bones. Pretty close to where we found Bitsy."

Sheila gave a low whistle. "I wonder if they're connected." Then she answered her own question. "Of course they are. They have to be."

"The medical examiner should be able to tell us more," Whitney said. Sheila kicked her boot toe into the gravel. "Sounds to me like Ambrose Allen didn't take off like they thought. Somebody killed 'em both. What an awful, terrible thing."

Priscilla couldn't agree more. "Is Gilbert around? I want to ask him about his relative, Evangeline. She used to work for the Parkers."

Sheila pointed to the fields. "They're down at the bog. I really don't have time to drive you down right now, but it's not a bad walk if you take the shortcut." She explained the route, which led on a path through the woods.

"Want to go? Jake would like it," Priscilla said to Whitney. She agreed, so Priscilla put a wool hat on her head, attached a leash to Jake's collar, and locked the SUV.

They set off, cutting across the field toward the trees on the other side. From Priscilla's previous excursion, she remembered how they'd stayed on the lane that wound through the property. But walkers wouldn't damage the fields or woods the way vehicles could.

The air was crisp, cold enough to make their breath show frosty white. Bare trees stood etched against a tender blue sky, the low sun touching the trunks with gold. Much of the previous day's snow had melted, but patches still lingered in the shade.

Jake cavorted with glee, running out to the end of the lead and then back, taking detours to bark at a squirrel or rustle around in fallen leaves. Not for the first time, Priscilla reflected on how much joy he brought to her life. At the very least, he always made her smile.

They heard the men working at the bog before they saw them. Machinery groaned as berries were loaded into a truck. Dressed in waders, the men shouted and gestured, working together as a team. Chowder spotted the women and signaled for the machine operator to cut the engine. The workers waded to shore and pulled out thermoses and lunch bags.

"Looks like they're using our arrival as an excuse to take a break," Priscilla said.

The men waved and smiled as the women approached. Jake of course had to introduce himself to each one. They slipped him pieces of cookie while Priscilla pretended not to notice.

"What brings you down here?" Chowder asked. "Taking a walk around the property?"

"Not exactly," Priscilla said. She regarded the three men, realizing they might not have heard the news. They were probably the only three people on the island still in ignorance. She took a deep breath. "We made an interesting discovery today."

They listened while enjoying their break, exclaiming and commenting while Priscilla and Whitney filled them in.

"We appreciate you coming down to tell us," Chowder Jr. said. "Any idea who the poor fella is?"

"Not yet," Priscilla said. "We don't even know if it's a man or woman." She turned to Gilbert. "If you don't mind, I'd like to ask you a few questions."

He put up both hands, his eyes comically wide. "I didn't do it." Everyone laughed.

After the merriment died down, Priscilla said, "I understand one of your relatives worked for the Parkers. Evangeline Jenks."

Gilbert's face grew wary. "What about her?"

Now that they were discussing Evangeline, Chowder Jr. and his father wandered away to look over the equipment. It wasn't a topic of interest to them.

Priscilla didn't see any point in beating around the bush. "Jordan Parker thinks the first skeleton is Evangeline. I don't agree, but when I looked through the ledgers, I noticed that Evangeline wasn't paid after Bitsy disappeared."

Gilbert eyed her for a long moment. "Evangeline got married and went out West. That's what I heard. She and one of the gardeners. Solomon Smith, his name was."

"Thanks, Gilbert." Priscilla took a mental note of the information. They could check marriage records. "Any idea where they went?"

He shrugged. "Dunno. California, maybe." He turned to check what the other two men were doing. "I'd better get back to work."

"And we'll let you do that." Priscilla thanked him for the information, and she and Whitney began walking back to the farm. Behind them, the equipment started up again with a roar.

Through the woods, they strolled along, letting Jake explore at the end of his leash. Then Priscilla heard the distinctive crack of a rifle. Chips flew off a pine tree several feet above their head. Acting purely on instinct, she pulled Whitney to the ground and called for Jake.

CHAPTER SIXTEEN

Priscilla closed her eyes and prayed, her nose filling with the scent of decaying leaves and soil. All remained quiet but she pulled out her phone and called 911 anyway. "What's your emergency?" the dispatcher asked.

"I'm in the woods at the Weller farm and someone just shot at us." Priscilla gave their approximate location in regards to the house. She tugged on Whitney's arm and indicated they should crawl behind a nearby boulder. Then the huge rock would be between them and the shooter.

"Someone will be right there," the dispatcher promised. "Do you want me to stay on the line?"

"Please. Just in case," Priscilla said, feeling like the call was a lifeline. The trio huddled in the shelter of the boulder, waiting with every nerve alert and on edge.

Thankfully the woods remained silent. Had it been a stray shot from a hunter? But Sheila's land was posted, so even if that was the case, someone with a rifle shouldn't be anywhere near this part of the property.

They heard the roar of the ATV approaching. No doubt it was Sheila coming to see what was going on. The vehicle stopped. "Priscilla? Are you out here?" Sheila called.

"The farm owner is here," she told the dispatcher. "So I'm going to put the phone down a second." Priscilla handed her phone to Whitney, then yelled, "Sheila. We're over here, behind the big rock."

They heard a rustling through the woods, then Sheila appeared. "Whoever that was took off. The men saw the truck drive away."

Relief rushed through Priscilla. She took the phone back from Whitney. "I have dispatch on the line. Any description?"

Sheila took the phone to speak to the dispatcher. "It was a late model Ford pickup truck, dark blue, with a matching cap. Didn't see the plate. It was too far away." She gave the phone back to Priscilla. "The police will meet us up at the house. Let's go."

They got on the ATV, including Jake sitting on Priscilla's lap, and zoomed back to the house. Every inch that took them closer to safety made Priscilla relax a little more. Sheila pulled up next to the kitchen door, and as they got off, a police cruiser came up the drive.

Officers Ed Sequeira and Teddy Holmes emerged from the cruiser. Priscilla had met them both before, and she was relieved to see their familiar faces.

"Got a report of a gunshot being fired," Ed said after greetings were exchanged.

"That's right," Sheila said. "I heard it, plain as day. So did Priscilla. She's the one who called it in."

Priscilla told the officers the sequence of events, careful to introduce Whitney as Anne. The police officers gave her curious glances but were more interested in figuring out who had fired the dangerous shot.

"This kind of thing happens sometimes during hunting season," Ed said. "It shouldn't, but unfortunately a few hunters are careless."

"They give the good hunters a bad name," Teddy added. He looked them up and down. "You really ought to wear orange vests and hats, even if you're in a place that's posted."

Ed broke in again. "Some hunters apparently can't read. Hopefully they're not color blind too." The officers laughed, their version of gallows humor, then Ed said, "But it's more likely he wandered across the property line and didn't realize it."

"But everyone's land around here is posted," Sheila said. "There's no hunting for miles."

While Priscilla initially believed it was a hunter's shot gone astray, now she wondered. The bullet had hit the tree well above their heads.

Had it been a warning? She slid a glance at Whitney, whose face had paled.

"We'll head down to the bog," Ed said to Sheila. "Want to take us down?" They hopped on the ATV and roared away.

"Priscilla, I'm scared," Whitney said. "I think that shot was deliberate." Jake whined and stared toward the woods, as if he agreed.

"Let's go inside and talk." Sheila had told them to make themselves at home.

In the kitchen, Priscilla put the kettle on for tea. Sheila would probably want a cup when she returned. Then she joined Whitney at the table, where she was petting Jake.

"Does Dalton Rogers drive a blue truck?" she asked.

Whitney kept her eyes on the dog. "I don't know. I never saw his vehicle."

Priscilla remembered Geoff Sanders, the agent who had been looking for Whitney. She hadn't even tried calling him, since she was afraid to tip him off. But maybe she could figure out if he was friend or foe.

It seemed like she and A.J. would never connect. Now she had an inkling of what Rachel was going through, especially since the pair was separated by distance as well as work.

"Want a cup of tea?" Priscilla found a basket of tea bags and set it on the table, then pulled out mugs. Once the kettle boiled, she filled their cups and sat down.

"I think I want chamomile," Whitney said. "I need to relax."

"Good thought." Priscilla selected an orange spice blend. "I'm going to see if I can track down Geoff Sanders." At Whitney's puzzled glance, she said, "The man who was asking about you in the bakery. He said he was an FBI agent."

Whitney's brows rose. "Oh. That guy. Tell me what he was doing again."

Priscilla did one better and showed her the picture again. Whitney couldn't conclusively tell if it was Dalton Rogers the first time, and she hadn't changed her mind.

Priscilla put her phone back in her pocket. "I'm wondering if that's Dalton or someone he's working with. I found it very strange that he didn't give me a business card."

"That is weird. Dalton had one." Whitney put both hands around her mug, shoulders hunched. "I think I shredded it." A ghost of a smile touched her lips.

"Let me get Geoff's number." Priscilla remembered that her handbag was in the SUV. "I'll be right back."

Priscilla was locking the SUV again when she heard the roar of the ATV returning. She lingered, wanting to talk to the officers. Sheila pulled up next to Priscilla's vehicle and parked, then everyone climbed off.

"I've got to get me one of those," Teddy said. "It'd be fun bumming around."

"As long as you stay on the allowed trails," Ed said, ever the stickler.

Teddy laughed. "Yes, sir. Of course." He turned to Sheila. "We'll keep our eyes open for the blue truck, patrol some known hunting areas. But without a license plate, it might be tough to find, though the cap might help." He turned to Ed. "How many blue trucks on the island? In the state?"

Ed shrugged. "Thousands, unfortunately. But if the guy shows up again, call us immediately."

Sheila scowled. "I'd like to do more than that. Idiot could have killed someone."

"Thanks for getting here so fast," Priscilla said. "It was truly frightening."

"That's our job." Ed pointed a finger at her. "Get some orange clothes, okay?" He nodded at Teddy. "Ready?"

Sheila offered refreshments, but the officers declined with thanks. "We've got to go do roadside duty," Teddy said. "There's quite a to-do over a skeleton at Joan Abernathy's place. Traffic is jammed up, and the school bus isn't going to be able to get through."

Ed's eyes narrowed. "You know anything about that, Priscilla?" He knew that she and Joan were cousins.

"I was there when the crew discovered the bones. Has the medical examiner arrived yet?"

"He's there now," Teddy said. "Buzzed right over from the mainland on a police boat, like we thought he would. I guess the people hanging around expect a play-by-play. But they're not going to get it."

They hopped inside their cruiser and left, while Priscilla and Sheila watched. "They're good guys," Sheila said. "We're fortunate the island has such a great force."

"We sure are." Priscilla had nothing but respect for the hard-working officers who kept them safe. "There's hot water, if you want tea."

"No, I'm going to get back to work," Sheila said. "This weekend is going to be super busy, since it's the last one before Thanksgiving. Tomorrow is the cranberry sale for the contest."

"That's right." Priscilla gulped. Sheila had just reminded her that she had a committee meeting in the morning. The contest was on Sunday afternoon, only two days away.

Inside the farmhouse, Priscilla turned the kettle on again and then sat to dig through her purse. "The police left," she told

Whitney. "They're going to keep an eye out for the truck, but it's pretty much a needle in a haystack."

"I figured as much. Blue trucks are a dime a dozen." Whitney hopped up when the kettle began to boil. She refilled both mugs.

Priscilla finally found the scrap of paper with Geoff's number. "Hopefully I wrote this down right. He rattled it off so fast." She punched the numbers into her phone.

The phone rang a few times. "Yo," a man answered. Priscilla pulled the phone back and stared at it. Had she dialed the right number? According to the screen, she had.

"Hi, I'm looking for Geoff," she said. "Geoff Sanders."

"I'm sorry he's not here right now." She heard the sound of jingling bells in the background followed by voices. People laughed.

"What number did I call?" she asked. It sounded like a store or restaurant.

"This is Barry's Bait, down on the harbor." A chuckle. "I'm supposed to give the store name but I forgot. Oops."

Priscilla wanted to laugh, but she managed to hold it together. "Can you tell me what time Geoff will be in?"

"Um, um. Let me check the schedule. He'll be here at four. We're open until eight tonight." The voices drew closer. "Gotta go." He hung up.

Now that the call was over, Priscilla gave in to helpless laughter. While Whitney and Jake watched in concern, she put her head down and howled. After the outbreak passed, she sat up and wiped her eyes with a napkin. "I'm sorry about that. But according to the man on the phone, our FBI agent works at a bait shack down on the harbor." Whitney's disbelieving expression triggered another bout of laughter. Once Priscilla was back in control, she said, "Want to take a ride?" She might as well confront Geoff Sanders in person.

Priscilla and Whitney tidied the kitchen then headed down to the harbor. This time of year, many of the businesses were closed, but a few remained open, including Barry's Bait Shack, which appeared to be doing a bustling trade, with trucks coming and going.

Priscilla's belly lurched when she noticed a few were navy blue. Was the shooter here? She took a deep breath. How long would it be before her nerves settled?

"What do you want me to do?" Whitney asked. "I don't think it's a good idea for me to go inside, in case he is in there."

"You're right," Priscilla said. She checked the time. Ten minutes until four. "Geoff should be showing up any minute. Let's sit here and watch."

She'd parked in a spot with a good view of the shop, a small building near the ferry wharf. According to a sign on the side, fishing charters were still underway. That explained the activity, since it was Friday afternoon and weekends were the busiest time.

Men and women went in and out of the bait shop, many greeting each other with laughter and jeers regarding fishing prowess. By quarter after four, Priscilla realized they must have missed Geoff when he arrived. "I'm going inside. Stay put, but if you see Dalton, send me a text, okay?"

Priscilla brought her handbag, the better to look as though she was a shopper. The small store was brightly lit, with shelves selling all kinds of fishing gear. Freezers and coolers along the walls held things she didn't want to study too closely. There were also some convenience store items, which made sense. Why not sell snacks to people going fishing?

She skirted the side of the room, not able to get close to the counter. A thin, wiry man was working the cash register, his hands flying as he punched in sales and bagged purchases. Next to a cooler holding tubs of fish parts was a refrigerator stocked with bottles of water and soft drinks. Priscilla grabbed two waters and joined the line snaking toward the register.

Finally she reached the front. She set the waters down. The man's shirt read "Alex" under the Barry's Bait Shed logo. "I'm looking for Geoff."

He cocked a brow as he ran the bottles under the scanner. "You the lady who called?"

She pondered the question, wondering if she should admit it. "Yes, I am," she finally said. "Is he here?"

The answer was a wry grin. "Better be. I'm leaving in two minutes." Without breaking stride, he yelled. "Geoff. Get out here, man." He totaled the sale and told her the amount.

Priscilla stared at the open doorway leading to an office behind the counter. A huge, burly man with a massive belly appeared. He wore a bandanna tied around his head, and a drooping mustache hung over his lips.

"Don't get your shorts in a twist," Geoff said. "I'm here, ain't I?" He reached up and adjusted his bandanna, then shuffled forward.

Priscilla handed Alex money for the water, hoping he wouldn't say anything. But no, he had to. "Hey man, this lady was looking for you."

Geoff eyed her up and down, his eyes lighting up. "Really? Now I know I'm going to have a good day."

"I'm sorry," Priscilla said, her face flaming. "I thought you were someone else."

Alex bagged her purchase. "You said Geoff Sanders when you called."

"I know," Priscilla whispered, clutching the paper bag. "But I had the wrong number." Actually someone else gave her the wrong number. And she sincerely doubted his name was Geoff.

"Too bad, ma'am," Geoff said. "Change your mind, give me a call." He winked.

Mortified, Priscilla practically ran from the store, all too aware of curious eyes watching. A thought made her hesitate. There must be some connection with the bait shed, or else why would Dalton have used that number and Geoff's name? She glanced over her shoulder at the sign. Maybe he'd gone on one of the charters.

Investigating that theory would have to wait. Right now she was getting out of here as quickly as possible.

Halfway to the car, her phone rang. She stopped to dig it out and was glad she did. "A.J. Finally." She heaved a huge sigh. "I've been trying to get a hold of you."

"I know," he said, his deep voice resonant on the line. "And I apologize. It's this case. I've been out of town." He chuckled. "Rachel isn't very happy with me either."

"Say no more. I understand." Now that she had him, she wasn't sure how to begin.

While she wracked her brain, he said, "So what do you have for me?"

Priscilla studied the SUV, where both Whitney and Jake were pressed to the window watching her. The words came. "I have Whitney Parker."

Although she couldn't see his face, she sensed his utter surprise in the dead silence that followed. "Say that again," he finally managed.

She glanced around to be sure no one was in earshot. "Whitney Parker is hiding out on the island. She came by Joan's house, lost, during that big storm, and then she stayed at a cabin owned by a friend of mine. We've been dodging a rogue agent ever since." To affirm how risky it had been, she added, "Someone shot at us today."

"What's this about a rogue agent? And who shot at you?" A.J.'s voice went up a couple of notches.

By now, she had reached the SUV. Whitney unlocked the door for her, and she got in. "I'll let you speak to her," she said. "She'll fill you in." She handed the phone to Whitney. "Agent A.J. Montgomery is on the line."

Whitney put the phone on speaker mode and placed it on the console between them. "Hi, A.J. I'm Whitney Parker. You're on speaker so Priscilla can listen."

"Whitney Parker," A.J.'s voice boomed loud and clear. "Nice to meet you. You've got a lot of people looking for you."

Whitney pressed her lips together. "I know that, and I'm sorry. But I don't know who to trust."

"What do you mean?" A.J. asked, his tone sharpening.

Whitney explained that Dalton Rogers had been her primary contact from the FBI. "Dalton and I met several times. He promised me protection if I would gather evidence for the case against the firm. Information about how they cheated people and then stashed the money in offshore bank accounts." Her voice cracked, and she blinked back tears.

"It's OK, Whitney," A.J. said, his voice soothing. "Take your time. I understand this is a tough situation for you."

Now her tears flowed freely. "It really is. My uncle and I were close. I was devastated when I found out about the scam."

Priscilla handed her some tissues, then started the car so they could get some heat. Maybe that would help ease Whitney's shivering.

"I'll bet you were. I know people in general have been shocked." He paused. "So back to Dalton. What happened with him?"

Whitney explained that she'd gathered evidence, only to become suspicious of Dalton. "We were meeting at my apartment when I overheard him talking. He didn't know I could hear him."

"And?" A.J. prompted. "What did he say?"

She squeezed her eyes shut. "He said, 'The bank account information is almost in the bag. Once she gives it to me, we'll be all set.' Then he laughed. 'Get your passport ready for our new life, funded by Parker & Warren.' I put him off until later that night, then I packed and took the ferry to Martha's Vineyard. It was the first place I thought of."

A.J. groaned. "Those are serious allegations, Whitney. Dalton is a well-respected agent. I can't imagine him doing what you're claiming."

Whitney's face paled, making a few light freckles stand out. "You don't believe me." She turned accusing eyes on Priscilla, her voice rising almost to a shriek. "I told you this was a bad idea." She reached for the door handle, obviously seeking escape.

Priscilla took hold of her sleeve. "Hold on. Please." To A.J., she said, "I'm sorry, but I believe Whitney. We haven't even told you what's happened here. It isn't good, so please keep an open mind." To her relief, Whitney dropped her hand from the handle.

"All right. Fill me in," A.J. said, caution coloring his voice.

"Remember how I said someone shot at us?" Priscilla reminded him. "It might have been a hunter but maybe not. The bullet hit a tree way above our heads." She let that sink in. "Then there's the man who's been looking for Whitney under a false name. If he's on the up-and-up, why would he do that?" She waited for a response.

"True," A.J. conceded. "Explain that, will you?"

Priscilla took him through the tale, surprising chuckles from both A.J. and Whitney at her description of the real Geoff. "I think he did that to divert anyone from knowing who he really was. He flashed that FBI badge so quickly we couldn't see the name."

"OK, two strikes against Dalton," A.J. said. "Maybe. Anything else?"

Whitney took up the story, telling A.J. about the threatening letter and the ransacking of the cabin. "There were boot prints, big ones, in the snow. And Dalton is a tall man. Someone was looking for something in my cabin. It doesn't take a genius to figure out what." Color flared in her cheeks, but she was calm and composed.

"Where is the information in question?" A.J. asked.

Whitney glanced at Priscilla, her hand on the necklace. Priscilla nodded. "In a safe place. Not the cabin."

"Fair enough." A.J. was silent for a few moments. "This is what I'm going to do. I will come to the island on Monday. I can't get there before then, unfortunately, because I'm...well, let's just say I can't. Hold tight until then."

"You aren't going to contact Dalton, right?" Priscilla asked. "Or tell anyone where Whitney is? Don't forget he has an accomplice. The person he was talking to on the phone."

"That's why I didn't contact the FBI sooner," Whitney said. "But Priscilla told me I could trust you."

Priscilla held her breath waiting for his answer. She'd convinced Whitney to talk to A.J., so she felt responsible for the results. While she understood his skepticism regarding the rogue agent, she hoped he would err on the side of caution.

"I won't speak to anyone until after we meet," A.J. said. "I'm kind of out on a limb here, but I trust Priscilla's judgment." He broke into their profuse thanks. "If anything else happens, day or night, call me, okay?" They assured him they would.

Priscilla put the SUV in gear. "Let's go get your car. Then you're spending the night with me again." She was going to do her best to keep Whitney close until A.J. arrived.

Then a thought struck. If A.J. came to the island Monday, would he bring Rachel with him?

She could only hope. She missed Rachel so much.

CHAPTER SEVENTEEN

S tay put, okay?" Priscilla slid one arm into her jacket, then the other. "I'll be home this afternoon." They'd driven in tandem from the farm last night, with Whitney at the wheel of her car. She'd then parked it out of sight in the garage. Maybe the prowler and shooter would think she'd left the island.

"Don't worry about me," Whitney said. "I'll be fine." She put a finger in her book to mark her place. "Where are you going again?"

"I have a cranberry sauce contest committee meeting this morning." Priscilla laughed. "Wow, that was a mouthful. Then I'm meeting my cousins for lunch." She studied Whitney with concern. "But I can skip that if you'd rather I stay here."

Whitney waved that off. "No, please. Go about your business." Her mouth turned down. "I've already disrupted your life enough."

"Jake doesn't think so." Priscilla pointed at the dog lying sprawled at Whitney's feet. "He should be all set for food. And he'll let you know when he needs to go out." Priscilla wound a scarf around her neck and slid on gloves. Although it was another clear day, the wind was brisk.

Priscilla set off for the Faith Fellowship parish hall, where the meeting was to be held. The event was tomorrow afternoon, after church. With Thanksgiving only a few days away, they'd been pressed to find a good time.

The committee was already there, seated around a long table in the spacious room. Gail glanced up with what looked like relief when Priscilla came in. "Hello, everyone," she said. "Sorry I'm late."

"No, you're not late, we got started early," Jordan said. The blonde beauty looked tired, with circles under her eyes. Even her usually immaculate hair was slightly disheveled and sticking up on top. "Help yourself to coffee."

Priscilla stopped at the table holding an urn and a plate of donut holes. She filled a cup then put two holes on a napkin. Enough for a treat but not so many that she would feel guilty about indulging.

The others had stopped talking when she entered, and they waited until she was settled to begin again. "As I was saying," Harper said. "I've put the event on social media, and it's been getting a lot of activity. We should have a good turnout."

"That's great to hear," Ida Lee said. "The food pantry is depending on our contributions to carry people through the winter."

Priscilla bit a donut hole in half and chewed. "Can you take me through the day's events? I'm a little fuzzy on how the contest will help the pantry."

Everyone's head swiveled to Jordan. She sat up a little straighter. "I'm sorry, I didn't realize you didn't know. But you are a latecomer to the committee." Her cold blue eyes rested on Gail briefly as though to suggest that she had been remiss in some way. Gail didn't respond, and Jordan went on.

"Everyone who attends pays a dollar," Jordan said. "They also bring a contribution of canned goods. The rule is one can per person but most people bring a lot more."

Ida Lee broke in. "That's so true. Last year we had hundreds of pounds donated."

Jordan slid a glance at Ida Lee. "Ida Lee is correct. In addition, we sell baked goods, mainly pies, but cookies and cakes too. Some people can their own cranberry sauce, and we sell the jars."

Priscilla ate the other half of her donut hole. "That's a great idea. It's just like canning jam or jelly, right?"

"Yes, exactly," Gail said. "On the contest entry form, we refer people to the safe canning rules from the university's Cooperative Extension."

"Many islanders know how to can already," Ida Lee said. "I have my mother's pressure canner, and that thing gets a workout every summer. I have a huge vegetable garden. Most of it ends up in my cellar."

Harper, who had been taking notes as the group's secretary, looked up. "I want to learn how to can. Will you teach me?"

"Of course," Ida Lee said. "The younger generation is starting to be interested. Old things are new again."

Jordan cleared her throat. "This is all very interesting, but we're getting off on a tangent. Any more questions, Priscilla?"

"Actually, yes. How does the contest work?" Priscilla had been trying to imagine how dozens of entries would be ranked and judged. All that cranberry sauce to taste.

"Good question." Jordan passed out sheets of paper. "And it just so happens to be the next topic." She waited for everyone to take a look.

Priscilla saw five teams listing five people each, plus at the top, a list of the three judges—Jordan, Candy Lane, and Gerald. She began to understand the magnitude of this event and all the volunteers required to pull it off. "Oh, I understand. The teams pick out the top entries, and the judges choose the winner?"

"You got it," Jordan said. "When contestants arrive, they sign in and give us a jar. We number each entry and pass the jar to our kitchen crew. They prepare the tasting bowls, labeled only with the number and the name of the sauce."

"So mine will say cranberry-blueberry sauce?" Priscilla asked.

The others groaned. "You shouldn't have told us," Ida Lee said. She wagged a finger. "They'll accuse us of favoritism if you win."

Priscilla's spirits sank. Maybe she should make the jalapeno recipe instead. Though Gerald liked the blueberry one better.

Gail reached over and patted her hand. "Don't worry about it. Last year we had three cranberry blueberry entries."

"Great, and here I thought I was so original." Priscilla laughed and the others joined in. She thought of another question. "What does the winner get, anyway?"

"A fresh turkey from a local farm," Harper said. "They're also donating turkeys for family boxes."

"That's a great prize," Priscilla said. The others chimed agreement, and the meeting went on.

An hour later, they adjourned. "Still coming to lunch?" Gail asked.

"Absolutely," Priscilla said. "I'll meet you there."

By the time she got outside, she and Jordan were the only two in the parking lot. "See you tomorrow," Priscilla said politely. "It should be fun."

Jordan sighed and rolled her eyes. "I don't mind telling you that I'll be glad when it's over. With all that's been going on . . ." Her eyes were distant. Then she shook herself. "But pretty soon I'll be heading to a warmer climate. That is what's keeping me going."

"It's a good time of year for a vacation," Priscilla said. "The weather has been horrendous." Although she liked the variety of four seasons, many people couldn't tolerate cold or snow.

"Sure has." Jordan unlocked her car. "Have a good day."

The donut holes had done nothing to dampen Priscilla's appetite, and she found herself thinking about lunch on the short drive to the Colonial Inn. Maybe she'd have that winter shrimp sandwich again. Her mouth watered at the thought.

While parking on the street, she spotted her cousins' vehicles— and a familiar black SUV. What was he doing here? He never ate here on Saturdays.

Before getting out, Priscilla called the cottage to check in on Whitney. She and Jake were fine, just getting ready to eat lunch, so with a spring in her step, Priscilla hurried inside. She might use the bitter wind as an excuse but she knew the truth. "I'm here to meet my cousins," she told the hostess.

"That's the big party in a booth by the window," Tilly said on her way by. "How are you, Priscilla?"

The hostess patiently waited while Priscilla paused to talk. "I'm great, thanks. By the way, I really appreciate you showing me Hazel's things. Really helpful."

Tilly folded her arms. "That's not the reaction I got from Franklin," she said with a sly smile. "He practically examined it all under a microscope before he'd accept it."

"Well, you know how it is. You get an idea in your mind and then try to bend the facts to fit." Priscilla tried not to do that. It took effort.

Tilly craned her neck, spotting something in the dining room visible only to her finely tuned senses. She patted Priscilla's arm. "Please excuse me. Have a good lunch."

The hostess smiled and nodded, then sashayed into the dining room ahead of Priscilla. The cousins saw her coming, turning to wave. Gerald was seated with them. She knew he was at the restaurant, but this was even better.

"Hello, stranger," he said, his eyes crinkling with warmth. "Trudy insisted I join you all."

Priscilla slid in next to Gail. "I thought you usually take Max for a burger on Saturdays." Max was Gerald's grandson.

He swirled his glass of iced tea. "I do. But the poor little guy is sick with a cold, so no burger today. Instead you ladies have to put up with me."

"We don't mind," Joan said. "The more the merrier."

"We're having the shrimp sandwich," Gail said. "Plus chowder."

"Me too." Priscilla slapped the menu shut. She picked up her water and sipped, not wanting to meet Gerald's eyes.

"I'm the exception that proves the rule," Gerald said. "Roast beef with cheddar for me. With fries." His grin was wicked. "If you ladies are nice, I might share."

Priscilla couldn't resist any longer. She was happy to see him and that's what mattered. Plus she loved french fries. "Deal. So what's new with you?"

He shrugged. "Not much. But Joan has something to tell us."

All eyes turned to Joan. "The medical examiner called me this morning, Priscilla," she said. "The skeleton is male, about thirty years old."

Ambrose Allen. It had to be. But then she remembered not to jump to conclusions. "Could they date it? Him?"

"They think he's the same vintage as the first skeleton," Joan said. "They found some personal items with him, but nothing for a positive identification."

"Ready to order?" A server eyed them with a faint expression of alarm. They told her what they wanted and she hurried away, promising to bring drinks right over.

"I think we scared her," Gail said. "Although when I was a waitress, I overheard a lot of strange conversations." Gail had waited tables in her younger years, like many island residents.

"Your discovery puts a new twist on the tale," Gerald said. "Priscilla told me all about it the other night."

"The story was always that Bitsy and Ambrose ran away, right?" Trudy asked. "But now it looks like they never left."

"That's what I think," Priscilla said. "But of course it's not that clear cut. It turns out one of the maids who worked for the Parkers left around that same time. Evangeline Jenks."

"Why does that matter?" Gail asked. "She probably quit."

Priscilla waited for their server to place drinks on the table before continuing. "Jordan Parker, Vernon Parker's great-granddaughter, says the female skeleton is Evangeline. According to one of Evangeline's relatives, she left the island to go somewhere out West."

Joan used her straw to stir her soft drink. "Then again, there's always the possibility the skeletons are people we've never even heard of."

The table fell silent while everyone absorbed that sobering truth.

Then Priscilla felt a kernel of determination harden in her heart. "I'm going to do some deep digging. If any of those people left town and settled elsewhere, I'll find them."

"That's the spirit," Gerald said. "The secret to successful investigations? Persistence."

If that was true, then she was all set, because she didn't have very much else in the way of hard evidence. She'd go to the museum that afternoon. Why wait? With that decision, she put the puzzles troubling her mind aside. She would focus on enjoying a delicious lunch with very good company.

Her eyes met Gerald's, and he smiled. Very good company indeed.

After stuffing herself and laughing so hard her sides hurt, Priscilla drove down to the museum. The Open flag was out but only Mildred's car was parked in the small lot, an indication it was a quiet day. Probably most people were busy getting ready for Thanksgiving. That reminded her. She had a batch of cranberry sauce to make.

Before going inside, Priscilla called Whitney again. Again, she reassured Priscilla that they were fine. She and Jake had gone for a walk and were now getting warmed up by the fire. Priscilla told her what she was up to, and promised to keep her phone on in case Whitney needed her.

Inside the museum, Mildred was decorating the dining room for Thanksgiving. She was placing one of the lovely donated china sets around the long table. "Priscilla. What brings you out on this frosty Saturday?"

"I'm still investigating the Bitsy Parker case," Priscilla told her while shedding her coat. "Did you hear about the new skeleton?"

Mildred paused, a pile of salad bowls held in the crook of her arm. "I did. Poor Joan. She must think she bought a graveyard instead of a house lot."

Priscilla brushed her static-laden hair into place. "It was a shocker, that's for sure. Anyway, the medical examiner said it's a male of about thirty, and it was probably buried at the same time as the female skeleton."

"Oh my." Mildred set the pile of bowls down. "So it was a double murder, then."

"Looks that way." Priscilla motioned toward the upstairs, where historical records were stored. "I'm going to look at some databases. Rumor has it that a servant who worked for the Parkers went out West around that time. I want to try to find her."

"You know the way," Mildred said. "Go ahead and use the computer. The log-in information is beside the keyboard."

As Priscilla climbed the stairs, she reflected on the good fortune of having Internet access to vital records, newspapers, and collections of historical documents. Research in the old days must have been tedious and time-consuming, and most likely necessitated travel to other places. It must have been much easier to disappear back then too.

The research room held the aromas of old paper, ink, and leather books, a mixture Priscilla found both comforting and exciting. As she sat at the computer and turned it on, she laughed at herself. How many people got excited looking through dusty old papers? But it wasn't the items themselves, although the sense of touching items from across time was thrilling. They were like windows into another time and place.

Priscilla logged in successfully, then sat for a minute, thinking. She pulled a notebook and pen out of her purse. It always helped to write down her thoughts.

She'd look for Evangeline Jenks and Solomon Smith first. Marriage and death records. Gilbert said the pair had gotten married before they left the island. She checked the Martha's Vineyard roster of marriages for 1932 and found nothing.

Perhaps he was mistaken, and they got married at their destination. Out West, he'd said. That only narrowed it down to, oh, about ten states. Then she found a lifesaver. A compilation of marriage records for the western states, starting in the 1800s.

Nothing came up for Evangeline Jenks or Solomon Smith. Maybe they'd gotten married somewhere else. Or they'd never left Martha's Vineyard. Maybe the servants had been murdered and Bitsy and Ambrose had run away. Though why that might have happened, Priscilla had no theories at all.

Discouragement swamped Priscilla. How were they ever going to know who the poor victims were? The ring and cuff links were the only concrete clues she knew of.

On a whim, she entered Ambrose Allen into the database, and got a hit. Ambrose Allen had married Elizabeth Morgan in California on October 14, 1932.

CHAPTER EIGHTEEN

Priscilla stared at the screen, not quite believing her eyes. Ambrose and Bitsy had run away to California. Why had no one figured this out before? She looked at the record more closely. A note on the site said that many records were being added daily. Perhaps this marriage hadn't been available before.

With a sigh, Priscilla slumped back in her chair. On one hand, she should be happy the pair had lived. But did that mean Solomon and Evangeline were the victims? If so, did Bitsy and Ambrose kill them? But if they had, would they have been so bold as to travel under their own names? And no doubt relatives of the employees would have raised an outcry.

Priscilla eyed her phone and dialed Joan.

"Hey, lady," her cousin greeted her. "Did you find anything good?"

"I found something, but I'm not sure if it's good or bad." Priscilla took a deep breath. "According to an archive I searched, Ambrose and Bitsy got married in California."

Joan gasped. "No. How can that be?"

"I don't know, but I'm looking at it in black and white." Priscilla heard the glum note in her own voice. "I really thought those skeletons were Bitsy and Ambrose. Now I'm thinking they killed Evangeline and the gardener, Solomon Smith."

"Someone was buried on my land, no denying that." Joan was silent for a moment. "If it was the servants, why didn't anyone say something?"

Priscilla had already thought of an answer. "Maybe Vernon told the families that they had eloped. Gilbert Jenks told me that Evangeline married Solomon and went out West."

"So two couples left town at the same time, according to Vernon? Only one didn't." Joan scoffed. "Something isn't sitting right with me about this. I say keep looking."

"But for what?" Priscilla asked. She was fresh out of ideas. So much for being persistent and determined.

"It's a long shot, but while you're there, see if you can find pictures of Ambrose and Bitsy in the town newspaper or archives."

Priscilla checked the time. She could spare another half hour. "All right, I'll do that. Hopefully we'll be able to rule out one set of possibilities." Even if doing so complicated the mystery. She had no idea who would kill Evangeline—and put Bitsy's ring on her finger before burying her.

The small California town had a historical society website that included an archive of photographs. What a trove. But when Priscilla tried to use it, she got an error message. She tried again. Same result. The database was down.

"Grrr!" She was tempted to hammer her fists on the keyboard in frustration. What now?

There was a phone number listed so she called. To her relief someone answered. "I'm so glad you're open on Saturday," Priscilla said. "I've got a research request. And it involves two skeletons on Martha's Vineyard, in Massachusetts."

That introduction got the woman's attention, and she promised to do a manual search of the database for Ambrose and Bitsy. "We had a paper index before we uploaded everything," she explained. "It may take a couple of days, since they might not be the primary subjects in the photograph. But I'll look from 1932 on."

Priscilla had to be content with that. At least she'd made some progress, and now it was time to go home. She needed to make cranberry sauce.

Halfway down the stairs, she heard a familiar voice drifting from the rear of the building. Franklin. He and Mildred were chatting in the kitchen. She glanced at her coat, thinking she could easily slip out without either of them noticing. But that wouldn't be right, her conscience told her. She needed to say goodbye to Mildred.

Her conscience winning, Priscilla turned right at the bottom of the staircase instead of heading straight to the coatrack. As she'd thought, the duo was seated at the kitchen table, cups of coffee in hand.

"Want to join us?" Mildred asked. "You know the routine." She nodded at the Keurig on the counter.

"Maybe just for a minute," Priscilla said. She picked out a flavor and popped the pod into the machine. "You're going to want to hear about what I found, Franklin. It's about Bitsy."

He draped one arm over the seat back, casual and relaxed. "I've parsed those archives thoroughly myself, but you never know. I may have missed something." The sardonic quirk of his brow said that he highly doubted it.

Priscilla gritted her teeth. Why did she persist in trying to help this man? He didn't seem to appreciate it. *Because it's the right thing to do.* The answer dropped into her heart, and she wasn't going to argue. She knew a Holy Spirit directive when she heard one.

Once the coffee finished brewing, she added cream and sat at the table. Without preamble, she laid out the research she'd done that day. The last bit of information was the printout of the wedding record.

Franklin picked it up and stared at it. His lips worked, and his brow furrowed. Priscilla had the distinct feeling he was trying to figure out how to respond.

She put him out of his misery. "They've only uploaded a few of those records," she said. "That's why previous searches were unsuccessful."

Franklin set the paper down and slid it to Mildred. He picked up his mug and sipped, still frowning. "This doesn't make sense."

"I had the same reaction," Priscilla said. "Gilbert Jenks said Evangeline went out West with her husband. I suppose it's possible they are the skeletons."

"And Jordan Parker is right?" Mildred's eyes shone with quiet amusement. She knew about the animosity between Franklin and Jordan, both stubborn and strong-willed.

"Bah. I can't believe that." Franklin scowled. "What motive would anyone have to kill those servants? I'm not even totally sure why Bitsy was killed, and if that is Ambrose you found recently, him either. Not after considering Hazel Snyder's diary entries."

"At least now we know that Ambrose didn't kill Bitsy." Priscilla couldn't resist tweaking him, since that had been his theory. "But perhaps you were right, and they were involved. So Vernon killed them in a fit of jealousy." She smiled to let him know she didn't believe it.

Franklin tapped his fingers on the table then pointed at the paper. "Not according to that. They were alive and well and married."

"Then there should have been a divorce," Mildred pointed out. "Otherwise Bitsy was committing bigamy."

"At that time, many divorce seekers went to Reno," Franklin said. "They had to live there six weeks to obtain the divorce. So the timeline works."

"Good point," Mildred said. "They ran off in August, supposedly."

Priscilla's heart sank. "We're in the same position as before. Nothing is conclusive. I just pray the historical society in California comes through with something."

"Me too," Franklin said. "Otherwise there will be a lot of rewriting in my future." His expression while contemplating that possibility was decidedly gloomy.

Savory aromas greeted Priscilla when she walked through the door of the cottage.

"Something smells good," she called. Jake came jingling to greet her, pushing his nose into her hand. "Did you have a good day, Jake?" She ruffled his fur.

Whitney appeared in the hallway, beaming with pride. "I made one of my special dishes. Chicken and dumplings."

"Oh, you found the chicken in the freezer?" Priscilla accompanied Whitney to the kitchen. "That's resourceful of you."

"You had everything I needed—onion, carrot, potatoes. I even found frozen chicken broth." Whitney checked a bubbling pan on the stove. "This can simmer until dinnertime."

Priscilla opened the fridge, thinking she might as well make the cranberry sauce now. They could eat a little with the chicken and dumplings. "Whenever I bake a chicken, I boil the bones with celery and onion. Then I save the broth for other meals."

"I never thought of that." Whitney filled the kettle. "Want tea?"

"Sure, that'd be great." Priscilla pulled out two pounds of cranberries and then reached for frozen blueberries. She might have competition in the contest, but it was too late to find a new recipe. It wasn't about winning, anyway.

"How'd it go at the museum?" Whitney asked. While waiting for the kettle to boil, she went to the windows and gazed out at the evening. It was almost totally dark, and several stars shone in the indigo blue sky.

Priscilla filled her in while chopping berries in half. "I almost fell off my seat," she concluded. "I was so sure that the skeletons were Bitsy and Ambrose."

"I have an idea." Whitney dashed from the room and in a minute, returned holding her tablet. "Let's check for Reno divorces."

That's what Priscilla should have done. But she had resisted the idea, perhaps wanting to hold on to her theory a little longer. Not that she wished the couple murdered, of course. She had committed herself to learning the truth about the abandoned skeleton when she and Joan found her. What was one more obstacle, after all?

Whitney made a sound of disappointment. "They don't have anything that far back. The earliest online divorce record is 1968."

"I suppose I could contact them directly," Priscilla said. "But I think I'll take a break until after Thanksgiving."

"Might as well," Whitney said. "A lot of people are taking the whole week off."

That reminded Priscilla. She should really touch base with Rachel. She would call her after dinner.

After the sauce was ready, she filled several eight-ounce jars with the cranberry mixture. One for the contest, and the rest for her own use and Thanksgiving. Once they cooled, she would store them in the refrigerator.

Whitney set the table and then served big, steaming bowls of chicken and dumplings. After saying grace, Priscilla dug in, her mouth watering when she tasted the delicious gravy and tender morsels of chicken and vegetables. The dumplings were light and melted in her mouth. "I want this recipe."

"No problem," Whitney said. "I know it by heart. It's another dish my nanny taught me."

"Tell me about your family." Priscilla realized she knew only the bare bones of Whitney's life.

Whitney told her how, after the untimely death of her parents, she'd been raised between her grandmothers, the unpretentious Grandma Bennett and the formidable Grandmother Parker. Her nanny was one of the only constants in her life, until she was a teenager and considered too old for one.

I spent most of my time with the Bennett side," Whitney said. "But somehow it was expected I would work for the family firm. They paid very well, so it was hard to say no."

"Were you and Jordan close as kids?" Priscilla had to admit curiosity about this. Judging by Whitney's avoidance of her cousin, she'd guess no.

Whitney scooped up a spoonful of chicken. "Not really. She was always into prestige—joining clubs, being a member of a sorority. I don't care about all that."

"She's certainly a go-getter," Priscilla said. Without Jordan's strong arm, the cranberry contest might well flounder. Although someone else would probably step up, once there was a leadership vacuum.

After dinner, they cleaned up. Then Priscilla excused herself to call Rachel. The call went to voice mail, to Priscilla's disappointment. She left a light message, saying that she was just touching base.

Before she even walked away from the phone it rang. "Sorry, Mom. I couldn't get to the phone in time."

"That's okay. Where are you?"

There was a brief, fraught pause. "I'm in Boston. Landed this afternoon." Rachel sounded almost terse.

Priscilla knew better than to press her sometimes prickly daughter. "Did you have a good flight? At least the weather was clear."

"I did." Rachel gave some details about the trip. "I'll be over on Tuesday afternoon." She named the ferry time.

Should she mention A.J.? Priscilla thought she'd better not. Let him break the news that he was coming to the island earlier than planned. "I can't wait to see you. Did you hear that we found another skeleton?"

Rachel's shocked gasp was gratifying. "No. How would I hear?"

"Well, it was on the news the first time. Anyway, some men were fixing Joan's stone wall . . . " Priscilla told her the tale and then about her research efforts.

"The whole thing sounds like a book," Rachel declared. "Maybe you should write one. *Priscilla Latham Grant and the Mystery of the Martha's Vineyard Skeletons.*"

Priscilla laughed. "No, I'm afraid Franklin Mayweather has that covered."

"That professor who broke into your house looking for gold?" Rachel scoffed. "He must be driving you crazy."

Although there had been a time when she would have heartily agreed with Rachel, Priscilla couldn't bring herself to do that now. "Yes, he can be awful. But I think he's just lonely. And socially inept."

"Mom. You amaze me." Rachel fell silent. "I want to be like you when I grow up."

Priscilla was touched. "You're already pretty wonderful." Tears clogged her throat, and for a minute she didn't dare say another word. Then she choked out, "See you soon, darling. Love you."

"Love you too, Mom. Can't wait for Thanksgiving with the cousins." Rachel gave her a kiss through the phone.

After hanging up, Priscilla found a novel she'd been meaning to read. Then she relaxed in front of a roaring fire with Jake and Whitney. She found herself whispering a prayer of gratitude. Life was pretty good despite the challenges and trials.

CHAPTER NINETEEN

Priscilla went over to the fellowship hall after church ended, along with Gail and Uncle Hugh.

"What are we going to eat?" he grumbled while they added their food donations to the growing pile. "I can't go without my lunch."

Gail patted her tote bag. "I brought sandwiches, Pop. You know the committee has to get there early, even though the contest doesn't start until two."

Another volunteer had thoughtfully made urns of coffee, cocoa, and hot water, and after getting drinks, the trio sat down to eat.

"Thanks for bringing something for me." Priscilla picked up half a ham and cheese sandwich. "I forgot all about it."

"I can never forget food," Gail said, jerking a thumb toward her father. "Not with this guy around."

"Three squares a day," Hugh said. "That's my secret."

Considering her uncle was still relatively healthy and certainly of sound mind, Priscilla had to concede that he could be right.

As they ate their quick meal, the hall grew busy with the arrival of volunteers. Priscilla saw Gerald come in and waved him over. "I hear you're one of the judges."

He patted the badge on his lapel, pretending to be proud. "They needed my refined taste buds, so how could I refuse?"

"I have refined taste buds," Uncle Hugh said. "They should have picked me."

"Maybe next year, Pop." Gail patted his shoulder. "You're on the list to help set up."

"All right." He turned back to his sandwich. "Whatever needs to be done, I'm your man."

Jordan entered the room, and Gerald said, "I'd better go check in." He winked. "May the best sauce win." He marched off toward Jordan, who was joined by the other judge, Candy Lane.

"Gerald's such a great guy," Gail said. "Trudy told me he's coming for Thanksgiving?"

Priscilla popped a chip in her mouth. "His family is going out of town so I invited him."

"Neighborly of you," Uncle Hugh said. "Thanksgiving is a time for open doors and open hearts."

Gail and Priscilla looked at each other in surprise, since Uncle Hugh wasn't often flowery. "Tommy and Marigold will be joining us," Gail said. She was referring to Tommy Townsend and his mother. Due to complications of Tommy and Gail taking care of their aged parents, their fondness for each other was covert. Only Priscilla knew about it.

"It will be good to see them." Priscilla glanced at Uncle Hugh, whose ears had reddened at the mention of Marigold. In an odd twist, the older couple also cared for each other, but this too was as yet unspoken.

There was going to be quite a crowd at Trudy's, and Priscilla was looking forward to the occasion. She was so blessed to have family to gather with.

Gail collected their trash. "Are you two finished? It's time to get started."

Under Jordan's direction, the contest began promptly at two. Carts bearing bowls of sauce were wheeled out to the waiting first round judges.

As one of the entrants, Priscilla watched with interest. Many of the judges hammed up their reactions to the sauces, which were varied. Jellied and whole berry, spiced and plain, exotic ingredients and additions—all had their own special charm. Each team finally chose a selection for the head judges' table.

"We're ready to judge the final entries," Jordan said. "They include ginger and pear, classic jellied, apple cranberry, cranberry cherry, and a cranberry blueberry."

Priscilla's palms dampened, despite her avowed disinterest in winning. Was that hers? She couldn't tell, since the entrants didn't know their numbers. She waited as the three judges sampled, considered, and made notes. Would Gerald recognize her recipe? Would that be fair?

Gail, standing beside her, gave her an elbow and a thumbs-up. "Interesting that so many entries use another type of fruit," she whispered in Priscilla's ear. "I might have to do that next year." Gail had entered a classic whole berry.

Finally the judges came up to the microphone. They'd appointed Gerald to speak. With a big smile, he gazed around the room at the onlookers. "It's so good to see you all here in support of the food pantry. Judging by the mound of donations, our families are going to make it through the winter in fine form." Everyone burst into applause.

Once it died down, he continued. "Today's contest was a very difficult choice. To our cranberry cooks, you outdid yourselves. Before we announce the winner, I want to point out the table of fine sauces and baked goods available for purchase. What appreciated additions to your Thanksgiving table they will be." More applause.

Gerald rustled a piece of paper and cleared his throat.

Here it comes, Priscilla thought, clenching her fists so hard she felt her fingernails bit into her palms.

"All the entries were superb." Did his eyes linger on Priscilla an extra beat? "But in the end, we judges agreed, nothing beats a classic."

The jellied cranberry sauce had won. Priscilla felt slightly dazed. "They always do that," Gail said. "They pick either plain jellied or whole berry. Tradition, don't you know?"

"Really?" Priscilla shook her head, trying to clear her thoughts. "Why does everyone go all out then?"

"It's fun, I guess." Gail scanned the crowd. "I'm going to get Pop and get out of here, after a detour by the baked goods table. I want some of those homemade rolls." She disappeared into the throng.

Gerald came up to Priscilla after she made her own purchases of molasses cookies and a small pumpkin pie. "I'm sorry about that," he said, speaking under the chatter echoing in the room. "Your entry was the best, but you know—"

"I know," Priscilla said. "Tradition wins. So it was my sauce up there?"

He put a hand on her elbow to guide her through the tight-packed bodies. "I recognized the superb flavor. Of course, I had to pay extra attention to the others, to be fair."

Priscilla laughed, loving the fact that he had been able to tell the sauce was hers. That meant he'd really paid attention when he'd tried it. "Thanks for that. Not that it made any difference."

They reached a quiet spot. "So I'll see you on Thanksgiving, if not before," he said. "Should be fun."

"I'm pretty excited too," Priscilla said. "Rachel is already in Boston. She's coming over on the ferry Tuesday."

He smiled. "I'm looking forward to seeing her again." He leaned forward and gave her a peck on the cheek. "Have a nice afternoon, my cranberry queen."

Smiling to herself, Priscilla headed for home. Although it had been fun, she was glad the cranberry contest was over. Events like that took a lot of energy.

At the cottage, when she opened the garage door to pull in, something seemed different. Then she realized—Whitney's car was gone.

Trepidation gnawing in her belly, Priscilla pulled in and parked. She checked her phone and didn't find any calls from Whitney, which would have come through from the house number. She had turned off her cell phone days ago so she couldn't be tracked.

Priscilla hurried to the house, moving as fast as she could on the icy ground. Holding her breath, she dug out her key and unlocked the door. What would she find inside?

Jake came running to greet her, tail wagging. He looked fine, as did the quiet house. "Whitney?" she called, knowing that she wouldn't get an answer. Without taking off her coat or boots, Priscilla trudged through the rooms, searching for her guest.

A note was on the table. Priscilla set the pie and cookies down and read, "I got bored so I went to the farm to work on the inventory. I plan to be back before the contest ends, but if you're reading this, it means I'm not." A smiley face and her signature followed.

The trepidation deepened to dread. Priscilla glanced at the clock. Despite her jaunty note, Whitney should have been back by now. She wouldn't want to worry Priscilla. She was too considerate for that.

Priscilla snatched up the phone and dialed the farm. Sheila had been at the contest early on but had ducked out. No one answered. Priscilla dug through her contacts and located Sheila's cell number.

Same thing. No answer. Next she bit the bullet and called Franklin. He answered right away, the sound of voices and laughter in the background. "Are you at the farm?" she asked him, knowing the answer.

"I'm not, dear lady," he said. "I'm grabbing a bite to eat at the Colonial Inn and Restaurant. Is there anything I can do for you?"

"No, there isn't, I'm afraid. Have a good night." She hung up the phone and ran with Jake for the door, every instinct in her body crying out that something was terribly wrong. Whitney was in danger.

CHAPTER TWENTY

On autopilot, Priscilla pulled out of the garage again and drove to the farm, Jake in the back seat. Her thoughts went back and forth between a vision of Whitney and Sheila drinking tea together to—what exactly? She steeled her mind, not wanting to picture horrible things.

Dear Lord, she prayed, *please protect my friends and keep them safe…* The refrain went through her mind in an endless, urgent loop. All the while she navigated the streets as fast as she dared. Night was falling and patches of ice had formed on the roads. If she hit one wrong, she could slide off and hit a tree. Or an oncoming car.

She also peered at every vehicle, hoping to see Whitney at the wheel. No Whitney, but she had to slow and move onto the shoulder to avoid a truck in the other lane, one that was taking its half out of the middle, as her husband used to say.

It was a navy blue pickup, with a cap. Her heart jumped. Until the shooter was caught—if ever—would she be afraid of every similar truck?

After what felt like eons, Priscilla reached the farm entrance. The light was off over the sign, indicating that the place was closed. Maybe Sheila had also gone off-island and was in a place with poor cell reception.

But even so, that didn't explain where Whitney was. Without Franklin and Sheila there to talk to, surely she would have come back to the cottage.

Whitney's car was parked by the barn, along with Sheila's truck. The light over the barn entrance was on, as were lights in the house. Priscilla parked, let Jake out, and went to the back door.

She knocked on the glass but no one answered. A half-curtain blocked her view, so she moved along to another window and peered inside. The kitchen was empty and clean, although she spotted a couple of mugs by the sink.

Feeling like an intruder, Priscilla tried the door. The knob turned easily, so she opened it and stepped inside, staying on the mat. Jake followed, sniffing the air eagerly. "Stay with me, boy," she said. Then she called, "Sheila? Are you home?"

No one answered. She listened, straining her ears for any sign of life. No footsteps overhead, no sound from a television or music. Besides, the house had the deserted feel of a vacant building. Nothing moved or breathed.

She crossed the floor to the office, thinking that by some chance Whitney might be in there, working so hard she didn't hear Priscilla come in.

The office was also empty, but Priscilla could tell that Whitney had made a lot of progress. She obviously had a knack for organization.

Whitney had to be at the cabin. Maybe she had gone to collect some things—fresh clothing and perhaps another book. Although why she didn't drive over, Priscilla couldn't imagine.

Priscilla thought she would try that herself. Why walk through the lumpy, frozen field in the dark? The fear in her belly had crystalized into a cold weight. Trying to keep her fears and speculations at bay, she went through the motions of starting the car, turning, and driving down the lane. Movement was the key, doing the next thing.

She parked beside the cabin, in the small dirt area at one side. No lights were on, which nipped her latest theory in the bud. But she climbed out anyway. "Stay here, Jake," she said, leaving the window cracked.

Keep moving, keep looking. On stiff legs, Priscilla walked around the cabin to the door. *Put one foot in front of the other.* At the bottom of the porch steps, her foot crunched on something. She bent down and picked it up.

The flash drive Whitney wore on the chain around her neck. Why was it here, in the dirt? Priscilla bent over and felt around, using the light on her phone to see better. Something gleamed in the grass. The chain.

She straightened, the flash drive clutched in her palm. How had Whitney become separated from her precious evidence?

A soft footstep thudded behind her. Awareness of danger swept over Priscilla like a wave of cold water. Someone was out there, creeping around in the dark. She darted around the cabin, to the far side. Thinking quickly, she texted Joan and Gerald.

Send police to Weller Farm ASAP.

Then she put the phone on silent and shoved it in her pocket. No need to announce her location.

The footsteps advanced to the porch, then retreated. She had barely allowed herself to relax, thinking he was gone, when something coarse-woven and smelling of grain was tugged down over her head.

Priscilla tried to scream, but the thick fabric muffled her voice. She flailed trying to get it off, but strong arms went around her.

"It will go better for you if you come quietly," a deep voice said.

She opened her fingers and let the flash drive drop. If this was who she suspected, why make it easy for him to get the information?

The man picked Priscilla up and slung her over his shoulder as effortlessly as if she was an actual bag of grain. The sack over her head was dense, magnifying the thunder of her heartbeat as he walked, every footstep jolting up through her body. One glove slid off her hand, and she let it fall. Another clue for someone to find.

She heard her captor shout. "Open the back."

Something squeaked and then Priscilla was unceremoniously dumped on a hard metal floor. The ridges against her back felt like the bed of a pickup truck. Frantic barking echoed through the trees. Poor Jake. He must be wondering what was happening.

"Get her phone," another man said. His voice was familiar and Priscilla strained to recognize it. Someone from the island, definitely.

A meaty hand foraged in her coat pocket and extracted the phone. Then the door of the cap slammed shut, and the rattle of a lock was heard. She was alone in the dark.

Or was she? Priscilla tugged off the sack. Something warm and soft lay next to her, groaning. "Whitney?" The truck started with a roar and jounced along on the rough lane leading through the woods.

Another groan. "Priscilla? What are you doing here?" A little light leaked into the truck from the taillights, enough that Priscilla could see her friend's wide-eyed face.

Priscilla felt along the back of the cap for the handle. She tried to turn it, and for good measure, pushed on the door. As she thought, it was locked. "Someone grabbed me and threw me in here. I'm guessing it was Dalton." She doubted the men could hear her over the engine, but she whispered anyway.

"It was." Whitney felt the back of her head. "He hit me on the head after I tried to fight him off." Grim satisfaction flashed across her features. "But he didn't get the flash drive."

"I know. I stepped on it. But it's OK," she added hastily at seeing Whitney's upset expression. "I left it behind. I also texted Gerald and Joan to get the police." Hopefully they would find the drive, the glove, and Jake.

But how would the police find *them*? "Where are we going?" she asked Whitney. The truck continued to lurch and bounce over ruts and rocks, bruising Priscilla's body on the hard floor.

"I have no idea." Whitney covered her face with both hands. "I'm so sorry, Priscilla. I shouldn't have gone back to the farm."

Priscilla agreed wholeheartedly with that statement, but she knew no good would come of recriminations. "It was a case of wrong place, wrong time. Let's put our thoughts, energy, and prayers into getting out of this situation. Hopefully help is coming."

"Can you pray with me?" Whitney whispered.

"Of course." Priscilla took her hand and prayed out loud, asking for God's mighty hand to save them, for His guidance and peace.

Whitney heaved a sigh. "I feel a little better, believe it or not."

"I believe it." Priscilla had utmost faith, but still, adrenaline was coursing through her body and all her senses were on high alert. God would help, but they still needed to do their part.

"Maybe I should have given the drive to him," Whitney said. "But then all that money would be gone. All those poor people."

And he might have killed her right then. Whitney was valuable because she was Dalton's link to the money.

The truck continued on. Priscilla tried to picture the island map in her head. There was a patch of woods and swamp adjacent to the Weller farm. This must be where they were, headed right into the heart of the swamp.

Gilbert Jenks owns a camp in the swamp. The truth sank into her mind like a pebble in a pool. The farmhand must be the other man with Dalton. How long had he been working with the rogue agent? No doubt he'd been promised his investment money back, and probably much more to help with a kidnapping.

The truck finally halted with a jerk that sent them sliding. The doors opened and slammed, and then the back gate squeaked open. "Come on out, you two," Dalton said. "I've got a gun so don't try anything."

"Why are you doing this?" Priscilla said. "Let us go. We haven't done anything to you."

Dalton reached in and tugged Whitney's leg. "This one has something I want. And until she gives it to me, neither of you are going anywhere."

Priscilla hoped and prayed the police would get there before Dalton got tired of asking. She knew that he might not allow them to live, even if she told him to look under the bushes beside the cabin.

Once they were standing upright, Dalton, who Priscilla recognized as the man pretending to be Geoff Sanders, prodded them along a muddy, rutted path into tangled woods. Up ahead, Gilbert held a flashlight to illuminate the way ahead. A rectangle of light shone through the trees.

The tiny cabin sat on a small rise overlooking a stagnant body of water. Priscilla couldn't see the details but the pungent stench of rotting vegetation was familiar.

"Go on, get inside," Dalton barked. Gilbert climbed onto the creaking low porch and opened the door. Whitney and Priscilla followed, taking cautious steps to avoid pieces of wood and other debris strewn around the dirt clearing.

The cabin was one room with a loft. On one side, a woodstove glowed with warmth, on the other was a kitchenette made from rusty metal cabinets. Fishing gear lay strewn around, and several rifles hung over the mantel.

Gilbert gestured for them to sit on the sagging sofa. Its only attraction was that it was close to the heat. Dalton stood facing them, the gun held at the ready.

"Why are you doing this?" Priscilla asked Gilbert. "We would have helped you." She tried to appeal to the man's latent sense of decency. He was an islander, a farm worker. Surely he had some values.

He scoffed, sticking his thumbs into his belt loops. "You gonna help me escape this place, go somewhere warm?" He sneered when she didn't answer. "'Course not."

Dalton paced, never taking his eyes off them. "You led me on a pretty chase, Miss Parker. You should have given me the information and saved me all the trouble."

Whitney's eyes flashed. "No way. I have a fiduciary duty to our clients."

Priscilla clasped her hands in her lap, praying. Surely Joan or Gerald would have seen her text by now and called the police. Hopefully they would be able to track them into the woods, once they realized nobody was at the farm. If they could hold these men at bay a little longer...

Dalton thrust his face close to Whitney's. "What a principled little thing you are. But you'd better get over it. Fast." Whitney shrank back against the dusty, faded cushions.

Priscilla reached for her hand and squeezed, trying to give encouragement.

The sound of another vehicle rumbled in the distance. Hope shot through Priscilla's heart. Then it sank when Gilbert said, "Think that's the boss coming?" He chortled at the surly expression that crossed Dalton's face. "A little too close to home, buddy?"

"Shut up." Dalton turned and strode to the door, peered out the window into the dark. "Go see who it is."

Gilbert slouched outside, sending the other man poisonous glares. Didn't he realize that Dalton might cut him out once he was no longer useful? There truly was no honor among thieves, Priscilla knew.

The trio left inside waited in uneasy silence. Dalton paced around the small space, still keeping the gun pointed their way. Priscilla studied the contents of the cabin, looking for something that could be used in self-defense. They had to get out of here.

Where are the police? And who is the boss? The questions whirled in her mind. When voices sounded, she knew that one question at least would soon be answered.

The door flew open again to reveal Jordan Parker. Dressed in a parka, rubber boots, and jeans suitable for the swamp, she still managed to convey elegant authority.

Whitney gasped. "Jordan. What are you doing here?"

Jordan gave Dalton a quick kiss. She laughed. "You didn't think I was going to go down with the ship, did you? I'm not that dumb." She tossed her head. "I have an MBA, remember?"

"But your dad..." Whitney protested.

Her cousin laughed again. "He doesn't know anything." Jordan preened. "I'm the mastermind behind it all." She leaned close to Dalton. "And Dalton is making sure we get away with it." Her smirk was wicked.

Hence Gilbert's nickname for Jordan. Priscilla slotted this new information into what she knew. Jordan had set up the scam and no doubt deceived other members of the firm to hide it. Once it came crashing down, she allowed her father to take the hit.

Whitney had shriveled into herself, obviously stunned by this betrayal. Jordan strode across the floor and stood right in front of her. "You need to give it up, Whitney. Face it, I've won. Your goody-two-shoes routine is over."

"What if I refuse?" Whitney stared up at Jordan, dredging some defiance from somewhere. "You're a thief and a crook. What would Grandmother Parker think?"

Jordan slapped Whitney. "Don't talk about Grandmother. I was always her favorite."

Whitney smiled. "Are you sure about that? She told me I was her favorite. She even let me play in her jewelry box."

"No way. She never let anyone play with her things." Jordan rested her hands on her hips, frowning. "You're lying."

Priscilla understood what Whitney was doing. She was distracting Jordan with family dynamics and rivalry, and buying time. Jordan had left the door to the outside ajar. That was good. Maybe they could create a distraction, make a run for it. Yes, it would be dangerous, but the dark woods would soon hide them.

But where were the police? The time had seemed to drag, but maybe it hadn't been all that long.

Dalton took a step forward. "Enough, ladies. Let's get back to business." Before he could say more, there was a scrabbling sound on the porch and Jake nudged open the door. Priscilla had never been so happy to see him.

"What's that dog doing here?" Gilbert asked. The words were barely out of his mouth when Jake growled and launched himself at Dalton. Biting and snapping, he ripped Dalton's sleeve, making him drop the gun. Then Jake went after his pant leg.

Priscilla jumped up and grabbed a weighted fishing net from a pile of gear. She threw it over Gilbert's head, forcing the man to grapple with the unwieldy bundle of ropes. Whitney tugged on Jordan's arm and pulled her down onto the couch. She threw another net over her cousin, who immediately became tangled.

"Come on," Priscilla said. "Let's go." She swooped down and picked up the firearm. Not that she planned to use it, but she didn't want Dalton to get it back.

Whitney on her heels, Priscilla rushed out of the cabin. She looked over her shoulder to make sure no one was watching and tucked the gun under a thick bush around the corner of the cabin, where it was completely hidden from view. She called to Jake and he burst from the cabin, galloping at full speed. He led the way down the path toward the lane.

Priscilla and Whitney followed, doing their best in the dark. "Do you think we should hide?" Whitney asked, gasping for breath. "They'll be on our trail any minute."

They had reached the parking area. "No, I have a better idea." Priscilla yanked open the truck door. No keys. Then she tried Jordan's sedan. The keys were dangling from the ignition. "Get in."

"They'll follow us," Whitney pointed out.

"True." Priscilla went back to the truck, popped the hood, and pulled off the battery connector. Her husband had taught her all about batteries. It wouldn't stop them for long but at least they would be delayed.

Whitney had jumped into Jordan's driver's seat and started the car. She backed up and turned to face down the road.

"Good girl," Priscilla said, opening the passenger door. Jake pushed his way past her and through the seats into the back.

"Let's go." Whitney put the car in Drive and shot down the road. The low-slung vehicle jounced and swayed, forcing Priscilla to grip the handle for dear life. A couple of times the car bounced so low it scraped the middle hump in the road.

Priscilla thought she heard shouts but then they sped around a corner and any sight or sound of the gang was lost.

The journey to the cabin had seemed to take forever, despite the speed. Finally the road widened somewhat, signaling that they were entering the farm property. A minute later they were racing past Whitney's cabin.

"Stop," Priscilla yelled. Whitney braked, sending them sliding forward. Thank goodness for seat belts. As for Jake, he was on the back floor, so he was okay. "I'm going to get your flash drive."

"How will you see it?" Whitney asked.

"Good question." Priscilla popped the glove compartment and found a flashlight. She turned it on. "With this."

It only took a minute or so to find the flash drive, right where she had left it. She snatched it up and hopped back into the car.

Blue and white lights strobed against the night sky, touching the trees. "Looks like help has arrived," Whitney said. She leaned her forehead against the steering wheel and closed her eyes.

"What are you doing?" Priscilla asked. "Resting? You sure deserve it."

"No. Thanking God." Whitney straightened up and hit the gas, laughing in sheer joy. Priscilla joined in, and even Jake got into the act with a howl or two.

The relief was certainly enormous, and Priscilla also sent up prayers of gratitude. The whole thing had gone off flawlessly, exactly as if they'd had help. Which was true, of course. God was faithful.

Police vehicles, Gerald's truck, and an ambulance sat in the farmyard. A throng of officers, Gerald, Franklin, and Sheila were gathered near the barn, along with Bosco. Sheila was holding Priscilla's glove.

The group turned to stare when they pulled up, the policemen standing on alert. Chief Hank Westin recognized Priscilla and told them to stand down. Whitney shut off the car and they climbed out, Jake barking and leaping in excitement. The chief took the lead. "Tell us what happened. We were just about ready to mount a search party."

"FBI Agent Dalton Rogers, Jordan Parker, and Gilbert Jenks are working together to steal financial information in the federal case against Parker & Warren." At Whitney's nod, Priscilla handed the chief the flash drive. "A.J. Montgomery, another FBI agent, is going to want to see this tomorrow. It has information about off-shore accounts, where Jordan funneled the stolen money. And I need to let you know that there's a gun behind some bushes at the cabin—around the right side."

"Dalton is a crook," Whitney said. "He wanted that information on the flash drive for himself. After he kidnapped us, we were able to get away."

"With the help of this guy," Priscilla said, giving Jake a pat. "He came to rescue us." But how had he gotten out of the car?

Franklin answered that. "I heard him barking inside your SUV when I got home, so I let him out. It's a good thing I did."

"All right," the chief said. "We'll issue a be-on-the-lookout for those three. Do they have a vehicle, Priscilla?"

"That one," she said, pointing to the pair of headlights emerging from the woods. "A navy blue pickup truck. I fiddled with the battery cable to give us a head start." The headlights stopped, then the truck did a three-point turn and raced back the way it had come.

The chief issued orders for pursuit, and the officers dispersed. "Priscilla, Whitney, I'm going to want full statements from you," Chief Westin said. "Can you wait here until I'm ready?"

"Come on inside," Sheila said. "I've got coffee brewing." She handed Priscilla her glove. "I guess we won't be needing this after all."

Priscilla tucked it into her pocket with the other one. "What were you going to do with it?"

"I was going to have Bosco track you," Sheila said. "Poor thing. He's so disappointed." Bosco, however, was busy running around the driveway with Jake.

Priscilla laughed. "He looks like he's gotten over it."

As they walked toward the house with Sheila, Gerald and Franklin joined them. "Disarmed a crook. Disabled a vehicle.

Escaped from kidnappers." Gerald shook his head. "Is there anything you can't do, Priscilla?"

"I'm thinking not," Franklin said. "Not only is she a crime-fighting machine, she is an incredible researcher. And to think she's not even trained as well as I am. What could she do if she were?" After making that remark, he hurried ahead to open the door for Sheila and Whitney.

Priscilla looked at Gerald, and they both laughed. "Leave it to Franklin," Gerald said with a headshake, taking Priscilla's arm.

"No kidding," Priscilla said. It was so typical of Franklin to temper a compliment with a nod to himself. "But it doesn't really matter." Franklin was—well, he was Franklin. Priscilla could tolerate him just fine. She paused to stare at the star-studded sky. "Right now all I can feel is pure gratitude."

CHAPTER TWENTY-ONE

Here comes the ferry," Priscilla told Jake. They stood on the docks waiting to greet one very special passenger. The afternoon was cloudy and small flakes were drifting down, but for once it wasn't windy.

Across the parking lot, Barry's Bait Shed was slow. Priscilla smiled at the thought of her encounter with Geoff Sanders. What must the man have thought? Once Dalton and the others were arrested, he'd confirmed to the police that, yes, he had assumed the innocent store clerk's identity. He'd gone on Barry's charters in the past and knew the gang at the store well. He'd also confirmed that he was the one who shot at Priscilla and Whitney in the woods, trying to scare Whitney into cooperating with him.

A.J. Montgomery had taken the first morning ferry and headed right to the police department. The chief had provided federal officers and agencies with a special room to use for the Parker case. Whitney was the star witness, as they say, and she had spent hours in interviews. A financial forensics expert had been called in to examine the flash drive and help build the case for fraud, diversion of funds, and numerous other charges.

Rachel hadn't come with him, since she was busy in Boston. Shopping, A.J. had said. But she was arriving now, on the last ferry of the day, and that was good enough for Priscilla. Priscilla had spent the day puttering around the cottage, cleaning, changing the guest bed, and preparing treats. In light of the harrowing events of the night before, such simple tasks seemed especially sweet.

The ferry slowed as it approached the dock, a familiar ritual. Workers on the dock and on board prepared to help the large ship slide neatly into its berth.

Priscilla's heart quickened. Watching boats go in and out of the harbor was always a thrill but especially when someone she knew was on board. She strained her eyes to study the passengers standing at the rail.

There she was, her girl. Rachel lifted a hand, her long hair blowing in the wind. As the boat drew closer, Priscilla saw she wore a trim navy blue coat and a bright scarf around her neck. Priscilla waved back, unable to prevent a huge grin from breaking across her face. Jake picked up on her excitement and reared up with a bark.

"Down, boy. She'll be here in a few minutes." Priscilla exchanged smiles with other people waiting. That was another thing she enjoyed, seeing the reunions on the docks. Sometimes her eyes welled up, sentimental fool that she was.

The gangway was lowered into place and the foot passengers began to stream off. Rachel politely stood back to let a family or two go by and then an older couple. Priscilla shifted from foot to foot, eager to greet her beloved daughter.

Finally. Rachel was in her arms, bringing the scent of cold sea air and light perfume. "Mom. It's so good to see you." She squeezed Priscilla.

For a moment, Priscilla experienced a visceral memory of Rachel when she was a child, so sweet in her arms. Her fine hair had tickled her nose then too.

She kissed Rachel's cheek. "Welcome to the island. Welcome home." Her voice was husky so she had to clear her throat. Jake jumped up on Rachel and yipped for attention, breaking the emotional moment with his comedic timing.

Rachel laughed and bent to give him his due. "I've missed you, Jake. I hope you've been keeping Mom in line." She grinned up at her mother. "I heard you had quite the exciting time last night."

A.J. must have filled her in on her involvement. The general story had gone out in the news of course, without her name, thankfully. Priscilla was grateful for that. "That's an understatement. When we get home, I'll give you the full report."

"I can't wait." Pulling her suitcase, Rachel strolled beside Priscilla toward the SUV. Her phone rang, and she halted. "Hold on. I'd better get this."

Priscilla and Jake waited while Rachel took the call. Not that she was trying to listen, Priscilla couldn't discern a thing—except the expression of joy that broke out across Rachel's features.

"Sorry about that." Rachel slid her phone into her coat pocket. "But I've just had very good news." She practically radiated happiness and satisfaction.

"What is it?" Priscilla asked, her heart swelling. She rejoiced in good news from a family member. From anyone, really. Bring on the good news. Life had enough of the opposite.

Rachel took a deep breath. "I know I've been a bit secretive lately, and I'm sorry. But I didn't want to say anything until it was final." She paused, making Priscilla's nerves scream. "I've just accepted a job in Boston."

It took a few seconds for the words to sink in. Then joy exploded in Priscilla's heart. "You're moving to Boston?" She launched herself into Rachel's arms, tears beginning to flow. Her darling would only be a few hours away. She could see her anytime she wanted. Well, as long as Rachel wasn't busy.

Rachel patted her on the shoulder. "Don't cry, Mom." Rachel's eyes shimmered with moisture, belying her words. "I wanted to be closer to you…and A.J." With his keen nose for news, the dog yipped again. "And Jake."

Priscilla threw back her head and laughed. Yet another wonderful thing to be grateful for. She'd be a blessings hog at Thanksgiving dinner, for sure.

"Smile, ladies." Gerald held his digital camera at the right angle to view the shot. "That's perfect."

The flash went off, momentarily blinding Priscilla. She was snuggled on Trudy's enormous couch with Trudy, Joan, and Gail, enjoying the pre-dinner lull. In the den, people were watching football, and around the spacious living room, other clusters of guests talked and laughed. In addition to Latham relatives, Tommy and Marigold Townsend were there, along with Whitney, Sheila, the Chowders, and Franklin.

Gerald wandered off to take a picture of Trudy's daughter talking to Rachel.

"What is he, our official event photographer?" Joan joked.

"He volunteered," Trudy said. "I think it's a nice idea. I always forget to take pictures until after everyone goes home."

"Hello, ladies." Sam Abernathy, Joan's son, sat in a nearby armchair, his wife, Alice, perched on the arm. "I wanted you all to know that the station is definitely doing a special on Bitsy Parker." Jovial and warm, Sam smiled at Priscilla. "I want you and Mom to be project consultants."

Franklin, with his sixth sense for anything that concerned him, wandered up. "I'm glad you asked them to help us. I'm planning to give them a mention in my book."

Sam's good humor didn't falter. After nodding at Franklin, he turned back to the women. "I understand you found some definitive proof regarding the skeletons?"

"Yes, we did." Priscilla pulled out her phone. "I'll show you the e-mails." The woman from the California historical society had gotten back to Priscilla on Tuesday. The photographs of Bitsy and Ambrose Allen were revealing, to say the least.

Priscilla found the e-mail and enlarged the first photograph, from a local paper's society pages. She handed the phone to Sam. "That couple is actually Evangeline and Solomon. They took on Bitsy and Ambrose's identities to start their new lives."

"No doubt with a big cash injection from Vernon," Joan added. "Solomon started a very successful nursery and gardening business."

"Click to the next photo," Priscilla said. "It shows the business." Solomon and several workers stood in front of a low-slung but attractive business, a work truck parked nearby.

Sam examined the pictures, with Alice looking over his shoulder. "They're still waiting on DNA results, correct?" Sam asked.

"Yes," Priscilla said. "We finally found some relatives. Both Bitsy and Ambrose were from off-island so it was a challenge." The police had found the resources in their budget to get the testing done.

"The way we're piecing it together," Franklin said in his sonorous teaching voice, "is that Bitsy and Ambrose confronted Vernon with his stock market shenanigans. Instead of repenting and making things right, he killed them in a fit of rage."

The group fell silent for a moment. "It was a terrible tragedy," Sam said. "We'll make sure they are honored appropriately." Priscilla had seen Sam's work, and he wouldn't put an undignified tabloid spin on the story, she was sure.

"We're going to make sure they are buried properly too," Gail said. "Donations have been pouring in for headstones."

People on the island were so nice, Priscilla reflected. Look at the way they'd taken her, and now Rachel, into their hearts. Her eyes met Gerald's across the room, and they shared a smile. Despite missing his kids, he appeared to be having a great time.

Trudy used her cousins' shoulders to push herself to a standing position. "You'll have to excuse me. It's time to get dinner on the table."

The other ladies joined her in the kitchen. While the turkeys rested before being carved, they reheated casseroles, rewhipped potatoes, and poured condiments into dishes. All the cousins had made cranberry sauce, so there would be four choices.

"Maybe we should take a vote at the table," Gail suggested, a teasing smile on her face. "See which of us made the best sauce." She dumped the ruby-red contents of a jar into a glass bowl.

"What's the prize?" Joan fired back. "It'd better be good."

"I know." Trudy wiped her hands on her apron with a laugh. "Winner gets out of cleanup."

"I don't want to win, then," Priscilla said. "I like working in the kitchen with you ladies." This statement was met with hoots, cheers, and hugs.

Soon the entire group was gathered around two very long tables. There were close to thirty people there, Priscilla estimated. Good thing Trudy had cooked two turkeys. In addition to two heaped platters of meat, bowls and platters filled with various yummy dishes lined the middle of the table.

Dan, Trudy's husband, led them in grace, then the platters and bowls went around. Priscilla was seated in the best spot in the house, she thought—between Gerald and Rachel. She filled her plate with a little of everything, conscious that it was all too easy to eat too much. But she took a big spoonful of Gerald's stuffing. That was only polite. He did the same with her sauce, she noticed.

After everyone was served, they went around the table sharing what they were grateful for. Priscilla loved listening to the gratitude for health, provision, and loved ones. All the while she was pondering what to say. She always had a tiny bit of stage fright in situations like this, silly as it might be.

Finally it was her turn, and she happened to be the last to speak. "At times I find myself complaining," she said. "So I resolved recently to be more consciously grateful." She saw heads nodding. "Right after I started, things immediately got more challenging." Everyone laughed.

"Been there," someone called.

"But all that did is make me pray more," Priscilla went on. "And make me more grateful for the good things in my life." She squeezed Gerald's hand, then Rachel's. "I'm going to quote Psalm 16, since it says it best. 'Lord You alone are my portion and my cup; You make my lot secure. The boundary lines have fallen for me in pleasant places; surely I have a delightful inheritance.'"

"Amen," Gerald said, echoed by Rachel. The others followed.

Then Dan lifted his fork. "Let's eat."

AUTHOR LETTER

Dear Reader,

Doesn't the idea of Thanksgiving on Martha's Vineyard evoke cozy images? Historic New England homes nestled among bare trees, fragrant wood smoke drifting from brick chimneys. As an early dusk falls, lights come on one-by-one, bright spots against the gloom. Inside, families prepare the annual feast and gather to break bread and give thanks together. It's truly a wonderful time of year.

In this story, which leads up to Thanksgiving, Priscilla realizes that she needs to be more consciously grateful. It's easy to let the annoyances and challenges of life overshadow all that is good. As the mother of grown children, I know what an adjustment it is when they become truly independent. Like Priscilla, I sometimes long for the time when my daughters were small and part of my everyday life. But I realized, as Priscilla does, that we are blessed indeed, in every season of life.

It's been such a thrill to write for this series, to join a wonderful, devoted lineup of writers and experience the sure guidance of our fabulous editors. Truly a team effort as we work together to craft the story lines. And the cover art! Oh my goodness.

May God bless you richly now and during all the seasons to come.

Elizabeth Penney

ABOUT THE AUTHOR

Elizabeth Penney lives in the White Mountains of New Hampshire, where she pens novels, runs a small farm, and cans lots of vegetables and jam. Active in their local church and community, she and her husband enjoy a clan of three children and five grandchildren. They are also under the management of a bold hen named Pearl and a very spoiled cat named Noah.

AN ARMCHAIR TOUR OF
MARTHA'S VINEYARD
Martha's Vineyard Cranberry Bogs

When I learned that cranberries grow on Martha's Vineyard, I had to include a farm in my Thanksgiving story. Cranberries are practically synonymous with the holiday, due to the Pilgrims enjoying them at the very first feast. Native Americans regarded the berries as a staple, using them fresh, dried, and for tea, much like we do. Some tribes even used the bright juice for dye. Extremely high in nutrients, cranberries are now considered a superfood, which is extending their consumption far beyond the holiday season.

While our first settlers may have seen similar fruit in England, it's our unique North American variety that has shaped today's $300 million industry. They had other names for the plant, including craneberry, fenberries, and bearberries. Bears like them too.

In addition to being delicious, cranberries require certain growing conditions, which is why they are found mainly in northern parts of the United States. These conditions begin with geology. Glaciers formed so-called kettle holes, and over time, pockets of clay became layered with rocks and other organic materials to form peat bogs. Add fresh water and an April through November growing season and you have a home for cranberries. A layer of sand also boosts production, growers learned in the early 1800s.

One interesting fact: the bogs are only flooded during harvest. The rest of the time the vines grow on dry ground, well-irrigated of course. Some vines on Cape Cod are over 150 years old.

An interesting project on the island is the Vineyard Open Land Foundation's restoration of a bog turned campground, called Cranberry Acres. Over the past ten years, they've been creating a demonstration organic cranberry farm. The goal is to teach organic techniques to farmers, botanists, and visitors while growing a crop that can help sustain the foundation's important work. Berries from Cranberry Acres are available during the season at farm stands and island markets.

With the continued interest in locally grown food and the importance of cranberries as a superfood, perhaps the once flourishing island industry will revive. Until the World War II labor shortage, there were many productive bogs around the island.

Read on for a sneak peek of another exciting book
in the series Mysteries of Martha's Vineyard!

Water Flows Uphill
by DeAnna Julie Dodson

Well, this should be interesting."

Priscilla Grant looked at the display in the shop's frosted front window. It was a fascinating array of sculptures and paintings with a variety of styles and themes, most of them a thought-provoking mixture of traditional and modern. There was a plaster bust of Shakespeare decorated with African tribal tattoos and sporting dreadlocks sitting beside one of Genghis Khan painted bridal white wearing a beribboned wreath of pink roses and baby's breath. Next to Genghis was a trio of plaster raccoons, one lime green, one neon yellow, and one electric blue. Beside them was an amazing painting of a wooden wall with graffiti carved into it. It looked so real, so much like actual carved wood with worn blue paint flaking and peeling off, Priscilla wanted to run her fingers over it to convince herself it wasn't. The brightly painted sign above her said Rayne Forster Gallery and Studio.

"Isn't that amazing?" her cousin Joan said, her dark eyes bright as she admired the painting. "I don't know how she makes it look so three dimensional."

"I'm a little surprised there's nothing holiday related in there since it's so close to Christmas." Priscilla grinned at the foot-high skeleton in traditional South American garb standing in the corner of the display. "She certainly has eclectic taste."

"I know, right? I never know what's going to be in here when I pass by."

"I didn't know you liked this sort of thing," Priscilla said. "I haven't seen any at your house."

Joan shrugged. "I don't know if it's my style to actually decorate with, but it's interesting to look at, don't you think?"

"Then we should look."

Glad to get out of the December wind, Priscilla opened the door, and they went inside. The gallery was warm and smelled of paint and sawdust and was lined with shelves filled with more art pieces. Some were colorful, some muted, some traditional, some modern, but most often they were a mix of at least two styles.

"I like to keep people guessing," said a melodious voice behind them.

Priscilla turned with a smile. "Are you the artist?"

The woman held out her hand, smiling too. "I'm Rayne Forster. Is there something I can show you?"

She was almost as tall as Priscilla but as slim and long limbed as a dancer. Her tanned skin was unlined except for the indications of frequent laughter around her eyes. If it weren't for the dramatic streak of white in the dark halo of her loose, natural curls, she might have passed for twenty-five or so. As it was, Priscilla guessed she was nearer to forty. Her lavish dangling earrings and the colorful scarf she wore in a band across her hair gave her the exotic look of a gypsy.

"We're just looking," Priscilla said, shaking her hand. Rayne's hand was strong but delicate, the hand of an artist. "I'm Priscilla Grant. I inherited the Misty Harbor Lighthouse along with the cottage when my aunt died, so I moved here from Kansas."

"Oh," Rayne said. "So that's you. I hear you have a museum in the lighthouse too. I really need to come see it. I'm thinking of doing some seascapes, and that lighthouse might just inspire me."

"I'd love to show you around," Priscilla said, and she gave her a card. "Call me when you have time to come by."

"I'll do that." Rayne smiled at Joan. "And you've been in here before."

"This is my cousin, Joan Abernathy," Priscilla said.

Rayne shook Joan's hand too. "I'm sorry I didn't get to introduce myself one of those other times."

"You were in your studio in the middle of something the two times I was here," Joan told her. "I didn't want to interrupt. But my cousin and I were going by, and I just had to show her some of your things. They're so different."

Rayne shrugged, looking faintly pleased. "As I said, I like to keep people guessing."

They stopped to look at a sculpture of a woman's head that had been very convincingly painted to look as if it were made of metal screen that you could look through onto a scene of a Parisian sidewalk café. But the café windows were cracked and broken, the awning hung in tattered strips from its frame, one of the metal chairs was turned on its side, and bits of newspaper and other debris lay on the sidewalk, the romantic scene neglected and abandoned. Priscilla was about to ask about the meaning behind it when the door opened, and a man came into the gallery. He was a little stocky, not very tall, just an inch or two taller than Priscilla, midfifties, she thought, but he was a natty dresser. When he spotted Joan, he turned on a smile that was certainly engaging.

"Well, hello." He swept the fedora off his head. "I didn't expect to see you in here again."

Joan's cheeks turned pinker than the winter wind had already made them. "Hello, Calvin. I didn't think you'd be back yet."

"I got to Lima in record time and found that my native craftsman has been working overtime." He winked at Rayne. "Do you have room for another shipment, honey? I think these new ones are going to sell like hotcakes."

Rayne laughed and shook her head. "I don't know how you always know what's popular, but I'll never argue with success."

"I told you everything would be snapped up in a day or two." The man grinned. "You be the artist, I'll take care of the imports, okay?"

She shrugged. "I'm just selling what you bring in. What you decide to ship over here is your own business."

"Nice and simple, just like I like it." He turned again to Joan. "So, what have you been up to since I left? Who's your friend?"

"My cousin, Priscilla Grant. Priscilla, this is Calvin Gallico. He imports artwork from all over the world."

"You two have met before, I see," Priscilla said.

Joan nodded. "When I was in here about a month ago, before Thanksgiving. Calvin was talking to Rayne about selling some of his imports from her gallery, and I was coming in as he was going out. Then a couple of weeks ago, we ran into each other again and started talking."

The man beamed at her. "You don't know how hard it is to find someone who can carry on a good conversation anymore, Priscilla. And to find out Joan here is an artist herself, well, it was just a pleasure to talk to her."

"Now, Calvin," Joan said, the pink in her cheeks deepening. "You know I'm just an amateur."

"An artist!" Rayne said. "What sort of things do you do?"

"Oh, it's not much. Not real art like yours."

Rayne chuckled. "I don't know about that. I guess some of my stuff is 'real art.' A lot of it is just fun. That's the stuff that seems to sell anyhow. People like my mash-ups."

"But you're a working artist," Joan told her. "I just do a few still lifes. Only for fun."

"You sold a couple," Priscilla reminded her.

Calvin's eyes lit. "You never told me that. That's great. I bet I could find some collectors who'd be interested in some of your work too."

"Stop," Joan said with a shy grin, and she pushed a lock of short brown hair behind her ear.

Calvin gave her an exaggerated wink, and that made her laugh. Was he flirting? And was she flirting back?

"So you're an importer?" Priscilla asked the man.

One hand over his heart, he made a slight bow. "I am. I deal in volume more than high price. Mostly little things anyone can afford, things folks can pick up on a whim and not worry about paying for. Interesting little things from all over. A lot of them handcrafted. I'll tell you what, honey, all those little nickels and dimes certainly add up after a while. I just have to keep finding artists who can keep up with the demand."

"Have you decided what you're going to bring in next?" Rayne asked.

Calvin nodded eagerly. "This guy I met is going to make more of the same kind of pottery I brought this time but bigger. Really impressive, you know? I think they'll sell well. In fact, I know several collectors who'll be really interested. Still want to carry them here? Same terms?"

"That will be great."

They shook hands on it, and then Calvin turned back to Joan.

"I have to meet a guy, but uh, I was wondering if you might want to have coffee or something. Maybe in the morning? And I heard the pond's frozen over. What would you say to some ice-skating sometime?"

Joan laughed. "Me? I haven't been skating in years."

"Me either," he said, his eyes twinkling, "so what could we lose?"

Joan laughed again, and then they both glanced at Priscilla.

"While they're making plans," Priscilla said to Rayne, feeling terribly in the way, "would you mind telling me about this sculpture? Is the woman dreaming of Paris? And what happened to her?"

"I hate to interpret anything for viewers," the artist said, walking with Priscilla toward the piece. "I think each person brings his or her own meaning to any creative work."

As she spoke about the variety of reactions her creations evoked, Priscilla couldn't help glancing over at her cousin. Joan and Calvin were chatting away about who knew what, neither of them seeming to notice that Priscilla and Rayne were on the other side of the room now.

After she and Rayne talked a moment more about the sculpture and Rayne's art in general, Priscilla took another look back at Joan.

"What's this about ice-skating? I always thought it was too warm here for anything but slush."

"Evidently not," Rayne said. "It's been cold enough for a long enough spell to make a good sheet of ice. It doesn't happen often, so it's kind of a treat when it does. Do you skate?"

"Not really. I do have some skates. I think. My husband and I went a few times years ago when one of the malls put in a rink. I'm not even sure if I brought them with me up here." Priscilla glanced at Joan and her friend and lowered her voice. "Have you known him long?"

Rayne shrugged. "A few weeks now. I don't know how much he really knows about art, but he evidently knows what sells. And I never turn down anything that brings in a paying customer."

"Do you know much about him?"

"Not really," Rayne admitted. "I know he's got a boat of some kind that he takes all over so he can pick up things to sell to collectors here. That's about it."

"Interesting." *Odd* was what Priscilla was really thinking, but she didn't say that aloud. Instead she smiled over at Joan. "Are we still going to the library?"

"Sure." Joan turned to Calvin. "It was good to run into you again. I'd love to hear about your last trip."

"Tomorrow at eight," he said. "Now don't you forget."

"I won't."

He nodded at Priscilla and Rayne. "Good to meet you, Priscilla. I'll be in touch, Rayne." He replaced his hat and turned up the collar on his coat. "Oh, I'll bring the new stuff over sometime tomorrow if it's all right."

"Just fine," Rayne said. "Anytime after lunch."

"Till tomorrow," Calvin said to Joan, "and Merry Christmas, everybody." Then he stuffed his hands into his pockets and hurried into the street.

"What's this about tomorrow at eight?" Priscilla asked, making her expression very arch.

"Just coffee." Joan colored again and then looked around the studio. "I do want to go to the library, but I haven't gotten around to looking at everything here yet."

"There are a lot of things to see." Priscilla gave her arm a squeeze, smiling. "And I hope you have a nice time with Calvin tomorrow."

Rayne was good enough to show them around the gallery and then give them a look at her studio. The former was artistically laid out, showing each piece to advantage. The latter could only be described as controlled chaos.

"I never know what I'm going to want to do next," Rayne said with a sheepish grin.

The large table in the center of the room was filled with her works in progress and covered with bits and pieces of just about everything imaginable. Around it was shelves full of supplies: paints and plaster mixes, various tools and brushes, and dozens of molds, classic and modern, austere and whimsical. Most interesting were the bins of what Rayne called "found stuff."

"Not that I found it at the dump," she explained, "not most of it anyway, but I did find it here and there, at thrift stores and antique stores and craft shops. Even office supply stores and beauty shops and a grocery store or two. I never know what I might need until I get started."

"Unless you have a commission, right?" Priscilla asked.

"Right."

"What kinds of things does Calvin usually bring in?" Joan asked.

"Oh, it depends on where he's been." Rayne walked them over to one of the shelves where there were several colorful items that looked like they were from South America. "A lot of earthenware lately. These handmade dolls have been very popular. I sold out of the alpaca-wool blankets he got on his last trip. It's always interesting to see what he comes up with."

"It must be," Priscilla said.

Rayne shrugged good-naturedly. "I'm just glad he knows better than me what will sell. Of course, I'd rather sell my own stuff, but this helps pay the bills."

"You never know when you'll hit it big," Joan said. "Or when your luck will change."

"Thanks for showing us around, Rayne," Priscilla said. "It's been nice meeting you. Good luck with your imports."

"Thanks." Rayne showed them to the door. "Come back anytime, and stay warm."

Priscilla buttoned her coat at the collar and pulled on the knitted cap she had in her pocket, and then she and Joan went back out into the cold. They made small talk on the walk back to the car and the short drive to the library. Once there, they returned the books they had checked out, chatted for a moment with Clara, the head librarian, and then checked out the books she had been holding for them.

"What do you think about stopping over at Candy's for some coffee?" Priscilla asked once they were back in the car.

Joan looked exaggeratedly thoughtful. "I don't know. Will cookies be involved?"

"They could be."

"Then I think we should absolutely stop by."

For Christmas, Candy Lane Confectionery was all glitzed up to look like a candy shop at the North Pole, and Priscilla couldn't help smiling at the little elf dolls that were peeping out of every available space. The shop was never very busy on a Tuesday afternoon during the winter, and she wasn't surprised to find most of the café-style tables available. She and Joan ordered coffee and chocolate chip cookies at the counter and then seated themselves at one of the tables near the window.

"Looking for something?" Priscilla asked playfully when Joan sat staring out over the harbor and the winter-gray sea beyond, obviously not hearing anything Priscilla had been saying.

"Sorry." Joan laughed half under her breath. "Just looking." After one more quick glance, she turned back to Priscilla. "How's Jake these days?"

Joan saw Priscilla's dog, Jake, all the time.

"Same as when you saw him on Sunday. How's Sister?"

Sister was the puppy Priscilla had given Joan last spring. Priscilla saw her all the time too.

"A bundle of energy as always," Joan said with a wry grin, "but I guess you knew that already too."

"So tell me what's really on your mind. Is it—"

Priscilla broke off as the girl behind the counter brought their coffee and cookies and left the check. Joan made a great show of putting sugar and cream in her coffee and then stirring it.

"Is it that man who was in the gallery?" Priscilla asked finally. "Calvin?"

"Is what him?"

"Is he what's on your mind?"

Joan shrugged. "Maybe. A little. I was just wondering which one of those boats was his."

"So he really picks up all his imports himself? That seems a little bit . . . inefficient."

"Well, I don't think he does all of it. He just gathers up different things he thinks his buyers over here would like and then, if they're interested in particular ones, he gets the artists to make up a lot of them to be shipped over. But he shows them the samples and takes their orders."

"Sounds like you and he have had time to talk," Joan said.

Joan bit her lip. "You don't like him."

"Hey, I didn't say that. I've hardly met him." Priscilla reached over and patted her cousin's hand. "I'm not trying to grill you or anything. I was just curious, and you seem a little bit distracted. You don't have to tell me about him if you don't want to."

"No, it's nothing like that. I just don't have that much to tell. We met at the gallery, and we talked for a while. Last time I saw him at Rayne's, we decided to have a sandwich at the Nautilus Café. It was nice. He's been a lot of interesting places, and we just talked."

"What did you say his last name is?" Priscilla asked.

"Gallico. Calvin Gallico. He lives in Boston, but he's always looking for artists who can make things he can import. With all the trips he makes, he says he's almost never home."

"No family then."

"Not really. No kids." Joan looked thoughtful. "He was married for seventeen years, but then she died and he hasn't met anyone since then. Sort of like me losing Allen."

"At least you have your boys."

Joan pressed her lips together. "That's not exactly a substitute, is it."

Priscilla should have bitten her tongue. Being a widow herself, she knew it wasn't. Motherhood was about preparing a child for a future and independence, for setting out into a separate life. Marriage was molding two separate lives into one. As much as she loved her daughter, Rachel, being a mother was no substitute for being a wife, for being a partner and a helpmate and a lover. It was no substitute at all.

"Sorry. That didn't exactly come out the way I meant it to."

"No, I'm sorry." Joan winced. "I didn't mean to snap at you. Anyway, I just had a sandwich with the guy. It's not like we signed a prenuptial agreement."

"Well, I think it would be nice if you met someone you liked. It just seems like it would be a hassle if he didn't even live on the island and was gone all the time."

"I don't know. I've gotten pretty set in my ways since Allen died. I may not be ready to have someone around all the time again. But it won't hurt to have a cup of coffee with him, right?"

"Or go ice-skating?" Priscilla teased.

"We don't have any definite plans for that. Yet."

"Keep your eyes open anyway," Priscilla said. "At least until you know more about him. Maybe he still has a wife in Boston."

Joan rolled her eyes.

"And another one in Brazil," Priscilla added with a grin.

"He was in Peru," Joan said primly. "Drink your coffee."

A NOTE FROM THE EDITORS

We hope you enjoyed Mysteries of Martha's Vineyard, published by the Books and Inspirational Media Division of Guideposts, a nonprofit organization that touches millions of lives every day through products and services that inspire, encourage, help you grow in your faith, and celebrate God's love.

Thank you for making a difference with your purchase of this book, which helps fund our many outreach programs to military personnel, prisons, hospitals, nursing homes, and educational institutions.

We also create many useful and uplifting online resources. Visit Guideposts.org to read true stories of hope and inspiration, access OurPrayer network, sign up for free newsletters, download free e-books, join our Facebook community, and follow our stimulating blogs.

To learn about other Guideposts publications, including the best-selling devotional *Daily Guideposts*, go to Guideposts.org/Shop, call (800) 932-2145, or write to Guideposts, PO Box 5815, Harlan, Iowa 51593.

Sign up for the
Guideposts Fiction Newsletter
and stay up-to-date on
the books you love!

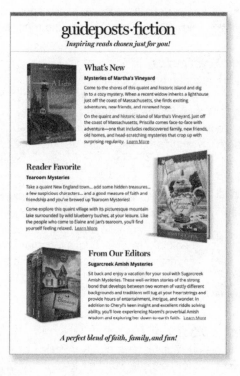

You'll get sneak peeks of new releases, recommendations from other Guideposts readers, and special offers just for you . . .
and it's FREE!

Just go to Guideposts.org/Newsletters
today to sign up.

Find more inspiring fiction in these best-loved Guideposts series!

Mysteries of Martha's Vineyard

Come to the shores of this quaint and historic island and dig in to a cozy mystery. When a recent widow inherits a lighthouse just off the coast of Massachusetts, she finds exciting adventures, new friends, and renewed hope.

Tearoom Mysteries

Mix one stately Victorian home, a charming lakeside town in Maine, and two adventurous cousins with a passion for tea and hospitality. Add a large scoop of intriguing mystery and sprinkle generously with faith, family, and friends, and you have the recipe for Tearoom Mysteries.

Sugarcreek Amish Mysteries

Be intrigued by the suspense and joyful "aha!" moments in these delightful stories. Each book in the series brings together two women of vastly different backgrounds and traditions, who realize there's much more to the "simple life" than meets the eye.

Mysteries of Silver Peak

Escape to the historic mining town of Silver Peak, Colorado, and discover how one woman's love of antiques helps her solve mysteries buried deep in the town's checkered past.

Patchwork Mysteries

Discover that life's little mysteries often have a common thread in a series where every novel contains an intriguing whodunit centered around a quilt located in a beautiful New England town.

To learn more about these books, visit Guideposts.org/Shop